Born and raised in Tokyo, Katherine Tamiko Arguile is a Japanese-British-Australian arts journalist and author. She migrated from London in 2008 to Adelaide, where she now lives beside the sea.

Besides working as an author, she co-owns and runs a coffee shop with her partner and writes arts reviews for various news outlets. She enjoys printmaking and other meditative pursuits whenever she can. Her award-winning short stories have been published in anthologies in the UK and in Australia. *The Things She Owned* is her first novel.

PRAISE FOR *THE THINGS SHE OWNED*

A beautifully handled story of a mother and daughter—the things that
bind them together and the unsettling forces that keep them apart.
Katherine Tamiko Arguile vividly evokes the cross-cultural experience
and what it means to occupy the uncanny space between worlds and
identities—and always with food and the preparation of food at its
fulcrum. In prose that just sings off the page, *The Things She Owned*
will leave you reeling, weeping, and then whooping ecstatically.
Simply gorgeous.

Molly Murn, author of *Heart of the Grass Tree*

Katherine Tamiko Arguile trains her ear to the reverberations held in
generations-old rice bowls and perfectly arranged oyunomi tea cups,
as she navigates the terrains of memory and trauma, a mother-daughter
relationship steeped in love and hate. *The Things She Owned* is absorbing,
compassionate, finely observed and wise. This is a story of
resilience and beauty.

Rebekah Clarkson, author of *Barking Dogs*

Katherine Tamiko Arguile has written a subtle tale woven from a double
layer of consciousness. Interleaved between cultures, histories and
relationships and anchored by melancholy objects, this is a vivid cabinet
of curiosities: words and things healing open wounds by creating new
sites of feeling and imagination.

Brian Castro, author of *Shanghai Dancing* and *The Bath Fugues*

Lives warped by war endure life-long emotional fallout, yet remain
suffused with Japanese culture's complex and delicate riches. From
the many exquisite dishes, exactingly prepared, to the final immersion
in Okinawan ritual and history, this haunting novel is bursting with
treasures, a magical feast laid out in lush, accomplished prose.

Carol Lefevre, author of *The Happiness Glass*

Affirmpress
books that leave an impression

Published by Affirm Press in 2020
28 Thistlethwaite Street, South Melbourne, VIC 3205
www.affirmpress.com.au
10 9 8 7 6 5 4 3 2 1

A catalogue record for this
book is available from the
National Library of Australia

Title: The Things She Owned / Katherine Tamiko Arguile, author.
ISBN: 9781925972610 (paperback)

Cover design by Alissa Dinallo
Internal illustrations by Katherine Tamiko Arguile
Typeset by J&M Typesetting in Adobe Garamond Pro 12 / 16.75
Proudly printed in Australia by Griffin Press

The
THINGS
SHE
OWNED

Katherine Tamiko Arguile

Affirm
press

For ease of reading, the author has included a glossary of Japanese terms in the final pages of the book.

In memory of my mother, Akiko Yonekubo, who was as far from Michiko as light is from dark.

South China Sea, August 1979

The sun is blinding. When Erika closes her eyes, its rays pulse white beneath her lids. When she opens them she sees her mother against blue sky, magnificent, like a goddess. Michiko is wearing a cream swimsuit, showing off sun-bronzed skin. Permed black curls tumble from a red and white polka-dot scarf around her head. Erika searches her mother's face. Sometimes she glimpses the eyes behind those huge Jackie-O sunglasses.

She stares at Michiko's crimson lips sipping from a martini glass. An olive skewered by a toothpick rests against its rim, which Michiko holds in place with a scarlet nail as she drinks. She empties the glass and plucks the olive from its stick with her teeth, glancing sideways at the men around her on the yacht. Julian rushes forward to refill it.

All afternoon Michiko drinks, reclining on the deck cushions, crossing and uncrossing her legs. She nods, giggles at the men. 'Hontō—? Usō!' she coos. *Really? Oh, you're such a liar!*

Erika wants to reach out and feel the icy glass the way her mother feels it. She wants to trace the outline of her mother's mouth with her fingertips. She moves close, and the heavy smell of sandalwood and spice envelops her. Her mother loves this perfume – Yves Saint Laurent's Opium. Erika touches Michiko's arm, feeling the sun's warmth in her skin. But her mother swats her hand away as if it were a fly.

Michiko laughs at something Julian says. He's acting the clown, entertaining his lover. He mimes walking the plank and goggles his eyes. He teeters into a handstand, leaps up to take a bow and struts about with his chest puffed out like a rooster. Michiko's friend Marit laughs too, though not as loudly. Erika is happy Marit is here – she and her husband have come to visit them in Hong Kong. Marit is kind to Erika. She has a way of making Erika feel she can be herself and not get into trouble for it.

As the sun falls towards the sea, Michiko grows quiet. Erika can see she's still smiling, though at no one in particular. Her eyes are focused somewhere beyond the horizon, her face pink and orange in the setting sun's rays. When she looks peaceful like this, she doesn't seem so frightening.

It's the right moment. Erika lays her head in Michiko's lap; Julian laid his head there earlier.

'Ugh! Hot and sticky. Go play!' Michiko pushes her off, pointing with the hand holding the glass, slopping icy vodka on Erika's legs. The cold cuts through the heat of her skin. The shock of it is strange, like a burn and an itch.

Erika heads to the prow to curl into the cushions there. She's never been on such an enormous yacht. She peers over the edge at the waves far down below, listening to the conversation and laughter behind her. She turns to look at her mother, who is holding out her glass again. One of the men, the blond one, leaps forward with a bottle.

The man stares at her mother as he pours. He has an odd expression on his face, and the glass is overflowing, the drink spilling into her mother's lap. 'Oh,' cries Michiko, 'so cold!' And he takes a fistful of napkins from a tray and mops her lap; she twitches at his touch. Erika watches her mother covering the cloud of injection marks on her thighs with her palms while he wipes, watches Julian crossing his arms, his face darkening. The man sits close to Michiko and drapes his arm over her shoulder. He leans into her, whispering to her in a peculiar way with his face turned to the side so his mouth is close to her ear and his ear close to her lips, as if he wants to trap every word. Everything goes quiet.

Erika is so absorbed by the sight of her mother with the man that when Julian looms over her she jumps.

'Hey kid! How about a swim?'

She loves swimming but feels a stab of fear when she thinks about being out here in the open ocean where her feet can't touch the bottom. Maybe everything will be okay if she wears her water wings.

Heart thrilling, she brings them to her mother and holds them out. The blond man is still curled around Michiko, murmuring. Erika waits for her mother to look at her.

'Come on, kid, we haven't got all day!' Julian sounds angry.

Erika wonders if her real dad would have been more patient. Erika doesn't know what he looks like because he left before she can remember, but she knows his name is George, which she thinks is a kind-sounding name. Her mother said that George left because he didn't want Erika, but Erika knows that sometimes her mother lies.

'*Mama*—?'

Michiko whips round. '"*Mama*" *wa dame! Michiko desho!*'

Erika holds up the floppy pieces of orange plastic. Her mother tuts and gestures to come closer. When she darts forward for them, Erika flinches, but Michiko just slips a wing onto each of Erika's arms, purses her lips around the valves and blows, leaving crimson smears. The blond man stays where he is, watching. Erika suddenly wants to push him away, hard, both hands against his chest, but Michiko has her arm gripped tight. Erika feels her blood pulsing as the wings grow fatter, and when her mother roughly runs a forefinger inside the inflated water wing, she catches the soft skin of Erika's inner arm. It hurts, but she makes no sound. She loves her mother too much at this moment, despite everything. She wants to sit close and put her arms around Michiko's neck. She wants to be where the blond man is, closer, even, so she might merge back into her. She basks in the imagined gaze of a mother's love, keeping very still, the way you'd keep still if you saw a deer in a clearing and didn't want to scare it off. But then Michiko slaps her bottom with a laugh. 'Go on, have swim,' she says. 'Julian take care of you.'

Erika heads for the long ladder that stretches all the way down the side of the yacht into the waves, but Julian picks her up from behind before she can reach it, grabbing her under the arms. He whirls her around.

'Wa-haay! Whoo!'

It makes her laugh. He plays with her like this now and then. It's fun, though it makes her feel a bit sick. It's the funniest feeling when he puts her down and the room keeps tilting and spinning even after she's stopped going around in circles. She can't work out where the floor is, or even where her own body is, and she'll fall over, laughing until her tummy hurts.

She sees flashes of sea, the sun, blue sky, her mother, the blond man, Marit, the other man, the deck, the sail, the sea, the sun, blue sky, her mother, the blond man, Marit, the other man, the deck, the sail ... She's flying.

'Yaaah! I'm gonna chuck you in! Here we go! Whoooshhh!'

She feels Julian stumble, and her heart skips. His breath smells of beer. He steadies himself. Now he swings her from side to side as he inches closer to the edge of the yacht; he's pretending he's going to throw her overboard. Erika's laughter turns to shrieks each time he swoops her up over the edge, when, for a moment, she feels as if she were lifting right up and out of his arms and can see the abyss of the dark shining sea far below. Each time, her tummy falls out from inside her as he scoops her back towards the deck, making her scream and laugh. Each time, she expects him to put her down so she can go to the ladder and climb down into the sea. But he keeps on and on, swinging and swooping and hollering. She starts to feel sick. She wants him to stop. She cries out, 'I want to get down!'

He keeps going, as if he can't hear her, and she squirms in his grip.

'No! Let me go!' She shouts louder. 'I don't like it!'

Still he doesn't stop. He keeps swinging her backwards, forwards, over the edge of the yacht, lurching. 'Wa-haaaayyy! Woo hoo!'

'Julian, put her down!' Marit's voice.

He doesn't stop.

'Julian!' Marit is shouting.

His arms grip Erika's ribs so tightly they hurt. She wants to cry, but knows it will embarrass her mother, so she bites her lip, her breath catching in her throat. She whimpers. She struggles once again to break free of Julian's clutches. Still he keeps on and on.

'*Julian!*'

On an upwards swoop over the edge of the yacht, Erika wriggles free. She feels the familiar lift out of Julian's arms, but then there's only the brush of his fingers against her ribs as she plummets, her body turning through the air as she falls, her stomach leaping to her throat. The rush in her ears, the white noise of the waves beneath her, is punctured only by Marit's long scream as she falls, headfirst, for what seems forever.

A Korean Cabinet

An antique reproduction of high quality, thirty years old, made to look two hundred years older. Crafted from dark zelkova wood, its top curls gently upwards at each end, like a temple roof. Its feet are carved curves. The cabinet stands waist-high and its width is that of a child's hug. It has two cupboards, one above the other, their sets of small double doors concealing larger spaces inside. The doors are fastened with ornate dark metal clasps: a ring to the right, two little catches to the left, over which the ring snaps tight. You can slide a bat-shaped brass padlock, decorated with red and yellow tassels, through holes in the catches. The rest of the cabinet is marked out in rectangular panels by thin bands of darker wood. Among them, if you look hard enough, you might find three that slide out to reveal secret drawers.

Erika

Erika spends her one day off a week cleaning her own and Lila Mackenzie's flats – three hours for herself and two for her elderly neighbour. She goes upstairs each Monday afternoon, taking a week's worth of casseroles and soups to put in the eighty-five-year-old widow's fridge, and when she's done she stays for a chat and a cup of tea and a biscuit. Mrs Mackenzie is frail and leaves messages on Erika's answering machine whenever she needs help with something, like opening a jar of honey or changing a light bulb. The relationship grew organically. There'd never been an official arrangement, but they'd assumed the roles of carer and cared for, settling into a comfortable companionship that bridged the fifty-five-year gap between them. Erika never tires of the stories Mrs Mac tells again and again as she reminisces over old photographs and prized objects. The old woman's memories are a robust and lively contrast to her brittle body. She sits curled and impeccably dressed in her enormous golden velvet armchair, her eyes sparking as she talks.

Mrs Mackenzie's stories reconnect an unidentifiable, broken thread inside Erika. She leaves, feeling restored somehow, clutching a shopping list and a purse of money from the widow's pension. She delivers the groceries before her evening shift later in the week, giving her a chance to check up on her neighbour. Mrs Mackenzie has two daughters and five grandchildren but Erika's never seen them visiting. The daughters are busy people and rarely seem to call, yet Mrs Mackenzie speaks lovingly of them, smiling at their photos above the mantelpiece. Erika wonders if they know how lucky they are, having this mother's unconditional love.

She's glad of the hours she spends cleaning the flat and tending to Mrs Mackenzie's needs. It keeps Erika from swimming into uncharted waters of empty time. Without these tasks, she'd happily work seven days a week. Before she got to know her neighbour, she'd even suggested this to her boss, André, the head chef at the restaurant where she worked. He said he'd be more than happy to let her kill herself working every day of the week if she wanted to, if it weren't for the miserable bastards at Health & Safety. He'd never had anyone complain about having time off, he'd said, and frankly, mate, Erika was a freak, but he'd forgive her because she was a fucking awesome sous-chef and had a nice arse. She'd grimaced before getting back to her station to prep her mise for evening service.

Erika navigates her day in a trance of tidying, dusting, polishing. Once her flat is clean, with everything in its place, she always feels better. It's a ritual of righting herself. If Marcus stays at her place more than three nights a week, things begin to unravel. Spoons get jumbled up with knives, the bar of soap becomes embedded with black curls of pubic hair, and mismatched socks emerge from the washing machine. She feels a tension growing inside her like a spring winding ever more tightly, until, despite herself, she shrivels and closes inwards. Eventually she can't look him in the eye anymore and has to ask him to stay away for a while. It doesn't happen often, and when it does, he doesn't take it personally. He has more important priorities: his son, Felix – his treasure, the love of his life. Erika has never met Felix. She doesn't want to, not until she's sure she and Marcus will stay together for the long haul.

The relationship suits them both. Erika's equally happy to oblige when Marcus is the one to ask for space. They loop away from one another, planets on separate orbits, knowing their paths will converge again.

Erika takes longer than usual to clean on this particular day. She works up a sweat, squinting against the glare of the late May sun. She balls up newspaper and gives her side of the glass a hard polish with vinegar, a tip from Mrs Mackenzie. She unscrews the smoke alarms from the ceiling to dust them, wobbling on tiptoe on a chair. She empties the kitchen cupboards and wipes down the shelves. She works through without stopping for lunch. She isn't hungry.

She vacuums the carpet on the other side of the dining table. The hose catches the edge of the dark antique Korean cabinet that sits in an alcove. She yanks it free and the machine topples on to its side with a whine.

'Fuck's sake.'

She stoops to right the vacuum cleaner and stands up too quickly. Dizzy, she grabs at the dining table to keep from falling. A piece of paper wafts off it onto the floor at her feet.

She bends to pick it up and a strangled sound escapes her. She kicks the off switch on the vacuum cleaner and sinks into a chair with the piece of paper, an unread email she's been avoiding all morning. When she first saw the subject heading and sender in her mailbox, it had filled her with such dread it made her nauseous. She'd printed it out to force herself to read it; holding it in front of her now she wills herself to focus. The Japanese words are typed in roman script, to make them easier for her to read.

Kei wants to visit her in London. She's been thinking about her aunt a great deal recently, she writes. Could she please visit Michiko Obachan's English grave? Is it near London? She's sure Erika hasn't meant to withhold this information, although it would have been nice to hear where her aunt's remains are buried. She understands that as Michiko Obachan's only child, Erika must feel a heavy sense of responsibility, but Kei knows she can trust her, as a descendant of the Takigawa clan, to fulfil it. She is sure Erika recognises her duties in accordance with the virtue of filial piety.

Erika draws a deep breath, forcing herself to read on.

Of course, Kei will stay in a hotel so as not to be any trouble. She is thinking of arriving towards the end of August to stay for about a fortnight. Would Erika please be so kind as to find her a hotel close to her house? She knows most of the hotels in her neighbourhood are expensive, but she does so want to stay near her cousin. Perhaps Erika would be good enough to find her one where the rates are not too high.

Erika decides to reply later, once she's calmer, once she's had a good night's sleep. She unplugs the vacuum cleaner and kicks the recoil button, the cable snapping as it reels itself in. She walks into the kitchen and opens the fridge, but she still isn't hungry. She puts the kettle on for a cup of tea. It's early but she's tired and ready for bed. She's spent longer than usual cleaning. She's run the duster across every windowsill, wiped down curtain rails and skirting boards. Every surface reflects the late afternoon light and glimmers cleanliness. The carpets are lint free; the bathroom tiles are shining and the kitchen cupboards are spotless.

Only the Korean cabinet, topped with its sombre arrangement of objects, stands neglected in its alcove. It's furred with a thick layer of dust. Erika hasn't cleaned it. She hasn't cleaned it in years.

An Onigiri Basket

A rectangular lunch basket with a well-fitting lid, it holds three onigiri rice balls, or five, if kneaded smaller, without fillings. It is made to look like woven wicker, allowing air to circulate within, but is a sturdy plastic of good quality. Its sides fold down to a slim rectangle so the base fits, snug, into its lid. It is kept in its nest of old Tupperware, creamy white in a sea of seventies orange, pea green and brown. It is practical, space-saving and made to last. It has held onigiri – and on rare occasions, neatly cut sandwiches – for more than thirty years.

Erika

'Oi-oi!'

Erika realises she's been dozing. Shrieks of kids high on summer holidays blast through the *shush* of waves over pebbles and smash into her consciousness. Frankie's baritone bellow is louder than all of the kids' combined. Erika's definitely awake now but keeps her eyes closed, screwing them up against the sun glaring red through her lids. Sweat trickles into one ear. She wipes it on her towel with an exasperated swipe of her head.

'Oi! Erika! Sarah! You coming in or what?' Frankie shouts.

She pulls the towel over her head, scrubs her mop of black curls and wipes her face. The summer's already making newspaper headlines as the 'Great Heatwave of 2003'; people have died all over Europe. In the oppressive heat, she feels her body constricting and prickling, as if it were trapped in a tightening vice. But it could never be hot enough to persuade her to go into the water.

Sarah is draped on the chair beside her with a floppy hat on her face. She flips up the brim and looks over. 'You're awake.'

'Yep. Fucking Frankie. I was having such a lovely snooze.' Erika swigs from her bottle of water and watches Sarah get up and strip off her wrap. 'You're not going in, are you?'

Sarah gives her a funny look. 'Course I am, I'm roasting. It's thirty-six degrees, for fuck's sake. Come with.'

'No, thanks.'

'You could just paddle.'

'No.'

'Come on, how often do we—' Sarah registers Erika's expression. 'Are you okay?'

'I'm fine. Really. I just ... I don't like going into the sea.' Erika hugs her arms and shivers.

Luca, Sarah's boy, sits on an inflatable li-lo on the pebbles between them, his face fierce with concentration. He's scribbling loopy shapes into a giant sketchpad with fat crayons. He flicks over to a new page with a dramatic flourish and draws a huge yellow oval in the middle.

Erika leans over him. 'Hey. What's that, a sun?'

He draws a black horizontal line across it and above that, two black dots, like hard pebbles. 'Nooo!' He chortles. 'That's you, silly!'

A frisbee glances off Erika's shoulder, spraying water everywhere.

Luca stands up. 'Hey! You wet my picture!'

Erika dabs at the sketchbook with her towel. 'Jesus, Frankie!'

The other chefs fall about in the waves, hooting and shouting. Frankie comes up the beach to retrieve the frisbee, arms outstretched and head cocked in mock supplication.

'Oh my god, Sarah, he's so fucking annoying.'

'You said a bad word. Naughty.' Luca bows his head over his sketchbook again.

'I did, didn't I, Luca. I'm sorry. Thank you for telling me off. I promise I won't do it again.' Erika pulls a guilty face at Sarah, who chuckles.

'Don't worry. I let it slip all the time. We have a swear box, don't we, Luca?'

Frankie stands dripping over them. 'Hey, Luca! Come and play frisbee with us in the water.'

'Can I, Mummy?'

Sarah rummages around in her beach bag. 'You need your wings on. Come here, baby.'

Erika watches Sarah blow air into the orange armbands. Luca's skipping a jig, impatient, slipping about on the stones. 'Just wait!' Sarah calls out between puffs. 'Stand still!'

Erika's heart beats faster. She looks again at Luca's sketchbook. The circle of yellow crayon is supposed to be her face, framed with a curly black mane. The line for a mouth and black dots for eyes are expressionless. She flicks back dog-eared pages. Great pink balloon faces with gaping red grins and blonde bubble hair. Blocky, bright cars with giant faces lolling from windows. Green scribble-trees, crooked houses with chimneys, orange smiley suns with red rays. She turns back to her portrait. Black lines for a body, arms and legs, and claws for hands. Behind it, a blue–black scrawl: the sea, empty of people or creatures, dark and seemingly endless. The solitary stick figure stands with its back to the waves, lipless mouth clamped shut. She breathes out. It's just a kid's picture, for god's sake.

Erika watches as Sarah walks Luca into the sea. Her mouth is dry; when she raises her water bottle to her lips, she notices her hand is shaking. Luca is knock-kneed with excitement, dancing his little dance, flailing his arms. The puffed-up wings make them look like spindly sticks. A wave breaks against him and he staggers and clutches his mother, squealing. Erika realises she's clenching her fists.

She slumps back into the deckchair. Maybe she needs another nap. It was a late finish to service last night – eighty-four covers. After desserts had gone out, they'd cleaned their stations, then spent another hour mopping and disinfecting the floor.

It had been an emotional evening and stinking hot too, in more ways than one. Just past midnight, André had screamed himself hoarse down the phone at Peter, the owner, about how that was fucking it, he wasn't fucking well opening his fucking kitchen again until Peter'd fucking well fixed the pile of bollocks drains and he wasn't going to stand in a putrid, stinking fog while trying to serve up fucking lobster fucking quenelles with fucking truffle velouté when everything fucking stank of shit. And he could fucking well consider his fucking restaurant closed until Peter got the fucking plumbers in and fucking fixed it, and properly this time. 'We are not fucking running' – here he'd paused for breath, red-faced and eyes bulging – 'a cocksucking Wimpy Bar.'

THE THINGS SHE OWNED

They'd continued to mop around him. Sarah mimed a cheer behind André's back and Erika had to stifle a laugh. They got the rest of the week off, perfectly timed for the biggest heatwave since 1976. At their usual post-service session at the Queen's Head, they'd clinked celebratory glasses and declared that the next day, given the forecast predicted a scorcher, they'd get the train to Brighton.

Erika must have dozed off again, because she doesn't notice Marcus standing over her until she feels his shadow cool her face. She opens her eyes and squints at his outline, black against the sun. His dark hair is plastered to his forehead with sweat.

'You're early.' She raises herself up to meet his kiss.

'The staff meeting this afternoon was cancelled. Too hot. They need to get air conditioning in that building, the tight-arses. Train could have done with it too; it was like a sauna all the way down from Victoria.' He kicks off his shoes, peels his shirt over his head and chucks it at Erika's feet.

She takes it and drapes it over her face to block out the sun. It smells, not unpleasantly, of his sweat.

'Come in with me. Just knee-deep.' He takes her hand.

She pulls it back. 'No.'

'It's shallow. Nothing's going to happen. You'll just cool down.'

'I said no.' She pulls his shirt off her face and squints at him against the sun. She hugs her knees to her chest. 'I can't.'

He doesn't ask why. Just smooths his fingers through her hair and down to her shoulder where a koi carp of red and gold ripples across her skin. 'Whatever, babe. I'm going in.'

Erika watches him pick his way across the shingle down to the water. He greets Sarah with a kiss, salutes the swimming chefs and exchanges a high five with Luca. Arms stretched out, he strides into the sea, bounding over the waves towards the others. He makes it look easy.

Like Erika, Marcus has never known what a conventional relationship looks like. He was twelve when his mother died. He was raised by his grandmother while his father worked for months at a time on the oil rigs. His grandmother had nurtured and loved him, believed in him. Maybe it's because of this unwavering love that, despite his unconventional childhood, Marcus has remained secure in himself. He and Erika differ in this way. Whatever storms cast Erika adrift, Marcus is her anchor – at least, for now.

There are so many day-trippers in Brighton today. She can hear them screaming as the rollercoaster thunders and rattles at the end of the pier.

Marcus is heading back out of the waves towards her. She stands up for a hug. The chill of his wet body cuts through the heat of her skin and makes her suck in air, her arms pocking up with goose bumps. She closes her eyes, feeling seawater drip off his chin onto her head. She holds onto him, feeling him breathing.

'Kei's coming.' She keeps her eyes closed.

'What?'

Her ears are squashed against his arms so his voice is muffled. 'She's booked her flights. I said she could stay with me. It's done.'

He leans back to look at her and the sound of waves on pebbles, the screaming, the rattling and the Wurlitzer on the pier all flood back with a roar.

'When's she coming?'

'End of August.' She draws away, flicking pebbles with her toes.

'Shit. What are you going to do?'

'Do about what?'

'You know, about the … thing.'

'There's not much I can do about it now.' She drops back into her deckchair. 'Even if I knew what to do.'

'Why did you say she could stay?'

'I didn't have a choice.'

'Of course you have a choice.'

Erika huffed, exasperated. 'You don't understand.'

'All I see is you getting really stressed.'

She tuts, pulls a book out of her bag and pretends to read.

'You could've said you were going to be away or something.'

She slaps the book down. 'Can we stop talking about this?'

He grabs a towel and scrubs at his hair. 'Suit yourself. Don't say I didn't warn you.'

When the rest of the group returns from the water Sarah spreads a picnic blanket over the pebbles along with a mismatched assortment of cutlery, plates and plastic containers. The chefs are cracking open beers. Luca sits on his li-lo, eating a Marmite sandwich. Sarah grabs two frosty bottles of beer from the icebox and sits back down in the chair beside Erika.

'Feeling better?' Sarah asks, offering Erika a bottle.

Erika nods, smiling, and pops the top. She takes a swig and sighs. Always the best, that first icy gulp; the rest is never quite as good. She pulls a cooler bag from under her chair and unpacks a tall steel flask filled with hōji tea, cups, a bag of nori-speckled rice crackers, an orange Tupperware container filled with seaweed-and-cucumber salad flecked with sesame seeds, a jar of bright-yellow takuan pickles, plates, and a cream-coloured plastic wicker box, its lid held in place by a rubber band. She opens it to reveal a neat row of black-and-white onigiri rice balls. She feels a twist of pain somewhere below her breastbone at the sight of them and replaces the lid. She cradles the box in her lap until Marcus takes it from her with a strange look.

He opens it and helps himself to an onigiri. 'What's up? You okay?'

She nods, wishing she could pull herself together. Luca hops about, examines his mother's picnic basket – 'Ooh, cheese strings!' – and skips over to Frankie. 'Urgh, what's that?'

'That, my little friend, is what's left of last night's Indian takeaway.' Frankie shovels a forkful into his mouth. Marcus loads his plate with another onigiri, salad and pickles. Erika pours hōji tea for them both and passes round the rice crackers.

'Is that all you brought, Erika? Nip food?' says Frankie.

'I don't like that word, Frankie.'

'Tasty,' says Marcus, his mouth full of rice.

'Aren't they those rice ball things they sell at the Japan Centre?' Frankie grabs one and takes a bite. He nods appreciatively. 'Not bad.' At the next mouthful he screws up his face. 'Christ! What the fuck is that inside?'

'Frankie! Mind your mouth,' says Sarah, gesturing with her head at Luca.

'Umeboshi. Salted plum. Delicious. Good for you too,' says Erika.

'Urgh. So's an enema.' He throws the half-eaten onigiri into his empty curry carton.

'Hey!' The tone in Erika's voice makes everyone look up.

'What?' says Frankie.

'You can't just throw that away!'

'But I don't want it.'

'It's rice. You can't just throw it away like that.' Erika's throat tightens.

'Well, you eat it then.'

'It's covered in disgusting rancid curry and your fucking spit. What kind of chef are you? Oh my god, you don't know anything!' She gets up.

'Jeez, Erika, it's just a goddamn rice ball. Lighten up.'

'Fuck you, Frank.' She's beyond caring what Luca hears.

She pushes herself out of her deckchair and stalks down the beach towards the water. At the waterline she sits down, her back to the others. The pebbles hurt her backside. She picks up a round white stone, stroking its smoothness before making a fist around it. The force of her rage shocks her. She rests her forehead on her arms. Out of the corner of her eye, she sees the tail of the koi carp on her shoulder. She shrugs, once, twice, making it twist and turn in the sun as if it were trying to swim free of her. She lets the sea foam tickle her toes. In one swift movement, she flicks salt water on her face, just in case tears come. No one sees her do it.

Michiko

Michiko had just been shy of her fourth birthday the night she saw the blazing chrysanthemum in the sky. The colossal bloom of flames had crowned the city, its petals of orange, red and gold unfurling and beating against the darkness. The dreadful brilliance of that all-consuming flower transformed night into day, and this vision, its smell, its roar, struck Michiko with such intensity that she could replay the exact scene in her mind for the rest of her life.

She bounced against her mother's back as the family fled towards the Imperial Palace moat, towards safety. As they ran, houses collapsed with snapping, creaking groans, opening up new and previously unseen vistas along their street. Michiko peered over her mother's shoulder. She wailed and buried her face again, but it was too late to unsee the horror now seared under her lids. Her heart drummed in her ears. Incendiaries flashed white through black sky, their shrieks punctuated by the juddering drone of silver-winged B-29s. A direct hit on a fire cart spewed searing globs, and the dull crump of the explosion travelled through the packed earth of the street, her mother's body and into Michiko's. The cart driver fell to the ground, his body alight, making sounds she'd heard no human make before. His horses bolted into the crowd, still tethered to the flaming cart, trampling bodies. The neighbourhood fire buckets stood steaming, filled in readiness, untouched. People stumbled over burning joists, choking and blinded, the fallen crushed by those fleeing behind. Michiko whimpered and the sound in her head blocked the screams of those who burned. She pushed hard against her mother's shoulder, rubbing her nose raw. Through the lilac of her mother's kimono, she breathed the muddy, black smell of burning houses, carts, clothes, mingling with the sweet indecency of singed hair and flesh.

At the crunch of gravel under her mother's wooden geta, Michiko opened her eyes and saw they were crossing the bridge over the Imperial Palace moat. The water sparked and glowed as if it were trying to swallow the fire and put it out. Beside the palace walls, they were jostled by the gathering crowd and she pressed one ear into the certainty of her mother's back, screwing her eyes shut.

At last, they stood still. With her right ear tuned to the outer world, she heard the dull roar of the inferno, the howling of the incendiaries, the low thrum of the silver bombers. A baby bleated a lament. With her left ear, she listened to her mother's internal world – the lungs drawing rasping breaths, the heart hammering a gallop – and as the wave of her mother's fear coursed into her, all reassurance, all safety, swept away. She gripped her fingers tight beneath her mother's throat until she felt the prick of pins and needles. The muscles in her mother's back moved, and the wisps of hair at her neck brushed Michiko's temple. Her mother was looking up. Michiko looked up too, and saw the vast burning flower, a giant sun god triumphant over the night, its dreadful roar filling her with terror and awe.

Her mother was weeping, rocking Michiko with her sobs. Closing her eyes against the lullaby of her mother's tears, she surrendered to oblivion. Exhausted, she slept.

Like Morse code, the sun's rays flashed on and off, on and off the surface of the water between green paddy rows as their train trundled along on its way back to Tokyo. 'That's rice,' her mother Chiyo said, and Michiko wondered how those delicate green grass-like shoots could turn into the bliss of a bowlful of steaming white rice. Michiko curled against her mother's body. As the train swayed them in unison, her head knocked against her mother's ribs. Gazing up at her profile, she still thought her lovely, even though her now hollow cheeks made her look too old, too weary.

They had not brought any rice back with them; all her mother had been able to trade for their bags of hōji tea were the same old tough, wrinkled sweet potatoes they'd been eating for weeks now. There was no more barley, and they hadn't been able to buy rice for months. If you knew where to look you could get hold of green vegetables, but they were always too expensive. There was no fish anymore.

Nobody knew how long this war would last. Michiko's mother searched for whatever she could to keep her family alive during this endless lack. The stock of tea from their shop was running low. Michiko and her siblings knew nothing of their mother's fears. They didn't know they might soon be reduced to eating grass, worms, and dumplings made with sawdust, as some of their neighbours had started to do.

'On the island where I grew up,' her mother would say, 'we grew our own food and caught fish to eat. We wouldn't starve if we were there.' And her eyes would grow unfocused, gazing at an inwards horizon. Michiko didn't ask questions because she knew her mother wouldn't talk about Okinawa when her father was near. She waited instead for the rare moments when her mother offered up her stories to Michiko and her siblings, like delicious treats. She knew Chiyo had been sent from Okinawa by a matchmaker, travelling over a thousand miles to marry Michiko's father in Tokyo. Her pale skin, her flawless beauty and her surprisingly generous dowry helped his family overcome their prejudices. 'She can pass as Yamato,' they had said. 'Nobody need know where she's really from.'

Michiko liked playing games inspired by their mother's Okinawan stories with Kensuke and Fusae, her older brother and sister. Their favourite was the creation story. Fusae played the goddess Amamikyū. She'd summon up the very first island, where their mother was born, with an imperious wave of her arm, then – *Pop! Pop! Pop!* – she'd create all the other islands, which were furoshiki wrapping cloths laid out across the tatami floor. Leaping onto the biggest one, she'd yell, 'Behold your goddess!' and make a swooshing sound to conjure up the first man, the king. This role was always played by Kensuke, though he also liked being the fierce sea-dragon god that ruled over the underwater realms. He'd change roles without warning, which made the game confusing, but Michiko didn't mind. She'd sit in the cupboard, wriggling with excitement and waiting for Fusae to call 'And now, the noro!' so she could slide open the door. She'd wait for Fusae to wave her arm again, and then, *Pop!* Amamikyū would create the first woman, a noro shamanic priestess, who would leap out of the cupboard. Being the noro was Michiko's favourite, because she could make anything happen with magic.

But now that only a thin layer of rice remained in the kitchen crock, saved for honoured guests, they'd begun swapping their Okinawa Game for a new one – the Eating Game. They'd haul off the crock's wooden lid and peer in, imagining the rice was to be prepared for them. Then they'd arrange their drawings on the table, images of bowls filled with earthy misoshiru with glossy, slimy nameko mushrooms, cubes of tofu and sweet green cress; of stewed pork and ginger; of spinach and pounded goma-dare sesame sauce. Next to these, they'd lay out pictures of dishes piled high with yellow takuan pickles and sweet egg omelette. These were the simple, familiar things they now craved. They would sit around the table with ochawan rice bowls filled with gravel from their father's garden – 'Careful not to chip your ochawan, now,' warned their mother – and take up their chopsticks. '*Itadakimasu!*' they'd cry, and pretend to tuck into a meal.

The layer of rice in the crock was so sparse they could see through it to the clay bottom. They hadn't eaten rice for a long time. A month ago, an important business associate of their father's had come to visit. The children had stared as their mother scooped a meagre cupful out of the crock and washed it carefully so as not to lose a single grain before steaming it in the smallest pot she had. They'd clustered around, inhaling the fragrant steam, getting in her way until she shooed them upstairs, where they made do with their imaginations, playing their Eating Game.

'Fusae, would you like a piece of my salmon?'

'Oh, yes please, that would be wonderful. Would you like some more pork cutlet, Kensuke?'

'Why no, I couldn't. I'm quite full, thank you.'

Their play was always shadowed with pain. Their stomachs were distended, tight as drums and tender to touch. It seemed odd that they should be so empty and yet look so full and round.

They'd grown so desperate with hunger that Kensuke had cried out down the stairs, 'Mother, if he leaves anything, can I have it?'

The guest had left his rice bowl and his pickles untouched, and though Kensuke's request had earned him a beating from their father, it was worth it for his morsels of rice. They had shared it, the five of them. At the end, one small portion had remained in the bowl. Michiko had reached for it with her chopsticks. In a heartbeat, her father had whipped a metal skewer from the hibachi full of white-hot charcoal and seared her fingers with it.

'This is for Kensuke,' her father had said, as Michiko howled. 'He's a boy. Stop your noise, Michiko, or you will be punished again.'

She'd cried silent, fat tears, the burn on her hand rising in an angry welt. The girls had watched their brother gulp down the rice, tears trembling at the edges of his eyes from the beating and from the pleasure of the rice.

After months of eating the same watery sweet potato gruel, Michiko's stomach struggled with the solidity of the rice. Soy sauce had once flavoured the watery mess of sweet potato, but now this had run out too. She was so tired of eating tasteless gruel that, despite the eternal gnawing of her hunger, she sometimes gagged as she ate.

Even so, as they swayed along in the train, Michiko looked at the furoshiki bundle misshapen with gnarled sweet potatoes in her mother's lap and longed for her day's meal when they got home. It was the only way to lessen the grinding ache inside. She imagined that one day her stomach and her back would end up sticking together, despite the bulge of her belly. Her mother had taken in her baggy monpe trousers so many times she'd given up, and they'd been held up with a belt of red string. Now her belly was so swollen, Michiko didn't need the belt any more.

There was shouting in the next carriage. Chiyo's body tensed against hers. Women got up, began wrenching open windows.

'The military police are on the train!' someone cried.

As they chugged past verdant hills and gleaming rice paddies, the women threw out their bundles. They rolled down the railway embankment, furoshiki popping open, sweet potatoes and cabbages rolling into muddy ditches, and then her mother was standing too, pulling at the window.

'Michiko! Pass me the bundle, quickly!'

She pushed it against the gap in the window, but it wouldn't fit, and it was too high for Michiko to reach. Her mother sat back down, breathing hard, and with shaking hands undid the furoshiki. Michiko passed the potatoes, one by one, to her mother, who hurled them out of the window.

They had barely emptied the furoshiki before three policemen burst through the door at the end of the carriage, herding a group of cowering women. One of the policemen bellowed, hands on hips, 'Black market trading is an imprisonable offence! It is an act of disloyalty to the Emperor. Let these traitors be an example to you!'

He shoved hard at the back of the grey-haired woman in front of him. Frail and gaunt, she crumpled onto her knees like a winter kimono slipping off its wooden rack.

'Get up!' he shouted, pushing at her so that each time she tried to rise up, she toppled over again. He yanked her off the floor by the neck of her overcoat, her geta clattering off her feet, and she began to cry. The policemen drove the women towards the front carriage. At the next station, they were taken off the train.

'Where are they taking them?' Michiko whispered to her mother.

'I don't know, Michiko. Nobody knows.' Her mother's dry eyes looked dead ahead, her mouth set tight. Only her fingers moved, curling and uncurling around the empty furoshiki cloth in her lap, tying and untying the corners.

That night they ate a broth of water boiled with a square of kombu seaweed her mother had already used for other pots of broth; in each bowl floated a single dumpling, made from sawdust, water and a little flour from a can of military supplies they'd traded on the black market. Michiko was so ravenous she nearly choked as she swallowed hers whole. Her mother had barely cleared the table before Michiko had run outside and vomited it up in the garden, earning a slap from her father for messing up his treasured flowerbeds. She used his trowel to bury the mess, her knees sinking into the dirt. She wondered if she should collect some of the burrowing earthworms to eat. Her mother was helping Fusae and Kensuke get ready for their bath. Her father was in his study. She watched a worm squirm and writhe and decided she couldn't bring herself to swallow it. She was not that desperate, yet.

With no one else in the garden, she crouched forward, lowering her forehead onto the earth, allowing its coolness to seep into the feverish red spots on her cheeks. The dirt muffled her sobs. She watered the garden with her tears and the soil stuck to her face, mingling with long strings of yellow snot. The immaculately pruned camellia branches scratched at her hair. The loamy smell of the earth between the smooth stones nourished and soothed her. It smelled good enough to eat. She pushed her lips into it and she licked what clung there. It was gritty, but she thought it tasted, somehow, of strength. Her father wouldn't let her mother grow vegetables or potatoes in this earth. She'd asked her mother why, and she had given Michiko a strange, sad smile and said Father wasn't prepared to rip out his camellias. They'd been growing there for generations, she'd said, tended by his father's father and his grandfather's father before that, and the camellias were their family heritage. The garden was full of poetry, her father had insisted, full of poetry and beauty. Poetry was eternal, while all living things were ephemeral. If he ripped the beauty out, what would be left?

A Casket

It is a box covered in pale golden brocade. The cover is topped with a cream curlicue knot, which holds its folded upper corners in place. It adorns a tab which, when pulled upwards, reveals the box of white Japanese pine beneath. The wood exudes a special scent, like incense. The box is not the treasure, however, for when its lid is removed there is an urn of polished black granite nestled inside, smoothly shaped with rounded edges and carved with kanji characters: a name, a date. Its weight, for something so small, lends it gravity. But the urn is not the treasure either, for the treasure lies within. The urn's lid is held closed, simply, with sticky tape.

Erika

The escalator deposits Erika in the arrivals hall of Heathrow's Terminal Two. She frowns at the board, checking to see if the flight from Tokyo has landed. Being late to greet Kei is not an option. It hasn't landed yet, thank god. Erika left home early but there've been delays; at Earl's Court the Piccadilly line platform was crammed with people. Earlier that morning someone had thrown themselves under a train. She blocked her mind from going where it usually tried to go whenever she heard the person-under-a-train announcement, and bought a magazine from the kiosk to distract herself for the rest of the journey to Heathrow.

It had been a hot, airless night and she'd barely slept. She'd fidgeted and sighed, kicking at the sheets, seeking relief in whatever cool spot she could find. Sometimes she'd dozed off to be ensnared in brief, claustrophobic dreams: Kei disembarking from her flight, smiling in anticipation as she passed through immigration and customs, the arrivals-hall doors sliding open for her as she stopped to scan the waiting crowds. Erika craning over the railings, so close she could almost touch her cousin. Erika shouting 'Kei!' over and over, waving, but her cousin looking straight through her, not seeing her. Erika watching Kei's face darken with disappointment. She woke herself up shouting, drenched in sweat. Too agitated to stay in bed, she'd got up to watch TV. Once she'd gone back to her room she'd slept, though fitfully, and woken again just before dawn. She watched the light creep between the curtains, bleaching the shadows from her room. She'd lain awake in bed, wired and exhausted, until her alarm went off.

Erika looks up at the board, sees the flight has landed, and the knot in her belly tightens. She needs to sit down and she needs a coffee. Kei will take at least forty-five minutes to pass through immigration, pick up her baggage and clear customs. Erika's mobile buzzes; she flips it open. A text from Marcus. *Hope today goes OK. Call me later x.*

She'd asked him to stay at his own place last night. She needed the solitude to calm herself, but now she wishes she'd asked him to stay over after all, even though she'd probably have kept him awake with her tossing and turning. He'd be in the staff room now, on his break. She heads for a coffee shop and calls him.

'Is she with you?' he asks.

'Not yet. I'm just getting a coffee.'

'You okay?'

She heaves a sigh. 'I wish I'd told her not to come after all.'

'I won't say I told you so.'

'You just did.' Erika reaches the counter. 'Black coffee please, triple shot,' she says to the barista. She points at her phone and mouths *sorry*.

'I'm sorry to be negative. I've been in a state since it sunk in she was really coming. There's that whole business with …' She trails off.

'Did you hide it?' he asks.

'I can't.'

'You realise you're making things difficult for yourself?'

She doesn't know what to say.

'Erika?'

'Forget I said anything. No point talking about it now.' She picks up her coffee, finds a spot at a table and takes a gulp, burning her tongue.

Now it's her turn to wait for him to speak, but he says nothing. She feels him pulling at her across empty space.

'I can't just stuff my mother in a cupboard, can I?' she says. The rhetorical adjunct floats in the silence. She forces a sharp, dry laugh.

'Well,' Marcus says at last, 'you'll just have to deal with it then.'

After Marcus hangs up Erika remains sitting near the window, watching Lilliputian airport ground staff swarm around jumbo jets. She hasn't flown for a while. The last time was to Japan twelve years ago. Her mind bounces off memories like a pebble bouncing off a frozen lake. She returns to the counter to order an apple danish, though she isn't hungry, and another coffee.

She isn't ready for this day. She was able to prepare the house for Kei's arrival, but she hasn't got a clue how to prepare herself. Erika has read her cousin's email over and over again to the point of paralysis. The thought of writing back in Japanese made her sick with anxiety, and she didn't trust herself on the phone. In the end, Erika had no choice but to write back that, of course, Kei could stay with her; that she'd take a few days off work so she could spend time with her.

She felt herself split into two halves, one fighting the other. What she wrote was the opposite of what she wanted, but another self had gone ahead with the invitation anyway. Kei had booked her flight, and that had been that.

Even then, Erika couldn't deal with the email's most difficult question; thank god Kei didn't ask again.

Kei should be in the arrivals-hall soon. Erika takes a final swig of her coffee and slops it down her chin and onto the white shirt she'd ironed so carefully the night before. *Shit.* She dabs at the dark stain with a napkin. *Shit!*

She follows signs to the toilets where she soaks paper towels under the tap and works the dark-brown coffee stain into beige. Now the whole front of her shirt is wet. Great. When she looks in the mirror, her bra is visible through the wet fabric. Worse still, the carp tattoo on her shoulder shows too. The knot in her belly twists tighter. 'Tattoos are for Yakuza whores!' Michiko had raged when, at seventeen, Erika had taken off her shirt to show her, knowing she'd get a kick out of her mother's reaction. She stoops under the hand dryer for as long as she can, plucking at the front of her shirt, waiting for opacity to return. Time is running out.

Back in the arrivals-hall, Erika panics at the sight of well-dressed Japanese travellers milling around. Tour guides hold travel-agency flags aloft. They bow and smile, calling out in high-pitched voices. Erika searches through the crowds and there, looking blank, with her suitcase at her feet, is her cousin. The stone in Erika's stomach turns into a boulder. Kei hasn't seen her yet.

Erika grips the strap of her bag with her hand to hide her tattooed shoulder and rearranges the dismay she knows is written on her face into a broad smile. She calls out. 'Kei!'

Kei wheels around and sees her. She smiles with her mouth, but her dark eyes flicker to the stain on Erika's shirt.

Erika's impulse to hug Kei falters and dies. It doesn't matter. A hug isn't expected now they're adults. She remembers their childhood reunions whenever she and Michiko went back to Tokyo – how Erika and Kei used to fall on each other in a half-wrestle, half-embrace, giggling with joy – and she feels a twist of sorrow.

'I'm so sorry,' Erika says. 'I was here waiting for you but I spilled my coffee and had to go clean myself up. I really, truly am sorry, I wanted to be here when you walked through the doors. I'm so happy to see you!' The Japanese words feel lumpen in Erika's mouth. She's gabbling.

'Well, I'm glad to see you too,' says Kei. 'It was such a long flight and there were huge queues at immigration. Then my suitcase was one of the last to come out on the carousel and I had to stand there for so long. I'm exhausted.'

The sight of Kei, immaculate even after her long journey, hits Erika with the stark reality of the next fortnight. How the hell is she going to get through this? The faux-pas of not being there to greet her cousin as she came through the arrivals-hall doors, of turning up with a stained shirt and a barely concealed tattoo, are nothing, nothing compared to the moment that's coming, when Kei will walk into Erika's flat and see the corner with the antique Korean cabinet, the corner that not even the ill-anticipated visit could induce Erika to touch. When they get home, Kei will no longer need to ask the whereabouts of her aunt's grave. She will see the answer right there, on top of the cabinet, under its thick blanket of dust. The black granite urn in its box of Japanese pine, covered with silk brocade. It holds fragments of Erika's mother's cremated bones, still uninterred after twelve years.

Michiko

To Michiko, this was the natural order of the world: heart-pumping dashes triggered by wailing sirens; the scarcity of food, of everything; rousing military songs of empty bravado; the frantic waving of Hinomaru flags to send young men off to war, boys only just out of school uniform. Every day, women grieved over news of a son's, a father's, a husband's, a brother's death; over the loss of children, friends and homes to bombs and tracer bullets fired from the sky. The hoods stitched from old futon quilts normally used for protection against earthquakes were now used – with preposterous hope – for protection from the never-ending bombing raids. Michiko's friend Maki-chan was killed with her brothers and sisters when a bomb fell on their house. No padded hood could ever have saved her.

Life had always been harsh and grey; adults had never smiled; everyone had always been afraid and hungry. Sometimes when she was playing, Michiko might forget about the world for a moment. But then the gnawing in her stomach or the fatigue would stop her from skipping or climbing and wrench her back to the dreadful heaviness.

Kensuke, born eight years before Michiko, told her it hadn't always been this way. He insisted there'd been a time when there was plenty to eat, when their mother used to throw back her head and laugh. On a summer's night, during the Obon festival, they'd danced with everyone from the neighbourhood under the glow of a hundred paper lanterns, stepping in time as they circled around the enormous taiko drum, the singer's quavering voice intertwining with melodies plucked by shamisen players. This was how they'd honoured the spirits of the ancestors who had returned to visit the living.

'If father wasn't nearby, mother would dance the Okinawan Kachāshi,' Kensuke told her. 'I wish you could have seen her. She stepped in time to the taiko drums and waved her arms in the air. Her hands looked graceful, like the tentacles of a sea anemone. Here, like this,' he said, and he lifted Michiko's arms and swayed them from side to side, showing her how to take the dainty steps forward, head tilted: toe, step, toe, step. 'It made Mother so happy. Sometimes, if she really got carried away, she'd whistle, or call out, like this: *Haaa-iya-sassa!*' Michiko echoed her older brother's high-pitched cry, and together they stepped across the tatami, waving their arms and hollering until their father thundered up at them from downstairs to be quiet.

Michiko asked her brother to tell stories about the old days again and again, as if hearing them released her from the relentless darkness of her world. She'd listen, lying with eyes closed as he sat cross-legged beside her, imagining herself in the scenes he conjured up. Fusae would join them, sometimes; though she'd been born before the war, she'd been too little to remember much of those days. Kensuke told of the kamishibai man who came each month on his bicycle with thrilling adventures about oni ogres, brave boys born from peaches and egg-sized princesses discovered in hollow trunks of bamboo. They'd listened, rapt, as he narrated along to colourful storyboards he slid in and out of the wooden frame strapped to the back of his bicycle.

The dagashiya was full of tempting treats, said Kensuke. For a few sen you could win a favour in a lucky dip: maybe a goldfish made of hollow tin you could float in a bucket of water, or a whistle that tweeted like a bird when you spun it on a string. The bustling neighbourhood rang with cries from street sellers, and the joyful din of brash charumera horns, bells and drums of chindonya wandering musicians in multi-coloured costumes.

Kensuke told how, the year before Fusae was born, he had travelled with their mother a long way south, on a ship, to Okinawa, the place she told them secret stories about. He'd swum with his cousins in a clear, bright-blue sea, their grandmother and aunts sitting with a picnic on white sand. He said it was a place of mysterious magic, an island where warm breezes blew through palm trees; an island lush with multi-coloured flowers, dotted with sacred groves and ancient rocks and trees. The sea was full of fish, he said, and its fields abundant with tasty vegetables. 'The island people live until they're a hundred years old,' he said. Michiko thought it sounded like one of those folk tales the old ones liked to tell. She couldn't believe that there had once been a life unburdened by panic and fear, sorrow and hunger.

She saw things a young child should never have to see: eviscerated dogs, their guts spilling into the road; soldiers missing both legs and covered in sores, crying and begging in the streets; women demented with grief, howling and ripping at their hair. Twisting into demons and ogres, these visions haunted her at night and she would wake up screaming. Her mother would crouch beside her. If Michiko didn't quieten soon enough, if she woke her father, he would bellow – '*Yakamashī!*' *Shut up!* – frightening her into louder sobs. Her mother would beg in a whisper, 'Please, Michi, stop crying, or you'll make your father very angry,' and when Michiko couldn't, he would rise from his futon with swift steps and loom over her, tall and dark. With the full length and strength of his arm he would strike her face until she fell silent.

They were not in the house when the bomb fell. The house appeared intact from the front, but the rear half was destroyed, roof tiles and splintered wood spilling into one end of the garden. Her mother had buried earthenware jars containing family documents, heirlooms and valuables in a corner of the garden for safekeeping, so they took only the things they needed and went to live with a nearby family. The Hasetanis' sons were away fighting in the war. Their father sat stooped in mute reverie every day, so his wife was glad of the company. She accepted packets of tea from the rapidly diminishing Takigawa shop stocks in lieu of rent. The room they shared was smaller than the old study at home. Michiko could not escape her father.

Sometimes he'd smack her head from behind as he passed, or tap out his pipe on her head, filling the room with the smell of singeing hair. Her mother might murmur something if she was present, but she knew better than to try to stop him. Michiko wished her father would go away to war like her friends' fathers, but Fusae said he'd already fought in another war when he was barely a man, the one in China, and that he'd seen terrible things. He wasn't fit to fight anymore. Traditional Japanese traders like him were encouraged to continue working as best they could. Even if nobody bought much tea these days, even if they had less and less stock to sell, there was still much to organise. Michiko's father planned for the time he knew would come, when Japan won the war. He sat cross-legged at a low table in the little room that was their temporary home, going over his ledgers, and Michiko knew to make herself very small and very quiet.

'You must be good, Michiko,' said Fusae, 'and not make father so angry. He works very hard for us.'

'Mother does too,' said Michiko.

Michiko liked it best when she was in the kitchen with her mother and Hasetani-san. She liked helping her mother cook the gruel by stirring it in the pot over the fire, or watching sweet potato skins blister and turn golden over glowing charcoal in the hibachi, but most of all, she liked to listen to the women's stories. Some of them were funny, like the one about Hasetani-san's youngest son, who got a bean stuck up his nose when he was in primary school because he'd wanted to see if it would grow there, and they had to go to the doctor to get it out. Other stories frightened her, though she couldn't help but listen. The most terrifying ones were about the war. The one about Hasetani-san's son-in-law gave her nightmares. He had come home with only one arm – the other had been blown off in Burma – and it was said that the Americans had found it in the jungle and eaten it. Americans liked to eat human flesh, people said, butchered from men they'd tortured and women they'd ravaged. She imagined American soldiers slashing at women with daggers until their insides burst out, like the dog she had seen on the street. She wondered why they didn't ravage the men too, but was too frightened to ask. The Americans must be monsters, even more dangerous and scary than oni ogres.

Everything felt impermanent and unsettled. Michiko didn't know when they could move back to their old house again. When she asked her mother, Chiyo said they would once it was rebuilt, but there wasn't any point in rebuilding until the war was over, because it might only get bombed again. No, she didn't know when that might be.

'But mightn't a bomb fall on this house too?' asked Michiko. 'And what if we are all inside? Will we die, like Maki-chan?'

But her mother just carried on scrubbing clothes in the wooden washtub.

Michiko was forbidden from going back to their bombed-out house, so she snuck away alone to play there in secret. She played make-believe, imagining she lived there with just her mother, brother and sister: a happy, peaceful life during the idyllic time before the war. She would sit under the smashed beams of the old room overlooking the garden. On the dusty tatami floor she would lay out plates of broken tiles filled with stones and camellia petals. She would pretend-eat this miraculous, endless feast with twigs for chopsticks. As soon as one plate emptied, it was filled again, like the enchanted rice bag the dragon princess gave Hidesato as a reward in the folktale 'Tawara Tōda'. But as dusk fell, she hurried back to the family's tiny room. She would swallow the same small portion of flavourless gruel she had every day, her stomach gnawing with hunger, and wait for something to happen.

One hot and humid day in August, news came of a terrible event in the south west of Japan. A bomb that shone more brightly than a thousand suns had fallen on a busy city. A second fell, three days later, on another. The bombs flattened a thousand buildings with typhoons of scorching wind, melting skin off people's bones. People who had been near the bomb simply evaporated, they said, leaving their shadows imprinted on the pavements and walls where they fell, like ghosts; others who had survived that day were now getting sick and dying slowly, their hair falling out, their skin oozing with sores, their noses bleeding. They said it was the worst atrocity in the history of Japan. There was going to be a radio announcement. Michiko listened to a small reedy voice speaking a language she didn't understand. 'What is he saying?' she asked, and her father roared at her to be quiet. They were gathered around the Hasetanis' tiny wireless with others from the neighbourhood, straining to hear the voice through crackling interference. That was the voice of the Emperor, Kensuke told her afterwards. He didn't understand what he was saying, either.

'Nobody's ever heard the Emperor speak before,' said Kensuke. 'Doesn't his voice sound funny?'

Michiko was surprised. Everyone knew that looking at the Emperor would make you go blind, because he was a god, a descendant of the sun goddess Amaterasu, and staring at the sun makes you blind. Surely hearing his voice should have made them deaf?

Her mother told her that the Emperor had used ancient, courtly words. 'That's why you couldn't understand what he said. It's like another language, not the everyday Japanese that we speak.'

Once the Emperor had finished – 'He rambled a little,' said their mother, 'it wasn't clear what he was trying to say' – the radio announcer explained that Japan had surrendered. Japan had lost the war. Michiko's father sat, silent, at his table in their room. He didn't speak for three days. She knew to keep out of his way.

Her father started repairs on their bombed house, shoring up the smashed rear walls to make it safe. He was determined to re-open the teashop. The carpenter and his son had still not returned from fighting in Singapore, so her father undertook to rebuild the house himself. Michiko asked her mother if her father might let them plant vegetables in the garden now, since most of it had been destroyed when the bomb fell.

'Just let him get the house ready first, Michi, and then we'll see,' she said.

The Emperor's radio speech was still the main topic of discussion a week later, when Michiko's father began to spend entire days repairing their home. He left the Hasetani house at dawn and returned at dusk, dusty and tired. His uncharacteristic three days of passivity had been replaced by fierce determination.

'I won't let the Americans stop me,' he said. 'Those barbarians know nothing about tea. In Japan, people will always want to drink good tea, war or no war. I will not be the one, after all these generations, to break the family tradition.'

Kensuke told Michiko that rebuilding the shop and the house was pointless because the Americans were probably going to kill them all anyway. There was speculation in the neighbourhood about what was to become of them. More men were returning from the war. Many didn't, killed or missing in action. There were those who killed themselves by seppuku after surrender so they would never return to face the shame of defeat. There were whispers too, about some who had returned who were no longer right in their minds. They'd been ordered to do terrible things or be condemned to death, they said, and were driven mad by their acts.

'The rice merchant's son just sits at the table staring into space,' said Hasetani-san. 'He won't eat or talk. His poor mother.'

At last the house was safe enough for the Takigawas to move back in. Despite the rubble in the garden and the still-unusable room overlooking it, their lives resumed a semblance of normality. One evening when her father sat cross-legged on the verandah, Michiko crept up to him, daring to whisper, 'Father, are the Americans going to kill us?'

He half-opened his eyes to look at her and said nothing. She flinched when he moved towards her before slackening in astonishment as he took one of her hands in his own. His fingers felt rough and calloused. She held on to this moment in her mind for a long time.

Later that week, she found her mother crouched in the garden, her apron over her head, crying. This frightened her more than the stories, more than the Americans. Seeing her mother helpless was unbearable.

Michiko wondered if Tokyo After the War would be the same as Tokyo Before the War. Japan would never be the same again, people were saying. They would have to get used to life with the Americans. That is, if they left anybody alive.

A Tea Service

It is a Wedgwood tea service comprising six cups, six saucers, six cake plates, a milk jug, a lidded sugar bowl (a small notch in its edge to accommodate a sugar spoon), a teapot and a cake stand. A cake slice with a matching porcelain handle also belongs to the set. The pattern is a popular and pretty classic of curled green-leaved stems, dusky pink five-petalled flowers and the tiny vibrant-red fruit of wild strawberries from which it takes its name. The cups are simple, shaped in pleasing proportion to their handles and saucers. The plates extend a margin wider than the saucers and are big enough to hold a modest slice of cake. The cake stand rests on a single conical foot, a little stage for whatever cake it displays. Arranged on a tray, the tea set exudes a sense of orderliness, of comfort, of life in an English country cottage.

Erika

The tail end of rush hour is a distraction from the awkwardness of their meeting. At Hammersmith they spill with the crowds from their Piccadilly line train and surge onto the Hammersmith & City line. Kei takes the last empty seat in the carriage, and Erika stands guard with the suitcase at the end of the row of seats, gripping the handrail until her knuckles turn white. Kei stares ahead, blank and disengaged: she's used to protecting her personal space in crowded places. Erika examines her cousin's profile, ready to avert her eyes if Kei turns to look at her.

The shining black hair on either side of Kei's ruler-straight parting has been smoothed into a neat chignon. She must have done it up just before getting off the plane. Her beige Burberry trench coat looks new. A thin gold chain glints somewhere below her collar, where Kei's slender neck disappears into the shadows. Her makeup is flawless, clean-looking – nothing on the eyes, just a slick of pale lipgloss. She looks fresh and energised, as if she's just stepped out of her Tokyo apartment instead of off a thirteen-hour flight.

Kei turns and catches Erika staring. Her face breaks into a blinding smile. Erika flushes, returning a hesitant imitation. And then, as quickly as it came, Kei's smile disappears. She turns away, returning to her look of blank absorption. Only the heat in Erika's cheeks proves she didn't imagine it.

The train rumbles alongside the Westway where towers rise up either side of the flyover, indifferent to traffic jams below. At Ladbroke Grove they shuffle off the train and out into the cacophony of the street. Double-deckers belch dirty fumes as they grind their way up the hill. Erika and Kei squeeze through a tide of schoolkids jostling and shouting at the bus stop; Erika feels the tension in Kei's bowed head and braced shoulders. Boys wear trousers slung dangerously low; girls' ties are knotted loose over open shirts, fake diamonds glittering in noses and ears. A tall girl shrieks in mock outrage, '*Tch!* Fuck *off,* Germaine!' and swings to thump a boy. The girl's book bag smacks hard into Kei, who makes herself small. Erika touches her shoulder. 'Are you okay?'

'Yes. How far is it to your house?'

'Not far.'

They turn into Cambridge Terrace. Parked cars and lampposts stand guard on either side of the street. Uniform rows of grey brick townhouses individualised with different-coloured doors. Window boxes here and there are blowsy with bright geraniums, trailing ivy or ferns, others are coffins holding brittle brown bones that had once bloomed. Grimy pigeons burst away from a squashed, half-eaten burger. The noise of Ladbroke Grove dims behind them and the rumble of suitcase wheels and click of Kei's heels grow louder, echoing off the high brick walls.

'This one, with the red door.' Erika's voice is too loud. They stand at the foot of the concrete steps. It's a dangerous threshold to enforced intimacy, a gate opening onto a minefield.

There's nothing Erika can do now. She heaves Kei's suitcase up the steps, bumping its corners on each one. Kei catches up with her and wrestles it away.

'It's okay, I can manage,' says Erika.

'I'll take it,' says Kei. 'It's brand new. And expensive.' She stoops to rub at the fresh scuffmarks with her fingers.

In silence, they make their way up four flights of stairs. Erika unlocks her apartment door and strides through the sitting room to open windows, letting in the air. Sunlight glints off the wooden floor.

Kei puts down her suitcase. 'This is nice,' she says, looking around. 'You have so much space. Aren't you lucky.'

'Here, come this way to your room. Let me take your case. I promise I'll be careful.' She ushers her cousin away from the sitting room with its dusty alcove and down the corridor to the bedroom she's taken great pains to prepare. 'There's space for your things in the wardrobe and drawers. The bathroom's the next door along if you'd like to freshen up. When you're ready we can have some tea.' The Japanese still feels awkward in her mouth. It's been a long time since she's spoken it.

Retreating to the kitchen, Erika puts the kettle on and leans her forehead against the cupboard above it. Kei hasn't seen the alcove yet but it won't be long before she does. Erika feels oddly calm, probably because it's too late to do anything about it. The tsunami is here. She may as well let herself surrender and be drowned.

Erika hears Kei come out of the bathroom. She picks up the tea tray she prepared before she left the house that morning. She'd found the act of arranging her mother's pretty pink-and-green Wedgwood tea set on it reassuring. The cups, saucers and plates, the teapot, sugar pot and milk jug, the cake stand and its cake slice – all matching – had exuded a solid reality that kept her anchored. And yet, looking at them now, these familiar objects suddenly feel strange and out of place, as if she's seeing them for the first time. There's a cloying scent in the air. Kei must be wearing Yves Saint Laurent's Opium – a lot of it. Odd that she didn't notice it before, especially since she knows the fragrance well. As she stares at the tea set, the wild strawberries tick across the porcelain as if they're searching for their lost leaves, like blind insects. She blinks, uncertain of what she's seeing. She feels unmoored.

Erika begins the ritual of preparing English tea, anchoring herself. She pours boiling water into the teapot, swirling it, holding it in her palm until it is hot. She empties it and dries it with a clean tea towel. One scoop of lapsang souchong, two of Darjeeling. The leaves warm against the porcelain, releasing their smoky perfume. She boils the water again and pours it over the tea, closes the lid and slips her mother's pink patchwork tea cosy over the pot. She pours milk into the jug and a token centimetre of sugar into the sugar pot.

Erika has baked a cake. Fresh English strawberries and whipped Jersey double cream are sandwiched in a sponge punctuated with tiny black full-stops of vanilla. She lifts it out of its Tupperware container, lays it on the cake stand and surprises herself by smiling. It looks good. 'Tea's ready!' she calls, and carries the tray through to the sitting room.

Kei has brought gifts. Bags of fine sencha and everyday hōjicha from the family tea shop. A box of mizuyōkan red bean paste jellies, Erika's favourite summer treat. Handmade writing paper from her aunt. Five rustic Hokkaido-style hand-thrown dipping dishes in blue and white from Michiko's old friend Sayuri Obachan. There are practical gifts, things not available in England: woven gauze dishcloths, a herbal remedy for indigestion, a high-tech duster. Erika lingers over each thing as she unwraps it, distracting Kei from the alcove as long as she can. Between each unwrapping, she asks questions: about Fusae Obachan and her ikebana class; about Kensuke Ojisan, Kei's father; about Hiroshi, Kei's older brother, his wife Akemi and his two kids. How's the teashop? Is business good? How's the neighbourhood? How's Kanagawa-san?

Kei gives short answers. She cuts the cake with her fork into tiny morsels, lifting them into her small mouth one by one; she takes delicate sips from her cup.

Erika's running out of questions. She wants it all to be over, but dreads the moment. She doesn't know how to get there. It feels like pulling a tooth.

'How is Jun-san? Doesn't he mind you coming here without him?' she asks.

Kei picks up her cup with a clatter and peers over its rim at her cousin. When she puts the cup down she's still looking at Erika, silent. She and Jun have no children yet, and Erika knows she wants a family;

perhaps Kei doesn't want to be reminded of that. It's obvious it's not a topic to be pursued.

'More tea?' Erika casts about for something else to discuss. She picks up her cup and gulps. Ah yes, Mrs Mackenzie. She brightens. 'I'll introduce you to Mrs Mackenzie upstairs on Monday. She's been looking forward to meeting you.'

Kei nods, still saying nothing.

Silence settles around them.

Kei puts her cup down, dabs her lips with a folded napkin. She reaches into the bag Erika had thought was empty and pulls out another package. 'This is the last one,' Kei says. 'It's a special gift from me. I got one for myself too.' She hands Erika a parcel the size of a large matchbox, carefully wrapped in paper branded with the logo of a well-known Buddhist-ware shop in downtown Tokyo. Erika swallows. She peels away the tape and takes off the paper, putting the box on her lap so she can fold the paper into neat squares. She takes her time. The weight of the box is surprising, given its size. When she lifts the lid, it reveals something hard wrapped in fine tissue.

'I wonder what it is?,' she says, to relieve the silence. She lifts the object out, feeling its cold solidity through the paper.

'Careful,' says Kei. 'Don't drop it.'

Erika rolls the tissue's contents into her hand. Its coldness becomes warmth as she holds it. It's a transparent cylinder of polished quartz crystal with a bulb at one end. A body and a head. It's marked with a few curved lines for eyes, brows and mouth, and she sees that it's a little jizō, a bodhisattva. It wears a sweet, beatific expression, eyes closed in meditation. It's beautiful in its simplicity. Her stomach clenches. She shouldn't have eaten that cake so quickly.

'It's gorgeous. Thank you, Kei.'

'I thought your mother's altar might be a good place for it.'

Erika stares at the jizō in her hand and feels her face flush. This is it. Here it comes, the tsunami.

'I'll put it there myself if you like,' says Kei, 'since I should pay my respects. To tell her I'm here. May I offer incense?'

Erika runs her fingers over the object in her hand. So smooth and hard. Cold, now warm.

'Eri?'

'Yes?'

'Where is it?'

'Just there, round the corner.' Erika points. 'In that alcove, on the antique cabinet. There are probably some matches in the little drawer underneath. Feel free. I'll clear the tea things.' She jumps up and begins to stack plates and cups. A teaspoon slides off a saucer and falls, chipping a cup. 'Shit.'

She carries the tray through to the kitchen and pushes it onto the counter with a clatter. She fills the sink with hot water, letting the suds bubble up. She washes the forks and spoons. She rinses them. She tries to calm her breathing. She catches a drift of incense. She washes the plates and saucers. The cups. She examines the chip she made and droplets of water run off it like tears. The strawberries have stopped ticking across the porcelain, as if they've given up searching. She imagines the tea service crying. Her mother owned it for decades. There'd not been a single crack or chip until now.

She senses Kei standing behind her. She washes the milk jug. Rinses it. She doesn't turn around.

'I offered incense,' her cousin says.

'Good. Thanks.' Erika empties the sugar back into its paper bag, puts it away in the cupboard. Puts the sugar pot into the sink. Washes it. Rinses it. There will be the remnants of the cake to deal with next. After that, there will be nothing left to wash up. She'll have to stop, and then she'll have to turn around.

'Eri.'

Erika pulls the plug and watches the water swirl away. She wipes the sink down with the dishcloth, wringing it out so hard she hurts her fingers.

'Erika.'

She turns around, pretending not to notice Kei's expression. 'I bought fresh mackerel at the market yesterday. I've salt-cured it. It'll be delicious grilled with field mushrooms. We'll have that for dinner with some baby spinach. Would you like some rice with it?'

'Erika.' Kei crosses her arms and frowns. 'This is not good.'

Erika can't think of anything to say. She stands and stares, waiting to drown.

'Twelve years, Eri. This isn't good at all. Why is it still on the altar?'

Erika looks at her feet, feeling like a child.

'Erika.' Kei's voice is sharp, demanding. 'It's completely covered in dust. What's wrong with you?'

Michiko

'They're here! They're here! The Americans are here!'

Terror had turned to excitement as the news spread quickly through the streets: the soldiers were not the monsters described in the military government propaganda; instead of murdering and torturing, they were handing out candy, cigarettes, and other unimaginable luxuries.

Kensuke, as the eldest, was leader of their little procession as they ran through the streets, holding hands. He tugged hard, yanking Fusae's arm. 'Come on! Hurry up!'

'It's not me, Onī-chan,' Fusae whined to her older brother, 'it's Michi, she's so slow!'

'Why did you bring her with us? She's too little.'

'If we'd left her behind she would have told Mother and she'd have sent someone after us. And then we wouldn't have any chance of getting anything.'

'Well, we won't get anything anyway if we're this slow.' He was cross, and close to tears. He wiped his nose with his sleeve. He scowled, making his sunken cheeks more prominent, his shaven head a skull papered tight with skin.

Fusae kneeled beside her little sister. 'Michi, you know those pictures of chocolate that we play with in our Eating Game? Well, if you run as fast as you can with us now, maybe you'll be able to have real chocolate to eat.'

Michiko's eyes widened. 'Really?'

'Hideo-kun next door got some from an American soldier and he said it's the yummiest thing he's eaten in his life. Wouldn't you like to try some?'

Michiko raised the tea canister lid she held between her bony fingers to her mouth, touching its smooth curve to her lips. It slid on her skin, lubricated with slime from her nose. 'Stop sucking that Michi, it's dirty. Give it to me.' Fusae went to grab it but Michiko growled and gripped it harder, pulling it close to her chest.

'No! It's mine!'

'Come on,' said Kensuke, hopping with impatience. 'Come on! We'll miss them. We won't get anything if we don't go right now!' He grabbed Fusae's hand and pulled, making her stumble.

'Alright! Wait.' Fusae took hold of Michiko's hand. 'Are you ready to run? Let's have a race! The prize for winning is a chocolate bar!'

Michiko nodded, and they were off again. She lurched along on spindly legs. Each time she fell, they dragged her upright again, grazing her knees. A geta fell off her foot. She cried out but they forged onwards, Michiko limping on one geta as they tried to keep up alongside other children running barefoot through the dirt. Running made Michiko's distended belly hurt.

'I fell down, Onī-chan!' Michiko began to cry. Her knees were bleeding.

Kensuke pulled harder at his sisters. 'Come on! We have to hurry!' His voice cracked with desperation. And he ran on.

Michiko tripped and fell again. Her other geta slipped off her foot as she landed hard on one bony knee. She dropped her tea canister lid and it hit the ground with a metallic ring. She watched as it rolled towards the roadside, bounced off the kerb, spun, and disappeared down a drain.

She howled. Fusae turned back to help but Kensuke jerked her away by the hand. 'Leave her!'

'We can't just leave her! What will Mother say?'

'We'll pick her up on our way back. We can get food for everyone if we carry on but if we keep her with us we'll get nothing. All we'll have is the same old disgusting sawdust dumplings we have every day.' His voice quavered and broke. 'I'm hungry.'

Michiko lay face down in the road, shrieking. Fusae pulled herself free from her brother's grip to help her up. She smoothed her sister's hair and wiped her tears, leaving dirty trails on her cheeks. 'Stop crying, Michi.' She shook her sister's shoulders. 'Stop now. Listen. You want chocolate, don't you?'

Michiko hiccupped and nodded.

'Can you be a big, brave girl?'

She nodded again.

'You wait here for us, and don't go anywhere, all right? We have to leave you here for a while.'

Michiko contemplated this for a moment. Then her mouth opened once again, an upside down U, and she began to wail.

'Stop it!' Fusae said. She shook her sister's shoulders. 'If you want chocolate, you have to stop now and do what you're told. Will you wait here for us?'

'My toy!' howled Michiko. 'My toy!'

'Get her to shut up, Fusae,' said Kensuke. 'She's hurting my ears. What toy?'

'She means her tea canister lid. She dropped it. It must be here somewhere.' Fusae looked around on the ground near them.

'Fusae!' Kensuke was shouting. 'We have to go, now!'

'If we find it for her, she'll be quiet. Just help us!'

Michiko continued to wail, pointing at the drain. Fusae dropped to her hands and knees; she saw a glint of metal through the grating. 'It's down here.' She pulled her sleeve up to her shoulder and tried to push her arm through, but even wasted to skin and bone it was too big to fit through the gaps. 'It's no use. We'll have to leave it, Michi. I can't reach it. We can get you another one.'

The wailing grew louder. 'I don't want another one! I want that one! It's mine!'

'Onī-chan!' Fusae clasped her hands to her head. 'What shall we do?'

In answer, he grabbed Fusae's hand and pulled. And he ran. She held back at first, but gave up resisting and followed her brother. She turned back to look at her scrawny little sister who stood bawling in the middle of the road and called out: 'Be a good girl and stay there. We'll be back soon, with chocolate. Imagine! Chocolate!'

After her brother and sister slipped away into the crowds, Michiko stood in the street and wailed. A woman with kind eyes asked where her mother was, but Michiko didn't answer. There were too many dirty-faced starving orphans abandoned in the city, and the woman patted her head with a sad smile and walked on. Tired from crying, Michiko squatted by the grating, her grazed knees tightening and stinging, and waited for her brother and sister to come back. When they came back they would help retrieve her toy. And she would have chocolate.

She could see the lid down in the shadows. She pushed her hands through the grating but it hurt her arm. Tears welled up. What if they didn't come back? She began to cry again, scrubbing at her eyes with tear-slicked fists.

She sensed a sudden quietening. She looked up. A face was descending towards her, very white, very strange, framed with hair that appeared to have no colour at all. There was a big nose in the middle of it, the biggest she'd ever seen. But the strangest thing about the face was its eyes. They were pale, the colour of the sky in summer. They frightened her; she recoiled: the eyes of a ghost! She covered her face so she didn't have to look into them. But she felt a hand rest on her shoulder, and the touch was gentle. She heard words she didn't understand but the voice that spoke them was soft and comforting. When she found the courage to look again, she saw the strange face smiling. It belonged to a man wearing a neat beige uniform and a peaked cap. He put his khaki bag on the ground and knelt beside her. A crowd gathered. A woman called out: 'Careful, little girl! It's the enemy!'

Michiko was mesmerised by the pale eyes that looked so kindly upon her. He had peculiar tan freckles on his cheeks, which gave him a golden glow. She saw now that his hair was not colourless, but golden too. He was still smiling and his face seemed to her like the spring sun, warming and soothing. He spoke words she didn't understand, and even after the words stopped coming, his mouth continued to move. He was chewing something, but not swallowing. He kept chewing and chewing. What was this magical, everlasting mouthful? the soldier rummaged around in his bag. He pulled out a small rectangle of dark-brown paper with big silver letters on it and shining silver edges. He offered it to her. She took it and felt its weight in her hand. He was saying something. She brought it close to her face and sniffed. It had a warm, delicious, sweet smell. She tore at the wrapping, its contents softened in the heat. 'Chocolate!'

The crowd surged forward. The soldier bolstered himself against the rush and reached again into his bag. Other soldiers – his comrades – were handing out packets of cigarettes, chewing gum, chocolate and stockings. There were wondering gasps. Packets of chocolate were ripped open and wolfed down, leaving sticky smears on cheeks. Women held up seamed stockings to the light; they hadn't seen such fine stockings in years.

The soldier turned back to Michiko, smiling. He was still chewing. She couldn't stop staring at his shining golden face. Without taking her eyes off him, she stuck her tongue out to lick a corner of the chocolate bar. It melted and spread, rich and warm, across her tongue. Oh! If happiness had a taste, surely this was it. She had never tasted anything so sweet, so delicious. He laughed at her wide-eyed, ecstatic expression. She took a nibble. And then she laughed aloud with him, for the joy of it. He watched her as she continued to eat.

Bliss took her somewhere far away. It felt as good as falling asleep wrapped in a soft blanket, cuddled by her mother. She closed her eyes. She took a big bite and her teeth sank through the softening mass with a satisfying *crunk*. The chocolate melted on her tongue, coating her teeth, filling her head with overwhelming pleasure. Tears trickled from her eyes. The tight knot in her chest unravelled and her sobs subsided, leaving only hiccupping remnants. Her mouth was messy with chocolate. She gazed into the face of this smiling man and wondered. What was he eating? He was still chewing. Was there an everlasting chocolate? It was like magic! Who knew what magic this man – who looked like the sun – could perform? He looked so strong, so healthy. Then she remembered.

'My toy!' She pointed at the grating.

The soldier spoke soft words that curved and rolled like the chocolate she was eating. She understood he was asking a question; he raised his eyebrows and wore a quizzical look.

She implored him with her eyes, crouching down to jab urgent fingers at the grate. '*Omocha. Omocha ga okkotchatta no.*'

He looked where she was pointing. He nodded. He understood. He understood everything. He patted her head, smiling. Her father had never smiled at her this way, and she knew this gaijin-san would make everything all right again.

The golden soldier beckoned to an old man with a walking stick. He took the stick from him and began to chew faster. The crowd around them was restless, jostling to see, speculating about what he was doing. 'Be careful!' someone cried, but Michiko was not afraid. When the soldier spat out whatever was in his mouth into his hand, the crowd muttered. Michiko strained to see what it was. He took the stick and did something to the end of it. When he let go, she saw he had stuck a small grey ball on it.

The soldier poked it, end-first, through the grate. He moved slowly and carefully, and Michiko could see how he manoeuvred it with tiny movements towards the glinting metal. When he found his mark, he pushed down, as if spearing a fish. He began pulling the stick out and the lid came with it. Her toy! Michiko held her breath. The golden man drew the stick up – slowly, slowly – and there it was, her tea canister lid, it was nearly out. But then the rim of the lid caught the edge of the dark opening of the sewer. It came away from the stick, falling soundlessly into the depths.

The chocolate in Michiko's mouth had melted away. She felt her face flush hot with tears but she stayed quiet. The man shook his head, his face sorrowful. He understood. The corners of her mouth quivered. She knew, somehow, that she mustn't show him her feelings, that she mustn't cry. She held herself in, very tight and very still, clenching her fists with the effort. A small tear spilled from her eye. The man cocked his head at her with a sad smile, speaking his soft words. Then he reached into his bag again.

He pulled out a photograph and crouched down to show Michiko, pointing at the little girl in it, then pointing to himself. She had pale hair and eyes like his, and her smiling face looked full and healthy. She had a big ribbon in her hair and wore a pretty dress covered with flowers, and she sat at a small table laid out with tiny teacups and plates of cake. In the three other chairs sat two dolls and a stuffed bear. He held the picture out to show Michiko. She stared in wonder at the magical tea party. So beautiful, that ribbon and that dress.

Then he took a little cloth doll from his bag. Michiko saw it was one of the dolls in the photograph. It had long, golden, woollen hair and wore a red-and-white gingham dress. Blue felt boots were tied onto its feet with white satin ribbons. Michiko had never seen anything like it. He held it out to her, nodding. She looked into his face, questioning. He nodded and gestured to her with it. It was the most beautiful doll she'd ever seen. She looked up at him again, wide-eyed. *Take it.* He pushed it into her arms. She scarcely believed it could be hers.

Other children clustered around, pushing. 'A doll! I want one too. Mistah! Mistah?' Michiko clasped the doll to her chest. She could not stop beaming. The soldier looked happy she had taken it, and at that moment she felt this man could conjure any miracle out of thin air for her. She wanted him to stay with her, so she would always be safe.

'*Arigatō. Arigatō!*' She squeezed the doll, held it to her face.

He kneeled down to ruffle her hair. He closed his bag. And then he got up and walked away.

She didn't want him to go, but didn't know how to ask him to stay. She wanted to go with him. Watching his receding back, she burned into her memory his smile, his soft words, his golden face which was like the sun, his eyes the colour of the sky. She would never forget him, never. Not for as long as she lived.

A Kitchen Knife

It is a knife, twenty-six centimetres long from handle to tip. It has a handle of dark-brown wood and its double-ground blade, fourteen-and-a-half centimetres long, has been honed on a whetstone many hundreds of times. Its edge has always been kept razor-sharp. The side of the blade, made of the finest tempered shirogami steel, is etched with the kanji characters KiYa, meaning 'house of wood'. It is a Kamagata-Japan, a hybrid European-style knife that became popular in Japanese post-war homes. When picked up in preparation for cutting, the handle fits snugly in the palm of the hand. Its blade and handle are perfectly counterbalanced, so that without resistance, in one smooth, unthinking motion, the knife will slice through fish, vegetables, meat and even through small bones.

Erika

Erika suggests an early breakfast at the Portobello market before they head into town. She can't face eating alone at home with Kei, the two of them silent at the dining table, the altar brooding in the alcove.

Erika hopes she's dodged the worst of Kei's response. The night before, she'd stood in the kitchen, unable to speak, while Kei searched her face for an answer. The long, wordless minutes Erika and her cousin stood facing each other were excruciating. Erika couldn't explain to Kei why she hadn't dealt with her mother's bones because she didn't know. The years had passed and yet here they still were, sitting on an antique Korean cabinet covered with dust.

Once it was clear an answer wasn't forthcoming, Kei had excused herself, citing her jetlag, and gone to bed. Erika felt the relief of a prisoner given a temporary stay of execution.

The cousins greet one another, still fuzzy with sleep, unspoken words lying beneath the surface like unexploded mines. Erika feels exhausted, but she needs to get herself and Kei out of the house and away from the altar. London has enough distractions to create a safe path through the minefield, for now, at least. The colourful bustle and noise of her local market will be a good start.

It's busy. Erika walks fast, pushing through gaps in the crowds, slipping between traders' stalls. She's almost at the Electric Diner when she realises Kei's not with her. Retracing her steps, she finds her cousin stuck behind a throng of Italian tourists; she's too polite to push past.

'I lost you,' Erika says.

'You're walking too fast.'

'Come on, or we won't get a table.'

Kei follows close behind. Each time Erika turns back to check, her cousin's head is bowed in apology to those she pushes past. Erika feels a rush of irritation but doesn't know why. She resists the compulsion to grab her cousin's hand and pull her along, and they arrive at the Electric Diner just in time for the last free table, squeezing between a group of chattering Spaniards and a couple sipping coffee, heads buried in newspapers. Erika orders coffee, fresh orange juice and blueberry pancakes.

'I'll just have coffee,' says Kei.

The coffees arrive. Erika leans back into her chair, cup in hand. Kei is making no eye contact and endlessly stirs her coffee, even though it's black with no sugar. There are people all around them, protecting them from the risk of excessive emotion. Erika manages a tight smile. 'So! What do you want to do while you're here?'

'I need to go to Fortnum & Mason to buy tea, for omiyage for our business contacts, and for friends.'

'Don't your friends get tea from you all the time?'

'It's famous English tea. People like the pretty tins, they're nice to use after they're empty. They're light and easy to pack.'

'Those gift packs aren't cheap.' Erika drains the last of her coffee. She needs to order another. 'You're paying ridiculous amounts just for the packaging.'

'It's the gesture that counts.'

The blueberry pancakes arrive. Erika drenches them in maple syrup, ignoring the disapproval on Kei's face.

'Whatever,' she says briskly. 'We'll go to Fortnum's and maybe the Royal Academy afterwards. There's a good exhibition on at the moment. How about a dim-sum lunch in Chinatown?'

'Whatever you want.'

The noise of the diner presses back in as Erika eats and Kei sips at her coffee in silence. Conversations in different languages flow thick and fast around them.

'Why not just buy omiyage for family and close friends?' Erika stuffs a big forkful of pancake into her mouth, dripping maple syrup on her chin. 'Why buy for people the shop hardly does business with, when you don't need to?'

Kei's lips tighten.

'Buying presents for people you barely know. It seems so meaningless, and such a waste of time and money.' One half of her could bite off her tongue, but her other half won't shut up. 'I thought you came to London to enjoy yourself.'

'I like going to Fortnum & Mason.' Kei takes another tiny sip of her coffee and dabs at her lips with a napkin. The sight of this makes Erika wild with irritation: again, she has no idea why.

Erika concentrates on piling blueberries onto her next forkful. They keep rolling off and bouncing onto the table. She stabs a stray one with her fork.

'Still the same Erika,' says Kei.

'Huh?'

'Selfish. Childish. Lacking delicacy.'

Erika wipes syrup off her chin.

'It's not your fault,' Kei continues. 'You don't understand how important giri and ongi are to things going smoothly. If you were Japanese you would understand it's your duty to fulfil obligations.'

'Excuse me, Kei, I am Japanese. I understand those things. I'm just asking what would happen if you didn't waste all that money and time buying omiyage.'

'What business is it of yours? I can go on my own if it's that much trouble for you. Anyway, you're hāfu. Hāfu is not really Japanese.'

'What?'

'You're more gaijin than Japanese. You always have been.'

Erika barks out a laugh. 'Oh, for fuck's sake.' She lapses momentarily into English. She closes her eyes, inhales loudly, counts to three, opens them again. Kei's frowning at her.

'You know what? I'd say my non-Japanese half gives me perspective you don't have. Why do you have to buy presents for people you don't care about? It's not exactly from the heart, is it?'

'There you go. If you had true Japanese sensibility you would never ask such questions.' Kei sips at her coffee cup, although it's empty. 'Anyway, what you think doesn't matter. Buying omiyage is important to me. Giri. Ongi. Those are the rules we follow to keep the family tea business going. Hiroshi's doing his duty now he's head of the family, and I have to put aside my personal wishes to do mine, which is to support him as his younger sister. It's not about you and what you want. It's about making things work by doing what's expected of you. Your duty, Erika. Order me another coffee, please.'

Erika waves the waiter over, glad of the respite.

'As for coming here to enjoy myself, that's not the only reason for this trip,' says Kei, eyes burning. 'I came to fulfil my obligations to Michiko Obachan. I came expecting you to have fulfilled your obligations to your own mother, but you're as immature as you were when you were a teenager. You haven't been in touch with us in the twelve years since she died, not once, and you've done absolutely nothing about her nōkotsu. It seems you're too much of a selfish child to have managed putting her to rest. You're thirty years old, for goodness sake. You should be ashamed of yourself.'

Erika feels the pancake solidify in her stomach. Her eyes prickle. She closes them for a moment to breathe away her cousin's words. When she feels ready, she opens her eyes, drains her orange juice and slams the glass back onto the table, making Kei jump. 'Dammit, there's a lot you can do in two weeks! I could suggest,' – she waves her hands in mock cheeriness – 'watching the Changing of the Guard. The British Museum. The Tower of London. Tate Modern. A Thames boat ride.' Her voice creeps up half an octave. The Spaniards next to them stop talking and glance over. 'Oh! And of course, you love to shop! Selfridges, Harrods, Harvey Nichols! Or how about a visit to Oxford, Henley, Windsor Castle?'

'Erika, stop shouting. It's embarrassing.'

Erika swigs from her cup but it's empty too, and the waitress hasn't brought her second coffee yet. She squashes a stray blueberry as she thumps the cup back on the table. 'You're here for an eternity, for god's sake.'

There's a long pause while Kei stares at her. The Spaniards start up their conversation again. The couple next to them read on, oblivious.

Erika wipes her eyes. 'You have no idea what Michiko was really like. None whatsoever.'

Kei says nothing, her expression indecipherable.

Erika waits for her response, and when there is none, she shoves her chair back with a clatter and gets up. 'Okay, fine. You know what? Nothing more to discuss. You just do what you want. I'm off.' Erika puts a twenty-pound note on the table. 'Here. Eat something. You look hungry. Enjoy shopping for meaningless gifts. I'll be at home to let you in whenever you're done.'

It feels good, speaking her mind, but it doesn't last long. Erika walks along Portobello Road, powered by fury and adrenaline, bumping past tourists. But her rage has worn itself out by the time she reaches Ladbroke Grove, and she wonders if she overreacted. She walks back to the Electric Diner to look for her cousin, feeling queasy with guilt, but Kei has already gone.

Erika calls Marcus. 'Maybe it's better if you don't come over tonight. Me and Kei just had a fight. I feel terrible and I don't know what to do. I don't think I can bear another day of this.'

'Maybe next time you'll learn to say no.'

'You're not helping. I told you, it's complicated. I can't say no; it doesn't work like that with us.'

'You're doing everything half-cocked, Erika. Choose one side or the other. Be a good Japanese daughter, be dutiful and behave the way you're expected to, or put yourself first and tell her no. I don't understand how you can tell her to come and stay without even bothering to deal with your mum's altar. It's as if you're deliberately provoking her. Why?'

'I don't know. I'm confused.'

'You're not wrong there. Make a decision. Do what's expected of you, or give it all up.'

'Mmm.' She feels sick.

'I'm still coming over tonight. I'll use my charm to dissipate the tension. Don't worry, it'll be fine.'

Just as Erika returns home with groceries for dinner, the intercom buzzes, making her jump.

'It's me.'

Erika presses the access button on the intercom without a word and unlatches the front door. She rushes to sit at the dining table, picking up a pen and shuffling through a pile of old bills, making herself look busy.

Kei appears at the open door, laden with shopping bags. 'I need a nap,' she says. 'The jetlag's bad today.'

The faint scent of woody incense from last night still hangs in the air. Erika had almost managed to forget. She opens the windows, avoiding Kei's gaze. To Erika's relief, Kei disappears into her room with the bags of shopping. Now Erika just needs to survive until Marcus arrives to provide a distraction; she's glad now he insisted on coming over. In the meantime, she has dinner to cook; the kitchen is her escape. She wonders how Marcus and Kei will get on. It'll be the first time he's met anyone she's related to.

Kei comes back out of her room and stands in the kitchen doorway as she did the night before. The sight of her tightens the knot in Erika's stomach.

'I thought you were having a nap?'

'I am. I won't sleep long. Just enough so I can stay awake this evening and be polite to your boyfriend.'

'I thought about telling him not to come,' Erika says. 'I didn't think we'd be in the mood for a convivial dinner.'

'Don't be ridiculous, Erika, we're not children. Is he still coming?'

Erika rolls her eyes. 'Yes, he's still coming. Go and have your nap. I can wake you if you want.' She slides a carton of eggs into the fridge.

'I've got an alarm clock,' says Kei. 'Half an hour. Then I'll help you prepare dinner.'

'Sleep longer.' Erika stops putting groceries away and draws back her shoulders. 'I don't need your help.'

'Any longer and I'll struggle to wake up.'

'Fine,' says Erika, forcing a smile that's closer to a grimace. 'Whatever. Sleep well.'

Once she's tidied everything away, Erika puts on her apron and begins her rituals. She takes her mother's kitchen knife and lays it ready on the chopping board. Michiko was always scornful of domestic chores, but cooking was the one thing she enjoyed, and she was good at it. She'd been discerning in her choice of knife: this is a fine one, good for both Japanese and Western cooking. Erika has continued to care for it as her mother used to, sharpening it regularly on a whetstone, and now she slides it in one smooth, easy movement under the descaled skin of the wide fillet of salmon she bought from the fishmonger. She removes the skin, salts it and puts it aside; she'll grill it later and turn it into crisp crackling. She runs her fingers over the oily pink gleam of the fish and feels her mind drifting away somewhere, empty.

When she comes to, she realises she's been standing there with the knife in her hand, unaware of long seconds ticking by. She shakes her head to bring herself back into the kitchen. She puts the knife down, and sets about deboning the fish with a large pair of tweezers. She washes it under the tap and pats it dry with kitchen paper, buries it in a stainless steel dish filled with sea salt, brown sugar and dill. She covers it and puts it in the fridge.

Cooking keeps her mind occupied. It stops her from doing, thinking and saying dangerous things. Erika pours herself into making something she can contain, something she can arrange on a plate and present to someone. More than anything, she gets a kick out of seeing people eating what she's cooked, although, hidden away in the kitchens, there isn't much opportunity for that at André's. She loves watching people's expressions, the movement of their mouths as they chew. They don't know they're taking in a part of herself, her offering. She feels complete when she sits with Mrs Mackenzie, watching her tucking into the soups and casseroles Erika cooks for her.

She's taken aback when she realises she's looking forward to feeding Kei. The closeness they shared as children is long gone; food might now be the only language they have left in common, just as it was with her mother. Whenever Erika cooked for Michiko, she felt able to unearth her love from the morass of ill feeling that had come to bury it over the years, and express it through the food she prepared. Tonight she's making semi-cured salmon carpaccio with crushed baby potatoes in caper butter and a side of blanched asparagus, a dish her mother loved.

Kei's half hour is almost up. Erika washes her hands and puts on the kettle. She fetches the Wedgwood teapot and puts it on a little tray with a matching cup and saucer and a jug of milk. No sugar. As she places a single piece of her matcha green tea shortbread beside the cup on the saucer, she hears the trill of Kei's alarm clock.

She knocks on Kei's door.

Kei's voice is thick with sleep. 'Come in,' she croaks. She sits up in bed. There are pillow marks on her face and she rubs her eyes like a child. 'I'm still so tired.'

'I'm sure your jetlag will get better soon.' Erika puts the tray on the bedside table. 'I've chilled some champagne. We'll open it when you're ready.'

The sun has disappeared behind clouds; there's a slight chill in the darkening living room. Erika draws the curtains, turning on lamps and lighting candles. She sets the table. The smell of incense has faded. She puts on a Keith Jarrett CD. The candlelight is reflected in the glasses, giving the folded white linen napkins a chalky glow, and a bouquet of creamy Stargazer lilies blooms luminescent in a cut-crystal vase on the table. The scene is soothing, like a spoonful of Milk of Magnesia; Erika drinks it in and holds herself still, breathing slow, quietening her mind so as not to fan the embers of her anxiety.

She hears Kei coming out of her room and takes refuge in the kitchen.

'Here,' Kei says, standing in the doorway, holding the tea tray, 'where shall I put this?'

Erika's mouth drops open. Her cousin is transformed. What she has on is simple, but it's not anything she'd have imagined Kei wearing.

'Do I look all right?' Kei asks. She wears a trace of eyeliner, a smudge of dark-red lipstick, and a crisp white shirt unbuttoned low to allow a single pearl on a gold chain to glisten through the shadows. Beneath this, she has on a pair of tight-fitting dark-blue Levis that reveal the figure she usually hides under her conservative skirts. 'It looks odd, doesn't it? Without shoes. I'd wear boots with these if I were going out,' she says, wriggling her toes inside her white socks.

'You look great,' says Erika, confused. The saucepan lid is chattering. She removes it; steam billows.

'What are you making?' asks Kei.

'Oh, salmon carpaccio, vegetables.' Erika takes a frosty bottle out of the fridge. 'Here, have some. God knows I'm ready for a drink'.

Erika grips the cork and aims the bottle at her cousin. Kei shrinks back into the doorway.

'Don't worry,' Erika says, grinning. 'I won't pop it.' The bottle sighs as the cork twists free. Erika half-fills two flutes. 'It's English,' she says.

'English!' Kei snorts a laugh.

'Taste it.' Erika passes a glass to Kei and watches her drink. How is her cousin so alluring all of a sudden? Kei tilts her head back as she drinks and Erika sees her throat bobbing as she swallows and her cherry-red lips through the pale bubbles in the glass. Erika feels her eyes sting. A feeling she can't identify wells up in her. It's not an unpleasant sensation, but she's afraid of keeping it unchecked. She whirls back to the chopping board, wiping her eyes, and looks for the knife. It's not on the board, although she's certain she left it there.

'It's delicious,' says Kei. 'I'm surprised.'

'It grows in the same chalky soil as in Champagne,' says Erika, flustered. She prattles on to fill the silence. 'The soil layers go under the Channel and up the other side into England. No borders.'

'Well.' Kei stares at Erika, sipping. 'Aren't you the clever one with all your sophisticated wine knowledge.'

Erika searches the counter tops and draining board for the knife. She eventually finds it stuck back on the magnetic wall rack. Strange. Maybe Kei put it there when she wasn't looking. She shakes her head to clear the fog.

'Marcus will be here soon. I'd better get on with the rest of the cooking. Why don't you go make yourself comfortable in the sitting room? Here, take these.' Erika holds out bowls of green olives and parmesan crisps.

Erika needs to get back to the safety of cooking. She shakes up a garlic-and-herb dressing in a jar and sets the water to steam for the asparagus. The squawk of the intercom shocks her back into the present.

'Could you get that?' she calls out. 'That'll be Marcus. I'll be there in a minute.' She empties her glass and grabs a fresh one for Marcus. She wanders to the living room with the glasses and the bottle in an ice bucket and sets them down on the table. 'Want some more?'

Kei holds out her empty glass, shifting from foot to foot as Erika pours. Kei takes a swig and straightens her shirt. 'Do I look okay?'

she asks again. 'He doesn't speak Japanese, does he? Will you be much longer in the kitchen? It's just that my English isn't so good.'

'Don't be nervous. You'll be fine.'

Kei gulps from her glass then sits back down on the edge of the sofa, knees together. 'I'm not nervous.'

'Marcus is easygoing. I'm sure you'll like each other.'

'It depends what you've told him about me.' Kei quickly presses the glass to her lips, as if she's trying to push the words back in. Her cheeks glow red and her eyes glisten. She's already slightly drunk.

Erika opens the door as Marcus reaches the top landing. They kiss, and she is aware of Kei standing behind them, as they remain locked together. Peeling away, she introduces him to her cousin.

Kei raises one stiff arm, hand outstretched, the other by her side. 'I am very pleased to meeting you.' She bobs her head. 'My name is Kei.'

Marcus bows low. '*Marcus desu. Hajimemashite.' Pleased to meet you.*'

'Your Japanese very good.' Kei laughs. She turns to Erika, switching to Japanese. 'You taught him something.'

'For you.' Marcus hands Kei the bunch of sunflowers he has in his hand. '*Dōzo.*'

Kei flushes and beams. 'Thank you very much.'

Marcus takes the bottle from the ice bucket. 'Would you like some more?'

'Yes, thank you.' Kei drains her glass and holds it out again.

Erika's glad to get back to the kitchen to finish preparing dinner; she can't bear this charade. She takes the knife and sharpens it with loud swishes on the sharpening block. She furrows her brow. Odd, how it sounds like someone crying. She rinses the knife and stares at the characters etched into its blade as if she's seeing them for the first time. They look different, somehow, as if someone stole the old ones and put new ones in their place. She must be tired. She cuts paper-thin slices from the salmon fillet she's exhumed from its marinade, biting her lip in concentration as she arranges them on a serving plate like petals on a camellia.

Marcus appears, leaning against the doorframe. 'So?' he asks.

'It's awful. We haven't argued again since this morning, but it feels like we're sitting on a bomb that's about to blow. I wish you could stay the rest of the time she's here.'

'You know I can't. I pick up Felix tomorrow.'

Erika turns back to her work. The sharp knife allows her to cut the salmon into such fine slices that the dill fronds she's arranged beneath glow green through the coral pink. She scatters drops of mustard-dill dressing and olive oil across the serving plate, tucking nasturtium, garlic flowers and small curls of purple cress among the slices. She stands back to admire the effect.

'There.' She wipes the knife with a damp cloth, but realises too late she hasn't covered the full length of the blade with it; she's run the cutting edge along the pad of her thumb. She doesn't feel it slicing her flesh, though goose bumps rise up on the back of her neck as soon as it does. She drops the knife into the sink with a clatter. 'Fuck!' There are a couple of seconds' delay before a small ruby hyphen wells up along the cut.

'What's up?' Marcus comes back into the kitchen.

Erika holds up her wounded hand; she's pressing a tea towel against it. 'Cut myself.'

'You want me to find a bandaid?'

'Sure, thanks. There should be one in the bathroom.'

He disappears down the corridor and she hears him open the bathroom cabinet. He brings the box of bandaids and empties it out on the kitchen counter to find the right size. 'You'd better put some Savlon on there first. Hold out your hand.' He squeezes a blob of ointment onto his finger and Erika lifts the tea towel away.

'Where is it?' he asks.

'Where's what?'

'The cut.'

'What do you mean, where? It's there, on my thumb.'

'I don't see anything.'

She blinks to see if she's missed something. There's no cut. No blood. It was a clean cut. Maybe the edges don't show easily once the blood's wiped away. She rubs her fingers across her thumb pad, pulling at the flesh. Nothing.

'That's crazy. I swear I saw blood. I felt it cut my skin.'

Marcus picks up the knife from the sink and examines it. 'Did you rinse this off?'

'Not yet.'

'No blood on the blade either. Let me see the tea towel.'

She looks at it in disbelief. Nothing.

'You must have imagined it.' Marcus wipes the Savlon off his finger with the towel and chucks it on the counter.

Erika feels a twist of unease at the strangeness of it, but the evidence is undeniable. No blood, no cut. It was a fraught morning. More stressful days with Kei still stretch out ahead. She's overwrought, seeing things that aren't there.

She takes refuge again in the preparation of food. Take action, put things together, get expected results.

'I'll do the soup.' She holds out the plate of carpaccio with its crown of edible flowers. 'Please could you carry this out to the dining table?'

'Beautiful,' Marcus says. He kisses her. 'The food doesn't look too bad either.'

Erika rolls her eyes, but she reaches out to stroke the nape of his neck.

'Kei's different from what I imagined.'

'Different how?'

'Not as scary as you painted her. And forgive me for saying this, but she's kinda hot.'

'Don't creep me out, Marcus. It's Kei, for god's sake.' She frowns at him. 'She judges me all the time. I can't relax when she's around. She's nice to you because she wants to impress you. Ever since we've been teenagers she's had a pattern of saying the occasional nice thing so I start to feel relaxed, and then she bites when I'm off my guard. It's like I'm dealing with a shapeshifter.'

Marcus pauses at the kitchen door, a plate in each hand. 'That's how you seem to me, sometimes,' he says. 'I never quite know where I am with you.'

'The food's pretty,' says Kei. 'I hope it tastes as good as it looks.'

'Go ahead, eat.' Erika picks up her fork. '*Itadakimasu.*'

'*Itadakimasu,*' echoes Kei.

'What was that?' Asks Marcus. '*Itada*—what?'

'It means, please to enjoying your meal,' Kei says, and giggles. She's definitely drunk. She's definitely drunk. She puts her hand on his arm. Her lipstick's smudged.

Erika fights her irritation, resisting the urge to ask Kei about her husband, but instead says, '*Itadakimasu* means "I receive". It's an expression of gratitude. You say it before you start eating, the way you'd say *bon appetit.*'

'*Ita-maki-daa* ...' says Marcus. Kei guffaws, covering her mouth with her hand.

'It's not that funny.' Erika scowls at her cousin.

'How do I say it again?'

'*Itadakimasu.*'

'*Ika-da-ma-saaaa* ...' He keeps repeating it, bugging his eyes as he bungles it each time, making ever more preposterous versions of the word. '*Imakapasataaa* ...'

Erika can't help herself and joins in with Kei's laughter. Maybe she's being paranoid.

'*Ipapamapapaaaa* ...'

Erika knows Marcus is trying to relieve the unease that's papered over by this fragile layer of conviviality. She watches her lover and her cousin joking and laughing, eating the food she's prepared for them. These are the two people who are supposed to be closest to her. She feels a strange mixture of emotions she can't identify. Edginess and pleasure perhaps, maybe fear too. She wonders whether it might even be love, whatever that might mean.

Michiko

'Oh, Michi! Wasn't he handsome? An absolute dream!' Sayuri clutched the movie program to her chest. The friends emerged, blinking, from the Nichigeki Theatre and hugged their coats tight, their breaths misting in the early February chill as they waited for the lights to change at the pedestrian crossing.

'Mmm.' Michiko closed her eyes to hold on to the magic of *Pillow Talk* a little longer. 'Imagine what it would be like to have a husband like Rock Hudson.'

'You'd have to look like Doris Day to be his wife, with blonde hair and blue eyes and a high nose,' said Sayuri, shivering with cold.

'That white evening dress was perfect. Everything she wore in that movie was so elegant. Those narrow silhouettes …' Michiko opened her coat to look down at her wide, petticoat-flounced skirt, at her bobby socks and two-tone shoes peeking out beneath. She'd made the skirt and petticoat herself, cutting a pattern from newspaper and sewing whenever her father was out of the way. She'd saved every sen she earned in the family shop for over a year to buy the shoes, her mother secretly giving her a little extra at new year so she could get them sooner. She'd been so ecstatic when she bought them three weeks ago that she hadn't been able to stop gazing at them, tying and untying the laces, sniffing and stroking the leather. She kept the skirt and petticoat neatly folded in tissue in her box of treasures, along with her precious American doll. She wore them only for special occasions like this. Looking down now, it all looked unsophisticated and old-fashioned. Michiko scuffed at the pavement with her toe and scowled.

'What's the matter? Why the glum face all of a sudden?' asked Sayuri.

'I wish I was American.'

'Shh! Don't say that.' The lights changed and, jostled by the crowd, they started to cross. Sayuri looked about and lowered her voice. 'Especially not now. People are really angry.' The week before, Prime Minister Kishi had signed a revised Anpo with the Americans, and there were riots and demonstrations brewing across the country.

'So what?'

'Michi, your mother is from Okinawa! Don't you care the Americans are still occupying it? Using it to fight more wars?'

'No. We're in Tokyo. Why should I care?'

'Michiko!'

'It's not fair. In America, girls our age don't have to worry about any of that. They have everything: shoes, clothes, fancy cars, supermarkets that sell all the food they want.' They'd crossed to the other side and were walking under the bridge at Yūrakucho, past rows of food stalls beginning to light up against the dusk. Michiko kept her head down, drawing her scarf around her neck. 'There's enough space in those huge houses for your own bedroom, your own wardrobe full of clothes and a big bed to sleep in. Imagine not having to share!'

'But Michi—'

'If I were in America I could have gone to college, if I'd wanted to.'

'My sister went to college,' murmured Sayuri. 'You could go here too. If your father didn't need your help in the shop, maybe he'd let you.'

'Ha,' Michiko retorted. 'He just wants to marry me off. But I don't want to be some mother-in-law's slave. American girls choose their own husbands. I'd marry someone who treats me with respect, someone with plenty of money so I wouldn't have to work myself to death. I'd have maids to clean the house and take care of the children so I could play tennis and go to parties with my husband.' They dodged a red-faced salary-man staggering out of an izakaya bar. 'You've seen how romantic American men are, buying jewellery and flowers for their women. How many Japanese men do you know who give jewellery and flowers to their wives? I don't know any.'

'That's just in the movies,' Sayuri broke in. 'I don't think Americans all live like that.'

'You've heard about the American Dream, haven't you?'

'Yes, but …'

'That's why I wish I was American. To have a future.'

'They're the enemy.'

'Were. They helped us recover.'

'Yeah, under occupation. After they bombed Hiroshima and Nagasaki. People are still suffering and dying because of that. And they haven't given Okinawa back.'

They'd emerged from under the bridge and stopped across the road from Fujiya's, scowling at each another. Then Sayuri nudged Michiko with her elbow and grinned.

'Hey, if you were a gaijin you'd have to soak in dirty bath water.'

The audience had murmured, aghast, at the sight of Doris Day soaping herself *inside* the bath, the suds running into the clean water she soaked in. But then you could forgive Doris Day anything. Michiko chuckled. 'I wouldn't care about dirty bathwater if I were married to Rock Hudson.'

Sayuri linked arms with Michiko. 'Come on, let's not spoil our day. We're almost there – here, you have the movie program first. We'll take turns with it. You can look at the pictures and imagine yourself as a gaijin, sitting in filthy bathwater with your jewels on.'

Upstairs at Fujiya's they talked unceasingly about the movie, sipping pink strawberry milkshakes from straws out of tall glasses topped with puffs of cream and maraschino cherries. Michiko laughed and chattered as if nothing had darkened her mood.

Afterwards, she floated home, her head filled with diamond necklaces, fur coats, fluffy beds and satin pillows. No suffering, no sorrow, just gorgeous technicolour.

That evening Michiko helped her mother prepare the family meal, humming the theme tune to *Pillow Talk*. Chiyo was talking about the rise of the Zengakuren. The student sit-in at Haneda Airport a few weeks ago had made front-page news. 'They tried their best to stop the Prime Minister from flying to America to sign that treaty, but the police dragged them all out,' said Chiyo, as she shaved a block of katsuobushi for stock. 'I say good for them. Somebody has to make a stand. Okinawa must be returned to us.'

With her head full of Hollywood dreams and her hands occupied, Michiko was untroubled by talk of treaties. She sliced and chopped in a blur, relaxed and at ease, as if it were the knife doing all the work. She scraped the vegetables off the chopping board into Chiyo's pot of winter misoshiru, then went to squat beside the hibachi, fanning the white-hot charcoal while salted mackerel fillets bubbled and browned. She dreamed through dinner, barely noticing what she ate, imagining instead the marvellous Western dishes she'd cook. She imagined eating off a fine china plate with a golden fork, sitting on a tall-backed chair at a mahogany dining table. When she took the dirty dishes into the kitchen and stood at the sink, scrubbing and rinsing with her mother and sister, they chattered without seeming to notice Michiko wasn't joining in. Even her father shouting at her for taking too long to bring his tea didn't break her out of her golden cocoon.

'What's the matter with you, girl? You're half asleep! I hope you were mindful when you made the tea!'

'I made it properly, Father, I promise. I'm sorry you had to wait.'

She laid his newspaper in front of him and poured his tea before helping her mother with the darning. Only once the plates had been put away and the rice washed and put to soak for next morning's breakfast, once she'd laid the family's futons out for the night and lit the fire under the bath in readiness for her father, who bathed first, did she again notice the shabby walls, the worn tatami matting, the threadbare blankets. She didn't dare look at the movie program while her father was still awake, turning instead to the diary her mother had given her at new year, along with the extra money for her shoes. 'If you write out your frustrations it might improve your temper,' Chiyo had said, not unkindly. Michiko may have already grown bored of her shoes, but she adored the diary, her only privacy. Each day she opened up its sky-blue cover to write on its crisp white pages. She could set down her life one day at a time, exactly the way she wanted it to be.

Michiko hummed a Doris Day tune as she wrote about the chilly winter weather, about *Pillow Talk* and her outing to Fujiya's with Sayuri – leaving out the disagreement they'd had in front of the cinema – and about the food she and her mother prepared for dinner. When she finished, she went back to the start of January to re-read all her entries. She hadn't missed a day yet.

The diary kept her occupied until it was her turn to bathe. As the youngest and as a girl, she was always last. She couldn't imagine rinsing dirty suds into the bathwater like Doris Day. Even so, as she sank into the deep old wooden tub she saw instead a long shallow one, glistening with tiles and framed with golden taps, filled to the rim with bubbles. As she crept into her futon in the dark, she imagined herself sinking into soft silk sheets, Rock Hudson at the end of the phone line. For a long time, she lay awake, listening to her father's snores. She felt darkness descending, blotting out the glorious technicolour images she'd held onto throughout the day. It eddied about her and crept into her core. When she finally drifted to sleep, it was as if she were falling into a fathomless hole that had opened up deep inside her. She slept heavily, and did not dream.

A Rice Bowl

Hand thrown in a rustic style, the chunky thickness of the bowl contrasts with its smooth, creamy glaze. Beneath this glaze – which renders it a soft and dusky blue – a simple pattern of curlicues, like snail-shell spirals, inside which gentle dots are corralled. It is possible to see the way the artist made these marks with the point of a brush. The dots are all even in size, but here and there, tiny traces of a darker blue show the point of pressure created by the movement of the artisan's brush. The bowl is a hollow hemisphere, not the conical shape more traditionally favoured. It is not too large, and has a pleasing weight in the hand. On its base, the artisan has inscribed a single character, his identifier. The bowl has had decades of use and, as is usual, has only ever had one owner at a time. Only rice is eaten from it, and always by the one who owns it.

Erika

The sky hangs low and murky, and Erika can no longer see the stars. As the boat lurches through storm-thrashed waves, the wind whips sea spray into her face, stinging and blinding. Flailing about for something to hold onto, she finds nothing. She grips the deck with her toes but it isn't enough to steady herself. Falling to her knees as the boat bucks and rolls, she's afraid she'll be thrown into the ocean and lost. Lying flat on her stomach, she clings to the deck, heart racing, sick. She can't tell whether the surging waves are those of the sea or if they're inside her.

Sensing a presence overhead, she turns on her back and sees a great bird. Its golden plumage blazes against the black of the sky so that when she closes her eyes she sees its imprint on the inside of her lids, like the afterflash of lightning. When she opens them again, she sees it hovering above as if it hardly notices the storm raging around it, its wings spread wide, its razor-edged talons trailing behind. Its sharp eye is on her, enormous, observing her. The bird is trying to tell her something. She tries to quieten the waves heaving inside her, doesn't dare blink or avert her eyes in case she misses a sign, but she can't figure it out. In frustration, she shouts out. The bird hovers above a while longer, then dips lower, almost touching her. It keeps its calm gaze fixed upon her. Then it flies up and away into the darkness.

An urgent nausea pushes her awake.

Erika makes it to the bathroom just in time. She vomits twice, three times until her stomach empties, and still she retches. She curls into a ball at the foot of the pedestal sink, cooling her cheek on the tiles. The floor still feels like it's rocking. The vomiting brings no relief.

She hears the door open.

'Erika? You okay?' Marcus's voice is muffled with sleep. He kneels beside her, stroking her back. 'Do you want some water?'

'Un-hunh.'

He rinses a facecloth under the tap, wrings it out, fills a glass with water. 'Here.'

She sits up to drink, groaning.

He wipes her face as she curls back onto the floor. 'Any better?'

'Nuh.'

'Poor you.' He remains crouched beside her, soothing her back with his hand. His warmth seeps into her on one side, the chill of the tiles spreading into her from the other. 'What do you think's brought this on?'

'Maybe dinner last night. You okay?'

'Absolutely fine.'

'Kei?'

'No sign she's awake.' He continues stroking Erika's back.

The nausea rises again. She heaves and crumples over the toilet, vomiting up the water she's just drunk. Bile burns her throat. She slumps back to the floor. 'Leave me here.'

'I can't go back to sleep with you lying on the bathroom floor.'

'Go away. Please.'

'Babe ...'

'I'll come to bed in a bit.'

Marcus rolls up a towel and slides it under her head. 'Sure?'

'Mmhh.'

'Shout if you need me.'

The cold solidity of the bathroom floor is reassuring. She drifts in and out of sleep, pushing herself up between feverish dreams to retch. She's at sea again, under the stars now, so cold out on the deck of the boat where she lies, and Kei comes to her, rising out of the sea, peering into her face with quiet indifference, then sinking back into the waves. Later she thinks she sees the figure of her mother at the helm. She can't see her face. It's turned to the horizon. Her back is solid and still. Both her hands are on the captain's wheel as she guides the boat through the waves.

Erika creeps back to bed at dawn. In the half-light she sees Marcus asleep on his back, mouth open, arms splayed. She moves slowly so as not to wake him, feeling the relief as she stretches her cold, cramped body out on the soft mattress. She dozes.

She wakes to a gentle knocking on the door.

'It's me. Can I come in?'

She looks at the clock; it's gone past eleven. The other side of the bed is empty. Marcus must have left for work hours ago.

'Sure.' She pushes herself up against the pillows.

Kei comes in with a tray, rice and tea bowls clinking, and sets it on the bed. 'Marcus told me you were sick in the night. He says he'll phone you later.' She stands beside the bed, making no move to leave.

'I can't go out with you today,' Erika murmurs. 'I have to get better in time for work tomorrow.'

Kei lays her hand on Erika's forehead. 'You don't have a fever,' she says. 'What made you sick? It can't be something you've eaten. We ate the same things.'

Erika pulls the quilt over her head.

After a moment, she hears Kei sigh. 'You're not pregnant, are you?'

Erika snorts. 'Absolutely not.' She sticks her face out from under the quilt. Kei is still standing over her. 'I have my period. Want me to show you?'

'Why are you so angry?'

Because you're here, she wants to say. *Because you think you're so much better than me, and judge me when you haven't the faintest idea what I've been through.* Her rage is inflamed by rising shame. Her eyes sting, and the bowls, teapot and cup on the tray blur into watery blobs. She blinks and scrubs at her face with her palms. She groans with frustration and pulls the quilt over her head again.

'I made okayu,' Kei continues. 'I hope you don't mind me going into your kitchen. I don't know if this is your rice bowl and chopsticks – did I pick right? I found the umeboshi in the back of the fridge. It'll help settle your stomach.'

Erika waits, but doesn't hear Kei moving from beside the bed. Half-chastened, half-exasperated, she flips the quilt back. The tray is laid with a folded napkin and a small teapot and cup. Kei has chosen the correct chopsticks: plain, made of hinoki cypress, Erika's own. The rice bowl on the tray is Michiko's. Its rustic hand-thrown curves are comforting. A soft clear glaze covers brush-point dot patterns the colour of the sea when it moves from shallow to deep. It is one of a pair. The other, Erika's bowl, is the same size and shape and similarly glazed, but girdled with two stripes, one muted blue and one dark red. Michiko bought both of them from a small ceramic shop in downtown Tokyo more than twenty years ago.

The wrinkled dusky pink of the pickled umeboshi plum sits in the centre of the steaming okayu rice porridge, a washed-out, shrunken rising sun. It's the only thing Erika could face eating at this moment, a dish consumed in illness and convalescence. Someone else – someone who knows what's needed and how to do it – has to make it for you. She hasn't eaten okayu since her mother died because there hasn't been anyone to make it for her, until now. She feels the stinging in her eyes again. Alarmed, she clears her throat. She doesn't cry; it's not what she does. She didn't even cry back then, when she was eighteen.

Erika rolls on her side and looks at Kei. 'I've always had problems with my digestion.' She scrubs at her face again. 'I get sick when I'm stressed. I'm run down at the moment too. I've probably caught some kind of bug. Thanks for the okayu. I'll eat it in a minute.'

'It's really hot anyway, you might as well let it cool down.'

Erika hears the kindness in Kei's voice and glances at her cousin's face. She almost looks like she cares. She's still not making a move to leave the room.

'Kei, I'm really tired. Would you mind leaving me for a while?'

Erika reaches for the tray and slides it onto the bedside table. Some okayu slops over the side of the rice bowl, and when she picks it up to wipe the spill, the sea-blue brush dots bleed down the side of the bowl along with the porridge, like tears, or raindrops trickling down a window. She lets go of the bowl with a clatter as if she's been burned, splattering okayu across the tray.

'What's the matter? Is it too hot?' asks Kei.

Erika feels a cold flush of fear. 'It's nothing. I think I just need to sleep. I'll see you in a bit.' She holds her breath. As soon as the door closes she curls into a ball under the quilt and puts a pillow over her head. She doesn't want to see that rice bowl; it frightens her. Her face feels full, the bones of it aching. Her eyes prickle. She stuffs her fist into her mouth and cries, soundlessly, for a long time. When she finally falls asleep again, she doesn't dream.

'It's a relief not to feel sick any more,' Erika says, slathering butter and honey on toast. 'I'm hungry.' She forces a brightness into her voice she doesn't feel.

Kei is at the kitchen table drinking tea. 'Are you sure you should be having that? That butter will upset your stomach again.'

Erika smears more butter on her toast. 'I'll be fine. Your okayu worked its magic.'

Later, they go for a walk in Kensington Gardens. It's Saturday and the park is filled with families playing ball games and racing toy boats on the lake. The leaves are starting to turn and the late afternoon sun is setting the golden trees aglow. There's a quiet chill in the air that hints at autumn. Erika tightens her indigo-dyed linen scarf around her neck. She catches Kei staring at it.

'Recognise it? It was Michiko's.' Erika crams the ends of the scarf into her face and inhales. 'Amazing. It still smells of Opium. Her perfume, I mean. Yves Saint Laurent.'

'You've not washed it?' says Kei, horrified. 'In all these years?'

'I've never worn it, especially not since ...' She forces a hollow laugh. 'I forgot I'd kept it. I was looking for something different to wear when we went out the other day and found it scrunched up in the back of the drawer. I like it. I just felt like wearing it today.'

On the far side of the boating lake, a child wearing a gold T-shirt with a glittery unicorn on it is trying to fly a kite. She runs with it until it's airborne, but as soon as she stops and turns to tug its string and haul it up into the sky, it flutters back to earth like a felled bird.

'Do you mind if we go back?' Erika says. 'I suddenly feel exhausted.'

Erika wants to order takeaway but Kei insists on cooking. She makes up a pot of ojiya, mixing barley miso, shredded ginger and chopped spring onion into rice porridge and whisking in a couple of eggs, leaving tendril trails of white and gold.

'This will be easy on the stomach,' she says.

They sit on the sofa slurping from steaming bowls with ceramic spoons, watching a comedy show. There's canned laughter and noise from the TV, but the room is heavy with their silence. She realises Kei isn't getting the jokes. 'Sorry, I guess you can't be enjoying this,' says Erika. 'Comedy's hard in a foreign language. We should chat instead, maybe listen to some music.' She reaches for the remote.

'No, don't switch it off. It's good for me to hear English.' Kei gets up from the sofa and collects the empty bowls. 'I'll get more ojiya. We can talk later, when it's finished.'

Erika watches the screen but isn't taking anything in. Maybe Kei just means talking generally. Talking about Tokyo, about what she wants to do tomorrow, about life. Just general, non-confrontational talking. She tries to focus.

Kei returns with refilled bowls. 'Here you go.'

Erika scoops a spoonful into her mouth and burns her tongue. She spits the mouthful back into the bowl.

'I heated it up again, sorry,' says Kei. 'I should have told you. Are you all right?'

Erika nods. It feels pointless continuing to watch the show but she stays glued to the screen until the credits roll.

'How's your stomach?' Kei raises her voice above the noisy adverts.

'Better, thanks. That ojiya was just what I needed.' Erika scrolls through the TV menu but there's nothing good to watch. There's no choice but to turn it off. The screen fizzes black and the sudden silence opens up a void in the room. Erika jumps up to collect the empty bowls. 'I'll make tea.'

Washing up in the kitchen, Erika remembers a book she once had, long ago, about a creature with a head at either end, each one pulling in opposite directions, having to negotiate where they were headed next. A Push-Me-Pull-You. This was how it was with Kei. They were taking turns to advance and retreat, advance and retreat, a tug of war. Kei's taken care of her and now it's Erika's turn to retreat. She returns to the sitting room, resolute.

'Okay. Let's talk then.'

Kei looks up, surprised. She takes the teacup Erika is holding out to her. 'What about?'

Erika falters, flushes. 'I thought you wanted to talk about … you know … about …' Kei waits while Erika forces words out. She may as well get it over and done with. 'You know, what's on the altar. The remains.'

Silence.

Get it over and done with, thinks Erika. Just get on with the lecture I know you want to give me. Her other half says: 'I did try to find a place to bury them.'

'Really.'

'There's only one Sōtō Zen temple in the UK. In Northumberland.'

'Where's that?' asks Kei.

'Near the Scottish border, near Hadrian's Wall. I went there a long time ago with Michiko and Julian to see that wall. It goes on for hundreds of kilometres across the moors. It was built by the Romans to keep out the Britons. When we went there it was really cold. There was thick fog so we couldn't see much, and it was pretty desolate. Michiko hated it and kept complaining. All she wanted was to find a pub with an open fire. She said the place made her feel sad, and she gave Julian a hard time for taking her there. They had a terrible fight. It's not a happy place.'

'You felt she wouldn't want her grave there.'

'It's so far from anywhere. I couldn't have looked after it. A whole day to get there and back. There isn't anyone but me here for her now, and I might not even stay in England. If I left, who'd look after her grave? It would be meaningless.'

'It would never be meaningless.'

'Yes it would, with nobody attached to it. I won't have kids. Any meaning will die with me.'

'How can you be sure you won't have children?'

'I know I won't. I don't want any.'

'Life changes in ways you don't expect, Eri. You still have time.'

'Believe me. I won't. Why is a woman always expected to have children? The planet's overburdened as it is,' says Erika. But she's encouraged by a gentleness in her cousin's voice. 'But do you understand? About the grave, I mean.'

'I think so.'

Something tightly wound inside loosens, just a little. 'In the West, people often have their ashes scattered somewhere beautiful, like the forest or mountains or the sea.'

'That's not appropriate. Michiko Obachan wouldn't have liked that idea at all.'

'No, she wouldn't. But since she's dead, does it matter? Come to think of it, being in a grave in Northumberland wouldn't bother her either. But I wouldn't be able to tend to it, that's all.'

'You're not tending to her now.'

Erika bit her lip. 'Do you have any idea what she was like as a mother? Do you know how she treated me?'

'That's in the past, Erika. You're an adult now.'

'Sometimes I wish I'd left all her bones in the family grave,' says Erika. 'But your father said I should have some of them so I wouldn't be lonely.'

'He did that on condition you interred them. Scattering her ashes is unacceptable. Remember how we had to get dispensation from the temple just to let you have some of the cremated bones? My father went to a lot of trouble for you.'

'Yes. But can't you see I don't know what to do? I thought I should leave them until I die. Then I'd have my own ashes mixed with hers.'

'That's not a good idea, Eri.'

'Why? There's no home temple here, nobody cares.'

'I care.'

'What do you care if some of my mother's bones are in an urn, here, with me, in England!' Erika feels her breath quickening. 'What difference does it make to you?' She stands up. Can we stop talking about this now?'

'Eri. I can stay here longer and help you sort all this out. It needs to be dealt with.'

She feels her cousin's hand on her arm.

'It's not only about your duty. It's – it's not good for you. I've noticed —'

'I have things to do. I have to think about what to cook for Mrs Mackenzie.'

'I've noticed something dark in you. You seem unhappy and lost. Even more than when we last met. I think it's because you're not dealing with it. It's been so long since Michiko Obachan died. Twelve years, Eri. It's not just about doing the right thing by the family, or by tradition, or even by Obachan. Until you deal with those bones, you aren't letting go of her. You have to move on.'

Erika pulls her arm away. 'Thanks for the psychoanalysis.' She's starting to feel sick again. 'I'm back at work tomorrow and I have a lot to do. Can I go now?'

Michiko

Michiko leaned her forehead against the train window and watched the swooping rise and fall of cables strung between telegraph poles as they punctuated the passing landscape with a flicking rhythm. This was her first cross-country train journey since she was a small child. On the first leg of the long journey, the shinkansen bullet train had travelled too fast for her to catch the view without becoming dizzy. But once she and her mother had switched to the slow country train in Osaka, Michiko had been able to absorb the landscape flowing by – the river of houses, the roads, the fleeting scenes of village life. Sunlight flashed on and off the water-filled rice paddies, and she saw from the way the green shoots sagged under the weight of their golden tresses that they were nearly ready for harvesting.

Michiko and her mother had eaten their onigiri; Michiko packed away the lunch basket and poured them tea from a thermos. At the next station she might have time to buy sweets or some fruit. Her mother loved peaches, and they were in season.

They had been travelling since early morning. A paunchy middle-aged man in a shiny suit, his few strands of hair slicked into place over a balding pate, sat in the seat across the aisle from them. He kept eyeing Michiko's legs, wetting his lips from time to time with a fat tongue. She almost regretted her decision to wear the mini skirt she'd made. It was her favourite skirt, camel beige and decorated with a pattern of large orange and pink flowers. She pulled the hem as far down her thighs as she could manage, but the slippery polyester kept sliding back over her tights.

She'd left the house that morning wearing a long summer coat that hid what she wore underneath. Michiko knew her father well enough to realise the futility of showing him the latest fashion magazines as proof that this was the way modern women dressed. Her father voiced his disgust whenever he passed a woman wearing a short skirt in the street.

'Like a prostitute,' he'd spit. 'Look at her, exposing her legs, the shame of it.'

Michiko, already thirty, was now considered well past marriageable age and her father, to Michiko's relief, had given up seeking a suitable husband for her. The family accepted her role as the unmarried spinster who, together with her new sister-in-law, took care of the family and the tea business, picking up the tasks that would have been her mother's had she been well.

Michiko was less accepting of her position, and quietly continued to dream of a different future. How she would attain it, she didn't know. But she'd always felt she was destined for greater things, and prepared herself as best she could for when the opportunity arose for her escape. She took care to dress as if she were already living her dream life; she had a good eye for quality fabric, and had become skilled with a sewing machine, copying designs from her beloved magazines. She didn't care that as a woman in her thirties she should be more restrained in what she wore. She knew she was beautiful. But now, trundling along in the slow country train towards Kagoshima, she worried that her city style would cause trouble. Her mother may have been sitting beside her, but since Chiyo was no longer present in her mind, she wouldn't be able to protect her daughter should the need arise. Michiko hoped she wouldn't be so out of place in Naha city, where she imagined girls wore the latest American fashions. She couldn't wait to get there.

Michiko twisted sideways in her seat to turn her back to the businessman and patted the back of her mother's hand, which lay limp in her lap.

'Mother?' She spoke slowly, deliberately. She put her face close to Chiyo's, gazing into her eyes with a smile. 'Mother? Do you remember that day we had to throw all the sweet potatoes out of the window? It almost seems funny now, doesn't it?' She watched her mother's blank eyes roll towards her, but they gazed at her without recognition. There was a smear of saliva on her lower lip. Michiko took a handkerchief from her bag and dabbed at it. 'There.'

Michiko often wondered why the neighbours hadn't just called for an ambulance instead of bringing her mother home after the accident. They'd lugged her into the back of the shop, unconscious, her hair matted and dripping with blood, her yukata folded back to reveal one of her legs splayed at a curious and impossible angle, a flap of flesh hanging open like a book, revealing white bone. In time, her visible injuries had mended, but the blow to the head she'd sustained as she fell on the road had left her mind broken. The neighbours said the car that hit her hadn't even been going very fast. The driver sped off, leaving the onlookers to attend to Chiyo's prone body.

Michiko had just turned eighteen at the time.

The doctors had told them that if Chiyo had been taken straight to hospital and treated sooner, she might have made a full recovery. She'd had a catastrophic bleed on the brain, and they'd had to operate to relieve the pressure in her skull. She had come close to death. Yet physically, she'd made a remarkable recovery. There was still a chance that her mind might repair itself, the doctors told the Takigawas, that she might regain some of her former self. They instructed the family to talk to her as they'd always done, about familiar things that might trigger some kind of awakening. But secretly everyone held little hope.

An already-planned match for Kensuke had been hastily concluded so that Mayumi, his bride, could take over Chiyo's duties in the household and the business. It was as elaborate a wedding as could be managed given how quickly it had to be organised; for Mayumi, this was more than made up for by the prestige of marrying the future head of a respectable family. It irritated Michiko every time she heard her father talk to her sister-in-law; he spoke to her with a kindness and respect he'd never showed his own daughters.

Fusae had left the household two years before their mother's accident, her match made. Michiko had wept for days at the loss of her sister. Busy with her new duties as daughter-in-law in a small town in Chiba prefecture, Fusae was rarely allowed to come and tend to her mother, as it took over an hour and several trains to get to the family home. She came less frequently now Chiyo no longer seemed to recognise her.

Michiko had been filled with dread once Fusae was married off; she knew the next visit from the matchmaker would be to make arrangements for her. It soon became obvious she was unlikely to be married into a family with status, and not just because she was the youngest daughter.

'Your beauty is compromised by your bad attitude,' Chiyo had told her after the matchmaker had visited, a few months before the accident. 'You must be more delicate,' she said. 'Not so impetuous and wilful. If you are to marry well, my dear, you must try harder.'

Michiko hadn't been interested in any of the boring young men presented to her, and she entertained herself by giving each suitor a scathing nickname in her diary. The movie stars she took home from the cinema to dream about at night – the Rock Hudsons, the James Stewarts, the Richard Burtons – made all the men she met in reality seem hopelessly inadequate. She knew too that wherever she went to be wed she would still remain a slave, but to strangers instead of to her own family. She preferred the tyranny of her father – at least she was accustomed to it – and as long as she was still at home there was a chance for escape. Fusae was relatively happy, married to the eldest son of a respectable family, her status elevated even further now that she'd produced two sons. But Sayuri and others who had been married off to younger sons of traditional families suffered. Bullied by their in-laws, ignored by their husbands – except at night when they tolerated their perfunctory attentions under the futon quilt – they slaved all day and were last in line after the rest of their new families for everything: baths, food, clothes, respect.

Michiko liked to cross her arms and slump over the table during her matchmaking introductions, yawning and picking at her fingers. If this didn't have the required effect, she'd ask her in-laws questions: would she really have to live with them, or cook for the whole family? How much allowance would she be paid, exactly? Would she have her own room?

'It must be big enough for an American-style double bed,' she'd add, 'as well as wardrobes, a tall swing-mirror and a dressing table.'

She liked cooking very much, she'd say, with a demure look on her face, but not the clearing up afterwards. 'And as for chores, well – please, do forgive my rudeness, it is inexcusable, I know – I won't do *chores.*'

She enjoyed emphasising the word 'chores' while pulling a face, steeling herself so she wouldn't laugh; it guaranteed a reaction. She chewed gum at one meeting, enjoying the look of horror on the potential mother-in-law's face. Time after time the same response came from the prospective groom's family, 'No, thank you, she is not right for our son,' and Michiko would take her relief and escape with it into her diary and the world of the silver screen.

'You will do as you are told. You're not too old for a beating,' her father had said after the fourth rejection, and as he walked away she shadowboxed behind him, enraged. Her mother had hugged her close, pinning her arms until she'd calmed down. 'If he sees you doing that! My dear, I just wish you would stop goading him.'

Michiko regretted the worry she had caused her mother when she was still well; about upsetting her father she couldn't have cared less. But when he ordered his daughter to accompany her mother on the long journey south to the Okinawan islands where Chiyo was born, Michiko happily obeyed. That spring, an agreement between President Nixon and

Prime Minister Satō had come into effect: Okinawa reverted to Japanese sovereignty after twenty-two years of American rule, though the US military presence would remain. They didn't need passports or American dollars to go there any longer. And despite the contempt Michiko's father held for Uchinanchū culture, which he dismissed as coarse and primitive, he had taken the earliest opportunity to send Chiyo to Okinawa in the hope that the landscape and people of her childhood might prompt something in his wife's mind. Michiko spent enough time with her mother to know this was wishful thinking, but for once, she didn't object. She'd always dreamed of visiting the magical islands she'd been told about since she was a child. The thought that it had still been a part of America only months ago made her heart beat faster.

The journey to Naha took four days. They'd made progress quickly at first, taking just three hours to reach Osaka on the Tōkaidō shinkansen. Michiko had seen pictures of the bullet train in the newspaper when the line had opened in time for the Tokyo Olympics in '64, and the carriages still looked new. The seats in front of them had little tables you could pull down. You could eat your bentō in comfort, and afterwards you could recline your seat with your feet on the footrests while you sipped hōji tea. The train travelled so fast the landscape passed by in a blur. Like flying in a plane, Michiko wrote in her diary. It had made up a little for the lack of glamour, but once they'd switched at Osaka to the slow train, Michiko had grown restless. She'd finished reading the magazines she'd bought at Tokyo station, and had to fight the impulse to roll one up and use it to hit the greasy-looking businessman who continued to ogle her, undeterred by her filthy looks. She draped her coat over her thighs, pulled her new floppy-brimmed hat over her face and tried to sleep.

In Himeji, their first overnight stop, Michiko helped her mother bathe at the minshuku where they had reserved a room, laying out their futon so she could leave her mother to rest before dinner. As she watched Chiyo sleep, she felt a gnawing darkness in the pit of her stomach that threatened to smother the excitement of the journey. She longed for a different past, one that mirrored the bright future she dreamed of. A past where her mother had never been in an accident so they'd now be chattering and laughing, embroidering happy memories over the distress of the last long journey they'd made together. There might even have been a past where there had been no war, no starvation, no distressing train journey. But here she sat, as good as alone. She wasn't sure her mother even knew who she was any more.

Michiko's father had hardly needed to insist they stop off in Ibusuki so that Chiyo could go to the suna-mushi sand baths. Michiko had always wanted to go. Even if it didn't live up to its reputation for curing all ills, it would be relaxing for them both.

Michiko loved hot springs. Before the accident, and before Fusae was married, Takigawa had allowed his daughters and their mother a few days away from the shop so they could take the short train journey to Hakone, to rest at the hot springs there. The three women had soaked in the outdoor rotenburo rock pool at least twice each day. Their ryokan had been perched high in the mountains, and as they soaked in the steaming waters they could see over the forested valleys to the snowy flat top of Mount Fuji. Michiko had laughed when they first saw it and said: 'Now that's what Fuji-san is supposed to look like.' It seemed closer, more imposing than it did from the top of Tokyo Tower, where it looked like a milky thumbnail in the haze of smog. The spaciousness of sky and mountain-grazed horizon after years of close-viewed city living made Michiko feel as if she were leaking out beyond the boundaries of her skin.

Steam had billowed as they'd sat perched on stools, soaping each other's backs, rinsing off cumulus clouds of soap suds with wooden bucketfuls of hot thermal water. Clean, they'd stepped into the bath, tenugui cloths wrapped around their hair, leaning their arms on the boulders ringing the pool to admire the view as they talked. When a rising *keeu, keeu, keeu* had echoed across the valley, they'd stopped their chatter and looked up to see a golden eagle turning through the sky. Nobody had said anything. They'd sat in silence, smiling, soaking in the soothing waters heated by the earth's core. If only Michiko had realised then how precious that moment had been.

At Ibusuki, Michiko watched as cheery women wrinkled dark by the sun, stooped and strong from decades of shovelling hot sand, had buried her mother up to the neck. Chiyo's eyes were closed.

She wished her mother could tell her how it made her feel, wished she could share this moment together the way they had done in Hakone with Fusae. But as they lay buried, their faces poking out of the black sand and shaded by tiny parasols, Michiko couldn't tell whether her mother was asleep or dead. There was a body, but her mother no longer inhabited it. Michiko closed her eyes too and felt tears form tiny pools in their corners. She sighed, her breath catching. The weight of the sand and the intense heat on her body dissolved something impenetrable inside her, and she felt herself surrender. Cocooned and immobilised in hot volcanic sand, she cried herself to exhaustion. As she drifted off to sleep, Michiko realised that for the first time in her life, she felt safe, as if the earth were protecting her.

When the old woman finally dug them out of the sand again, Michiko felt as light as clouds.

Neither of them was seasick, like many of the other passengers were, on the overnight ferry crossing to Okinawa. Michiko sat with her mother on the deck as they sailed through the day, wrapped against the wind and watching the bow unravel a churning wake of milky green as the ship heaved though the waves. She had only been on boats on the Sumida river, or on rowing boats on the Imperial Palace moat. She had seen the sea once, years ago, on a school trip to Enoshima. She had never been out of sight of land until now.

They were lucky with their timing; a typhoon was due to pass through in a few days' time, and the wind was its herald. It whipped at her freshly permed curls, teasing, then with a sudden gust snatched the scarf she'd tied around her head and blew it out to sea. An offering to Ryūjin, for safe passage across his waters, Michiko thought, as she watched it flutter and tumble into the waves. It was only a cheap thing she'd bought for twenty yen anyway. She suddenly remembered the money her father had given her for her mother's care. She'd buy another in Naha.

The ship continued to work its way south, discharging passengers and cars at one small island port after another as the waves smoothed into a mirror and the water paled to turquoise. Michiko stood on the deck and held her mother's hand. She shaded her eyes as she watched the sun sink into the horizon, a giant, shimmering blood-orange, staining everything it touched pink and crimson. It blazed bright as it dissolved into the sea, fighting to the last, refusing to be extinguished.

A Lacquer Tablet

It measures five centimetres wide and eight high. Small dots of mother-of-pearl are embedded in its elegant, simply carved legs. It is feather-light in the hand. Hiding a slender inner core of wood, it has been painted over hundreds of times with layers of red and black lacquer and left to harden to a matt sheen. Its edges are highlighted with thin lines of gold. The gold paint has also been used for the kaimyō – the posthumous Buddhist name given to the deceased – inscribed in kanji characters on the front of the thin panel that rises up from the legs. On the reverse, the name that was used in life and the date of death are etched into the black lacquer to reveal the red beneath. It sits inside a red lacquer cabinet just large enough to hold it. In the morning, its doors are opened up and incense offered. At night, they must be closed again to keep the spirit from wandering.

Erika

It's Sunday, and there are over seventy covers. Frankie's done his back and rung in sick; André cuts Erika little slack despite her having to take on Frankie's sections as well as her own; she endures a savage slating after misreading a docket and plating up two lobsters instead of three. The humiliation distracts her from the flashes of panic that keep cutting through the blanketing numbness she's been feeling all day. She isn't going to get home until after midnight, by which time Kei will have gone to bed. Until then, her cousin will be in the flat alone. What at first had been a relief – to be at work, away from Kei – turns to apprehension.

During her break she phones Marcus. 'Please could you take Kei out on one or two evenings this week while I'm at work? I'm nervous about her being in the flat alone.'

'I can't, you know I've got Felix this week. She's already seen the urn, what else is there to worry about?'

'I don't like her alone in the flat while I'm working, that's all.'

When Erika gets home, the Korean cabinet and everything on it has been dusted. There's a small bunch of white chrysanthemums in a vase. It looks like a proper altar instead of a dump for neglected objects. Closing her eyes and breathing, Erika wills away the threat of nausea.

She has a shower and gets ready for bed but she's too wired to sleep. She fetches a bottle of eighteen-year-old malt whisky from the cupboard and its cork gives way with a satisfying *blonk*. Settling into an armchair, feet up on the coffee table, she sips from her glass. The liquid traces a burning path down to her stomach, distracting and soothing.

'You're back.'

Erika didn't hear Kei come into the sitting room. 'I'm sorry, did I wake you?'

Kei squints in the lamplight and rubs her eyes. 'I couldn't sleep. Jetlag still, I guess.'

Erika waggles the bottle at her. 'Want some?'

Kei sits opposite her and accepts a glass. Gesturing at the Korean cabinet, she says, 'I hope you don't mind.'

'Thanks for cleaning it up.'

'It looks better, doesn't it?'

Erika finishes her drink and pours herself another.

Kei speaks as if she's been rehearsing the words. 'I know you said you didn't want to talk about it, but …'

'Did you have a good day? What did you do? Did you cook something here or go out?'

Kei hesitates, starts to say something but seems to change her mind. She sips her whisky. 'I went to the National Gallery. I bought groceries on the way home and made chāhan for dinner. I made some for you. Are you hungry?'

'No, thanks.'

Kei moves over to the Korean chest. Her fingers slide over the front of the cabinet and linger over the metal clasps. 'What's inside these cupboards, anyway?'

'Just stuff.'

'What sort of stuff?'

None of your business, Erika wants to say. Instead she says: 'Michiko's stuff. The cabinet was hers. It's as she left it. I looked through it once when I got it home after clearing out her house. I can't really remember what's in there. Mostly junk.'

'Erika, could you do me a favour?'

'What?'

'Could you please stop calling Obachan by her first name? It's not right. Could you call her Okāsan, at least?'

'She didn't like me calling her that. She made me call her Michiko.'

'Yes, I know. We all thought it was strange. But she's not here now, so could you just … not? It sounds too odd, as if she's not your mother.'

Erika empties her glass and gets up. 'I'm off to bed.' She takes the glass and the whisky bottle and starts heading for the bedroom, and then pauses to turn around. 'Goodnight.'

Kei is frowning.

Erika flushes with guilt and adds: 'I'll be cleaning for Mrs Mackenzie tomorrow afternoon. Come upstairs when I'm done and join us; we always have a cup of tea and some cake. She wants to meet you. You'll like her.'

Erika starts cooking at dawn, bleary-eyed and hungover. Two small fish pies in foil cartons ready for the oven, a Lancashire hotpot and a crock of Scotch broth. At the last minute Erika decides to bake an old-fashioned Victoria sponge cake to have with their tea. Raspberry jam in the middle and a dusting of icing sugar on top. She's washed, chopped and bagged up the vegetables ready for Mrs Mackenzie to microwave. Kei has gone clothes shopping on Kensington High Street. The flat feels lighter; Erika can breathe again, can better channel her care into the food she's cooking.

It's all ready by ten o'clock. Erika's repertoire for Mrs Mackenzie is limited – by request. The curry Erika once made had remained uneaten. 'I like my food plain, my dear,' Mrs Mackenzie had said, patting Erika's hand apologetically. So, cottage pie, beef casserole, toad-in-the-hole, the occasional roast chicken. Haggis, neeps and tatties on Burns Night. At Christmas they eat roast turkey and stuffing together. It makes Erika happy.

Three hours to clean her own flat. Erika includes the Korean cabinet in her rounds this time and feels blank as she dusts the box containing the granite urn with her mother's bones inside. It makes a muffled rattle when she moves it, and she is surprised to feel nothing.

She wonders how she's going to get through the rest of Kei's stay. At least there's Notting Hill Carnival coming up soon over the long August bank holiday weekend to distract them; this year Erika and Sarah have been given time off for it. Barriers and portaloos will soon be manoeuvred into place, and excitement will start to brew in the neighbourhood. Erika's invited Sarah to stay over; her presence will dilute any tension. Marcus will join them on the Monday while his ex looks after Felix; Sunday is Children's Day, so he'll bring his son separately then. Erika's apprehensive at the thought she might bump into Marcus while he's with Felix. Two million people will be packing the neighbourhood over the weekend, she tells herself. The chances of that happening are slim.

Erika doesn't hear Kei letting herself in over the sound of the vacuum cleaner. She jumps when Kei taps her on the shoulder, smiling, laden with bags. After putting one of them on the table, Kei disappears into her room before returning to wrest the vacuum from her cousin. 'Let me.'

'No. Give it back.' Erika pushes her cousin away, and when Kei heads back to her room she regrets sounding so irritated. She calls out after her: 'Thanks though. I'm almost finished.'

The cleaning done, Erika finds Kei reading in her room. 'Ready to go upstairs to see Mrs Mac?'

'There's something I want you to open first.' Kei fetches the red bag from the sitting room and holds it out. 'Go ahead.'

Erika pulls out a small box and flushes with shame. It's from a local jeweller.

'Don't worry, it's nothing expensive.'

Inside is a necklace with a tiny silver pendant in the shape of an angel. It isn't really the sort of thing Erika wears – she's not into angels – but it's pretty.

'I wanted to get you a protective omamori, but since you can't get them here I thought I'd get you the Western equivalent. It's a guardian angel. Here, let me.'

Erika wants to tell Kei that she can't buy her way into favour, but feels something inside her come undone. She's glad Kei has moved behind her to fasten the chain, so she can't see her face.

'I want us to start again,' says Kei. 'I'd like to help you organise getting Michiko Obachan's remains interred while I'm here, if you'll let me.'

Erika's stomach lurches. No, you can't, she wants to say, but keeps quiet.

'I know we don't really get on, but could we try? We're family, after all. We grew up together. You and me, we're very different. But we need to do the right thing by Michiko Obachan. All this strife is making me sad.'

Erika fingers the angel around her neck and clears her throat. She waits until she's composed herself and turns to her cousin. She smiles. 'It's lovely. Thank you,' she says, and means it.

'That was delicious, my dear,' says Mrs Mackenzie. Her quavering head is permanently bowed, her back stooped and twisted, but she peeks up from under her snow-white fringe with milky blue eyes and a girlish smile. 'I'll have another slice, if I may.'

'I do it,' says Kei, reaching for Mrs Mackenzie's plate. She cuts another slice of the Victoria sponge cake.

'Thank you, darling girl, you are kind. It runs in the family, I see.' Her warm Scottish burr wafts comfort.

The cousins sip their tea and Mrs Mackenzie eats her cake, her shaking fork scattering crumbs. An easy silence descends.

Kei gets up to look at the bookshelves before moving to an oak sideboard where various objects are on display. 'Many beautiful thing,' she says.

'I'm afraid they're rather tedious for Erika to dust, but I'm rather fond of them,' says Mrs Mackenzie. 'That's a lifetime of trinkets on there. They all tell a story.'

Kei is staring at a grey stone statuette about ten centimetres high. 'This is Kannon-sama?' She turns to Mrs Mackenzie.

'That is a statue of Kuan Eim.'

'Same goddess, different names,' says Erika. 'Guan Yin. Goddess of compassion and mercy.'

'William, my husband, brought it back from Thailand. He went there for a special reunion a few years before he died.' She gestures to Kei. 'Would you bring it to me, dear?'

Mrs Mackenzie turns the statuette in her hands and is quiet for a moment, her eyes unfocused as if drawing out memories from dusty corners. 'William was a POW in Kanchanaburi,' she finally says.

'P-O-W,' Kei repeats, turning to Erika, confused.

Erika sees she'll have to pick up the thread of Mrs Mackenzie's story. She's heard it many times before, though it never ceases to upset her, leaving a heavy weight in the pit of her stomach.

'Mrs Mac's husband was a prisoner of war,' Erika says quietly in Japanese. 'In Thailand. He was one of the soldiers forced to build the Thai–Burma Railway. The Death Railway.'

'I've never heard it called that.'

'It's because thousands of men died building it.'

'Thousands?'

Erika peers at her cousin. 'You don't know?'

'But Mrs Mackenzie's husband came back alive, didn't he?'

'William was a bag of bones when he returned home,' says Mrs Mackenzie, as though she'd understood every word that passed between the cousins. 'He caught dysentery and malaria while he was in the camp. He had scars on his back from all the beatings, but it took longer for his spirit to recover than his body. Nightmares, you know. But he would never talk about it. He was one of the lucky ones

– at least he survived …' She trails off, gazing at the statuette, her face mirroring its sad, gentle smile.

In the silence, Erika turns again to Kei. 'He came home traumatised,' she whispers. 'He was probably tortured.'

'By who?'

Erika gapes. She's heard this, that people don't know, but she didn't realise Kei was one of them.

'What did they teach you about the war in school?' she asks. 'About Burma and Thailand and the Allied prisoners of war? Nanjing? Korea? Okinawa?'

'We heard how awful the war was, of course. The firebombing of Tokyo, the atomic bombs in Nagasaki and Hiroshima. Everyone knows about those.'

'Those thousands, those POWs, they were starved, beaten and tortured. They died of diseases. They were worked to death building that railway. By the Japanese army.'

Kei looks shocked.

Mrs Mackenzie hands the statuette back to Erika. 'I don't want her to be upset,' she says, glancing kindly at Kei. 'Tell her I bear no ill feeling towards the Japanese people. It was the warmongers who were at fault. William forgave, in the end, and found peace of mind. That's what the statue was about – a reminder about mercy, compassion and forgiveness.'

Erika nods, feeling her eyes sting as they fill with tears.

The food put away in the elderly widow's fridge and freezer, the flat tidy and clean, the cousins go for a drink and some Moroccan food on Golborne Road. It's a warm afternoon, and people are spilling out of the pubs onto the pavement in anticipation of sunshine and a long weekend of partying.

They eat together in a silence that's not altogether uncomfortable, but Erika can't relax. She feels strangely restless, as if she might be compelled at any moment to jump up and run away.

The waiter clears their plates, and Erika orders baklava and mint tea. Kei pours herself another half-glass of wine, downs it, then props her chin on her hand to gaze at her cousin.

'What?' says Erika with a nervous laugh.

'We were friends, once. More than just cousins,' says Kei.

'I know. But we were children. It was easy then.'

'And now we're adults we have to be enemies?'

'Not enemies. But you used to like me when I was a kid, and now you don't. I feel like you came here to torment me and judge me about what you see as my failure to fulfil my obligations.'

'Erika, I came here to get away too. It's not always about you. You have no idea what's been going on at home.'

'I have no idea because you never tell me anything. You and your brother shut me out after Michiko died. You disapprove of me so much; why would I make an effort to get in touch?'

The waiter brings the baklava and makes a show of pouring mint tea in great steaming arcs from silver pot to tea-glass and back again without spilling a drop. Kei watches, mesmerised, as if Erika hadn't said a word. When the waiter ends the ritual with a final flourish, pouring perfect portions of tea into glasses he sets in colourful saucers, she claps her hands in quick, excited applause, like a child. He bows before leaving the table.

Kei gazes after him for a while, then blinks, sighs and says: 'I don't know why you find it so hard to deal with the urn, Erika. You just have to do it, and then you'll be free.'

'Free? From what?'

'Your suffering.'

'I'm not suffering.'

'You seem miserable. I want to help you.'

'I'm not miserable. I don't need help. Stop patronising me.'

Kei sits back and crosses her arms. She looks tired.

Erika sighs. 'I'm sorry, I shouldn't have snapped at you.' She refills their glasses, emptying the bottle. 'I just don't feel ready to talk about it yet.'

'You're going to have to deal with things sooner or later, Eri-chan,' says Kei. 'I hope you'll feel ready while I'm still here. You're not alone, you know.' She smiles and raises her glass. 'Here's to dealing with things.'

There's a softness in Kei's voice that makes Erika dive under the table for her bag so she can rummage inside it for her wallet. She doesn't want her cousin to see the tears in her eyes, because if Kei speaks kindly to her again, Erika knows she won't be able to keep them from spilling over.

If I start crying now, Erika thinks, It'll all be over, because I don't know if I'll ever be able to stop again.

Later that night, Kei and Erika sit rosy-cheeked on the sofa, another bottle of wine between them. Erika is worn out from all the emotion, but feels strangely at ease for the first time since her cousin arrived.

Kei gets up to light two sticks of incense for Michiko's altar. Erika watches as she tings the brass bell, puts her hands together and moves her lips in silent supplication. She goes to join her. When they finish, Kei says, 'Let's offer Obachan some whisky.'

Erika snorts. 'Oh yeah, she'd love that.'

Kei doesn't pick up on the sarcasm and goes to rinse out the offering cup in the kitchen. When she returns, Erika meets her with the bottle and pours a tiny amount into the cup.

'At least this won't hurt her now,' Erika says.

'What do you mean?'

'You really have no idea, do you? Did you know she could get through a whole bottle of vodka in one day? And you know she had diabetes, right?'

Kei shrugs. 'I know she liked a drink now and then. There's nothing wrong with that. She was always so cheerful when she'd had a bit to drink. Those funny stories she told!'

'Yeah, hilarious.'

Kei doesn't seem to be listening. She squats down and opens the top cupboard of the cabinet. 'Do you mind if I look inside?'

Whatever. What the hell. 'Go ahead.'

Kei pulls out a box. She opens the lid and lifts out a hard brown glasses case, a cedarwood box about six centimetres wide, a red faux-leather address book with a world map inside its covers and a wooden darning mushroom decorated with painted flowers. At the bottom is a silver pillbox inscribed with the initials MU, which rattles when Kei shakes it. She opens it.

'Is this her wedding ring? Oh, and her engagement ring. Emeralds. How beautiful. What's this for?' asks Kei, holding up the wooden mushroom.

'For darning.'

'It's so pretty with its painted flowers.'

'I guess she thought it was a good thing for a housewife to have. I never saw her use it.'

'Darning seems too unglamorous for her. I never thought of Obachan as a housewife,' says Kei.

'She wasn't. The only thing she was prepared to do was cook.'

Kei opens the little cedarwood box. It holds a tiny plastic bracelet with a white clasp, a strip of pink paper sealed inside. She reads what's written on it. '"Underwood, Erika. 3.2 kilograms. 18 April 1973." Oh, your hospital bracelet from when you were born! It's tiny.' Kei laughs. 'It's a bit loose, but it almost fits around my thumb like a ring, look. How sweet she kept it. I don't think my mother kept mine.'

Erika feels the same shock as when she first came upon the bracelet, just after her mother died. That Michiko had kept it was unexpected and utterly incomprehensible. A wave of dizziness washes over her.

Her vision distorts, as if everything is reflected in a fun-house mirror. Steadying herself on the cabinet, a movement catches her eye. The doors of the miniature red lacquer cabinet housing her mother's spirit tablet are opening, almost imperceptibly, like curtains on a tiny stage. She blinks. Inside, the golden kanji characters of Michiko's kaimyō tremble and swim on the tablet as if she's seeing the words come to life through a smear of Vaseline. Then, a startling flash of gold.

She rubs her face with her palms, not sure what she's seeing. She wonders if Kei has seen it too, and looks over at her. From Kei's relaxed expression, it's obvious she hasn't. Erika needs to lie down, get some sleep.

'Feel free to keep looking,' says Erika. 'I'm going to bed.'

The next morning, they eat breakfast together. Erika is alarmed to see a stack of notebooks from the cabinet sitting on the table. She's glad Kei has put the rest of the things back inside it; the objects seemed different from the last time she'd looked at them, altered by a new sheen of strangeness. The sight of them saps her strength. She doesn't know what to do with them; she can't bring herself to throw them away. She wishes they'd just disappear so she doesn't have to think about them. Maybe she should just give everything to Kei.

Kei's rubbing cream into her hands; she's taken off her rings and put them on the table but her wedding ring isn't among them. How could Erika have missed it? She's caught off guard when Kei speaks.

'Those are her diaries. And some letters. Have you read them?' asks Kei.

'Not really.'

'Aren't you curious?'

Erika butters some toast. 'Don't you think it's inappropriate?'

'If she didn't want them to be read, she would have destroyed them. Especially since she knew she was going to …'

'I don't want to talk about that, Kei.' Erika's voice is glassy.

112

'I'm sorry. I didn't mean to bring that up.'

Erika bites off a hunk of toast and takes her time chewing and swallowing. Then she says, 'I skimmed through them, but I can't read them properly because of the kanji. And what I can read looks banal. It's about where she went, what she wore, what she ate. Not much detail about what was going on inside her head.'

'Even less reason to feel bad about reading them then,' says Kei. 'Obachan had such a glamorous life. I'd love to read about what she did every day. Wouldn't you?'

Erika didn't expect this of Kei. She doesn't need to feel guilty about trying and failing to read them back then after all. 'Feel free,' she says.

'Really?'

'Yes.'

'Do you want me to transcribe the hiragana against the kanji so you can read it more easily?'

'There's almost thirty years' worth of diaries.'

'I don't mind. I'd enjoy it. I could skim through and pick out entries that look especially interesting. I can work on them while you're at the restaurant then take the rest back to Tokyo to finish.'

Erika forces a smile. She can't help but question Kei's motives. Curiosity, certainly. But is that enough to sustain what will surely be days of transcribing? Where will Kei find the time? The family business is thriving, despite the recession, and then there's her husband. Doesn't she have anything better to do?

Her husband, Jun. What's happened to Jun-san? Kei avoided Erika's question about him when she first arrived and hasn't talked about him since. Erika takes another bite of toast. It's not the time to push.

Each day for the rest of that week, the cousins eat breakfast together before Erika heads out to work at André's. Over toast and coffee, Kei talks about her plans for the day – shopping at Covent Garden or taking a river boat to Tate Modern; going to see the Cindy Sherman exhibition at the Serpentine Gallery or taking the Tube to Kew Gardens – and Erika chips in with recommendations for unusual places worth seeing, or good spots to eat nearby.

By the time Erika returns late each night she finds Kei gone to bed and an ever-growing pile of transcribed diaries on the dining-room table. With only an hour together each morning, the right moment to ask her cousin about Jun never quite presents itself. It seems Kei hasn't found an opportunity to broach the subject of Michiko's remains, either, much to Erika's relief. Erika hopes the distraction of Carnival on the weekend will keep Kei from bringing it up again.

The following Sunday morning, the sounds of whistles and horns announce the arrival of Carnival as crowds of people start to flood into the neighbourhood.

'You'll be so sick of that sound by tomorrow night,' Erika says, grinning. In the distance they hear the first booming bass beats of the procession beginning at the top of Ladbroke Grove. The smell of jerk chicken wafts in through the windows.

Sarah arrives. 'Hello! Kei! I've heard lots about you.'

'Nice to meet you,' says Kei, looking sideways at Erika.

'Where's Luca? It's Children's Day today.'

Sarah makes a guilty face. 'I know, I know. But I won't be able to relax with him out there in the crush, even if it *is* Children's Day. He's with Meg. She's taking him to Hamleys. He'd much rather be toy shopping with his auntie. Just as well, really,' she says, winking theatrically as she pulls a small baggie and some papers out of her pocket. She rolls a joint and lights it. 'Time to get into the spirit of Carnival,' she says, squinting through the smoke and passing it to Kei.

'No, thank you,' says Kei.

'Is Marcus coming?' asks Sarah.

'He's bringing Felix with him today, but we won't be seeing him.

I'm staying out of the way. He'll come over tomorrow.' Erika takes a few tokes and holds it out to Kei. 'You should try some. It's part of a religion for a lot of people around here.'

Kei laughs uneasily.

'I'm not kidding. Rastafarians see it as a key that opens a gateway to self-understanding. Sacred ganja that reveals truth.'

Kei shakes her head. 'I don't want any. I don't do drugs. I don't have tattoos, either,' she says, staring with disgust at Erika's koi carp. Kei goes over to the window and looks out. Something in the slope of her shoulders makes Erika feel sorry for her.

'You're sucking on that thing like it's your last breath,' Sarah says, laughing. 'Pass it over here.' She notices Erika's expression. 'What's up? You okay?'

Erika shrugs and gestures at Kei's back.

Sarah moves over to Kei by the window. 'Carnival's great! I promise you'll have fun. It's for the whole community. It started after the race riots here, to promote harmony and diversity.'

Kei nods, though Erika's sure she doesn't have a clue what Sarah's saying.

'She's upset about this,' says Erika, pointing at her tattoo, 'and about the weed.'

'I'm sorry, I didn't mean to upset things by bringing it ...'

'It's Carnival. She'll have to get over it. And there's nothing I can do about the tattoo, so she'll have to get over that too.' She passes the joint back to Sarah.

'I don't know why you're so reluctant to meet Marcus's son,' says Sarah, blowing out a plume of smoke. 'You've been together now, what, two years? Don't you think it's time you met him?'

'I will, once I'm certain Marcus and I are going to stay together. I don't want to fuck up his kid. Marcus is fine with that. He doesn't want to fuck his kid up either.'

A bass boom of a dub beat from a sound system below rattles the glass in the window frames. 'Here we go,' says Erika.

'That is very loud,' says Kei. Competing beats begin to bounce around the streets. She sticks her head out of the window. 'Wah ... very many people!'

'Just wait until tomorrow,' says Erika.

'Come on,' says Sarah. 'The parade's started.'

Spilling downstairs, they emerge blinking into sunlight hazy with delicious, dense smoke wafting from food stalls lining the street. They order jerk chicken, rice and peas, salt fish and ackee. Clutching heaped plates, they push through heaving crowds towards Ladbroke Grove.

'Kei, hold my hand!' shouts Erika. 'Just keep pushing through.' The jubilant sounds of steel pans shimmer, almost palpable in the air, bass beats thump up through their bellies and into their throats. 'The parade's passing through, come on!'

The spicy smoke-clouds of grilling food and ganja, the glittering colours, the heat and the pounding, urgent beats swirl around them in an intoxicating haze. An electric thrill surges through the crowd, passing from person to person; grinning faces everywhere, whooping and whistling, hands in the air, couples kissing, children with balloons, dancing policemen, people pushing wheelbarrows piled high with ice and cans of drink, grizzled Rastas with long greying dreads blissing out on lolloping reggae. Erika looks back at her cousin whose hand she holds tight and sees that Kei's feeling it too; the excitement is infectious. The crowds grow densest along the barriers lining Ladbroke Grove, and breaking through at last, Erika presents it all to Kei with a glorious wave of her arm – the parade jumping and grinding along the street like a giant pulsating creature; the beaming, exultant dancers in sequins and feathers and rainbow colours; the open-sided trucks bouncing as steel-pan players jump to the beat of soca; the MCs blaring blurs of sound; the crowd blowing whistles to the pounding beat. Erika sees Kei's mouth moving, but her voice is lost in the overwhelming noise. Erika and Sarah start jumping in time to the beat of the steel-pan bands, swinging their hips. Erika takes Kei's hand. Kei tries to pull it away, but Erika holds tight, drawing her in so she can shout into her ear: 'I don't want to lose you.' She grins at her cousin, taking bites from her jerk chicken sandwich in the other hand, sauce dripping down her chin as she bounces along with the crowd around her.

'Come on!' she shouts, and she swings Kei's arm as she dances.

Kei pulls a face and reluctantly starts to move. 'I feel silly.'

'Nobody cares! Listen to it! How can you resist?'

The river of people and bass beats flows past them, and as one float's entourage and music thin out, the clashing beats of the next begin to merge with it in a sonic soup. Calypso, reggae, soca, samba; on and on it flows against the bass-beat backdrop of the neighbouring streets' sound systems. Sarah pulls another joint out of her ponytail, lights it and holds it out to Kei, eyebrows raised in question, and to Erika's amazement, Kei takes it. Erika watches, mouth open, as her cousin holds it gingerly between her fingers and takes a tentative puff. She splutters smoke. Her eyes water as she coughs, but she waves away Erika's pounding on her back. Sarah offers her a swig from her water bottle. Kei takes another puff and holds it in this time. She grins, eyes wide and watering, and passes it to Erika. *Wah!* she mouths. She's already softening, morphing, eyes closed, and before long she begins rocking her weight from foot to foot. She opens her eyes and sees Erika watching. She beams, pulling her close, her lips up against Erika's ear.

'I can't believe I had some!' she shouts. 'Please don't tell anyone back home.'

'I can't believe it either. Do you like it?'

Kei just laughs, like a child, and raises her arms above her head as if she's just won something.

Sarah and Erika respond wordlessly, each putting an arm around Kei's shoulders, Kei the filling in their sandwich. They bounce together up and down to the beat.

'Group hug, woo hoo!' yells Sarah. They close together in a tight circle, pressed in by the mass of people, their bodies synchronised by the pulsing vibration of the passing procession. Erika and Kei haven't been physically close like this since they were children. It feels marvellous, strange and familiar all at the same time, as if something stagnant has washed away to reveal something good that's always been there. Erika hears Kei again in her ear.

'Thank you,' she says.

Back at Erika's apartment, as the volume outside begins to subside and night descends over London, Sarah turns up the stereo, loud.

'Won't Mrs Mackenzie mind?' asks Kei.

'She isn't upstairs. She's gone to stay with one of her daughters, like she does every Carnival weekend.'

Kei slumps on the sofa. 'That's good. Well, I had fun today. Although ... ow ... my feet.' She takes off her socks and massages her toes.

Erika sits on the floor beside her and takes a foot in her hand. 'Here.' She begins kneading.

'Nice,' says Kei, surprised. 'I suppose you do this for Marcus.'

'Never.'

'Really? You never massage his feet for him?'

'Should I?'

'It's a nice thing for a wife to do for a husband,' says Kei.

'And a nice thing for a husband to do for a wife. Anyway, we're not married,' says Erika.

'I used to do it all the time for Jun. Though it made no difference in the end. He left me.'

Hearing Kei give this information up so easily is a shock.

'He left me for somebody else. I had no idea he'd been having an affair.'

'Oh, Kei. I'm so sorry.'

'Is everything okay?' asks Sarah, sensing the change in mood.

Kei looks at her sadly, head swaying a little. 'My husband. He leave me.' The three of them process this information for a moment.

'He's a very silly man,' says Sarah. 'Leaving a lovely woman like you. What an idiot.'

Erika translates.

Kei shrugs and accepts another joint from Sarah. Massive Attack's 'Unfinished Sympathy' plays out its melancholy on the stereo, broken sporadically by the sound of whistles blown by drunken Carnival-goers on their way home.

'It must have been difficult for you,' says Erika. 'I'm so sorry. I didn't know. Why didn't you tell me?'

'If he were still with me he wouldn't have let me come to London, Eri,' says Kei, ignoring the question. 'He was very controlling. He didn't let me do things if he decided they were things I shouldn't do. You have no idea how lucky you are, with your choices, and your freedom.'

'Well you're free now; you made the choice to come here. And you have all that security, Kei. Even if you are divorced, you're still a part of that family. The family takes care of you. Everyone in the neighbourhood looks out for you. '

'In return for my freedom,' says Kei. 'I still have to go back to a cage, Eri. I'm still trapped. I don't have that many choices in life.'

'Everybody has choices.'

'Not if you're an abandoned wife in Japan. No choices. I thought I'd feel free now that Jun isn't around trying to control everything. But back home, everybody disapproves of the divorce. Everyone in the neighbourhood gossips about me, wondering what it was I did that made Jun leave me for someone else. They just think I'm a bad wife, and they never seem to think he might have been the one at fault. The only way I could get away from all that was by coming here. But I still have to go back. Family duty.'

Sarah returns from the kitchen with cold beers and passes the bottles around.

Erika clinks bottles with Kei. 'I know it's a strange question,' she says, 'but why did you come to London? I mean really?'

'I hadn't seen you for so long. And also because I wanted to get away from everything after Jun left.'

'So it wasn't to check that I'd organised a grave for my mother's bones?'

Kei looks at her. 'That was just one reason. I came because I hadn't seen or heard from you for such a long time. And I've been working so hard in the family business, I needed a holiday. And the whole thing with Jun. Like I said, I had to get away. It was all too much.'

They fall silent again. Sarah is horizontal on the sofa with her eyes closed, nodding her head in time to the music.

'I had fun today,' says Kei. 'For the first time in ages I felt I could forget all the bad things.'

'Me too,' says Erika. 'I'm glad you were here for Carnival. You timed your visit well.'

'I wish I could come again next year.'

'Well then, come.'

'I told you, I don't have the freedom you have. I can't just drop everything and come because I want to have fun. You're so lucky and you don't even know it.'

'I don't feel lucky,' says Erika, taking a swig of beer. 'I belong nowhere. I have no country. No family. Michiko never wanted me and my father left me.'

'You've got Marcus,' says Kei. 'He seems like a kind man.'

'I don't want to rely on him. You can't rely on anyone for your happiness.'

'You can do what you want, go where you want,' continues Kei. 'I can't do much other than what's been planned and expected for me, especially now I'm divorced. The family takes care of me, and I serve the family. You have no ties. So yes, you're very lucky.'

'Hey, what are you two talking about?' asks Sarah, squinting at them from the sofa. 'I don't like those long faces.'

'I'm sorry,' says Erika. The cousins look at one another, still serious. But Kei has a twinkle in her eye and Erika can't help but smile. When Kei smiles back, something passes between them, like a lifeline thrown from one foundering ship to another in a storm.

Michiko

The ferry sailed into Naha harbour at last. The sight of dark, oil-slicked water, grimy concrete buildings and industrial cranes was disappointing; Michiko had hoped for the azure waters and white beaches she'd seen in pictures. As the ship drew closer she saw dark-green army jeeps parked on the dock with the familiar star insignia painted on their sides. She shivered, despite the oppressive heat and humidity, the sight of them triggering mixed memories too complicated to deal with. She distracted herself by waving back at the crowds lining the wharf.

A distant cousin of Chiyo's – a widow with two adult daughters, her father had said – met Michiko and her mother at the bottom of the gangplank. Ayano Kinjō was a robust, smiling woman of about seventy, head and shoulders shorter than Michiko, short hair strikingly white against her sun-darkened face. It was the first time Michiko had met anyone from her mother's side of the family.

Michiko knew that when Chiyo was a young girl, the Kudakas had moved from Kudakajima, the island they'd been named after, to Mabuni, forty minutes by bus from Naha city. It was their house in Mabuni where Kensuke had stayed with their mother before the war, spending days swimming at Komesu beach nearby. After the chaos of the war was over, Chiyo discovered that her parents, her two younger sisters and her older brother had lost their lives. The American offensive had reached the southeastern corner of the island, and everyone had fled towards the cliffs that rose high above the crashing waves. Government propaganda had been explicit about the horrors of what American soldiers would do to them if they were caught. Okinawans were supplied with grenades and bottles of cyanide-laced milk, and urged to end their lives quickly to avoid capture.

Chiyo never spoke about how her family had died, but everyone knew the name Americans gave to that stretch of the coastline: the Suicide Cliffs. The only thing Chiyo ever said was that the family might have lived had they stayed on Kudakajima. When they'd moved to Mabuni, they'd taken their entire household with them, and all of it had been destroyed in the bombardment, leaving no trace of the Kudaka family home: no altar, no documentation. After Chiyo's accident, none of the family had known of other relatives in Okinawa until their father made enquiries through a business associate based in the south.

Michiko introduced herself as to a stranger, addressing the woman as Kinjō-san.

'You needn't be so formal,' the woman said, laughing. 'Just call me Obā.' She turned to Chiyo and grasped her hands. 'Chiyo-chan! It's me, Ayano. I still know you after all these years. We were young girls when we met, do you remember?' But Chiyo showed no sign of recognition.

The woman had a heavy accent. She was speaking Japanese, not Uchināguchi, but it still took Michiko a moment to figure out what she was saying.

'I'm sorry,' Michiko said, 'I'm afraid my mother doesn't ...'

'It's all right. Your father explained everything. Here, let me help you with your bags. I'm parked just over there.'

The little car was dented and rusted, but Michiko was impressed. 'My father won't get a car,' she said.

'You don't need one in Tokyo, with so many buses and trains,' said Obā, flipping their suitcases into the boot as if they were feather-light. 'There aren't as many options here, not as many roads. It used to take me nearly an hour to get to work by bus, but now it only takes thirty minutes. My employer gave me this car.'

'Gave you a car? For free?' said Michiko, helping Chiyo into the back. She moved to the front to get into the passenger seat and hesitated, confused. 'Why's the steering wheel on the wrong side?'

'American road rules. They haven't changed things back to the way they were before the war.'

Obā pulled away, following a convoy of army trucks out of the port and onto a busy main road. 'This car used to belong to my employer's son. He was killed last year, fighting in Vietnam.'

'I didn't know Okinawans were fighting in Vietnam.'

'The family I work for is American. They're stationed at Futenma military base up at Ginowan. I'm their housekeeper.'

Michiko sat up. 'What are they like?'

'I never see the husband. He's a platoon sergeant, away in Vietnam. The mistress is kind to me, though she grieves terribly for their son. He was only eighteen. I care for their two younger daughters. The mistress gives me clothes they've grown out of, for my grandchildren. I'm lucky to have a decent job. It's hard to find work here.'

It felt good to have a two-way conversation again. Michiko was already adjusting to Obā's Uchinā accent, picking up traces of it herself. Chiyo sat silent in the back as they drove along a long, straight street lined with a mixture of low, traditional tile-roofed shops and modern buildings three or four storeys high, bristling with signs for shops, cafes and bars.

'We're on Kokusai Dōri, the longest street in town. It cuts all the way through to Makishi. Look, here's the market, closed for renovations. It's where people traded food on the black market during the war, before things got too bad to be out in the open.'

Michiko felt as if she were in another country. There were hedges of red and pink hibiscus everywhere; palm trees rose up between buildings and lush green vines tumbled over stone walls. There were plenty of Okinawans going about their daily business, but Michiko had never seen so many foreigners mingling with the crowds.

'Are these gaijin all American?'

'Mostly.'

'It's not really "Kokusai" then, is it? They should call it Amerika Dōri.'

Obā cackled so loud and long that Michiko had to join in, even though she didn't think what she'd said was all that funny. 'Oh, my dear, they probably should. You'll find most of the bars are full of American GIs.'

Michiko peered down side streets lined with clusters of unlit neon signs advertising late-night bars and 'Girls Girls Girls'. She stared at a group of young American soldiers, handsome in their uniforms. 'There are so many bars,' she said, craning her neck.

'Those places aren't safe, especially at night. Drunk soldiers making the most of things before they're sent to Vietnam. The only women you'll see in those places are the ones selling themselves for money. A young woman was raped and strangled to death here only a few months ago. The soldier who did it was only a boy. He was about to be sent to Saigon.' Obā sighed. 'War makes such monsters of men.'

The traffic was thinning out.

'Do you think I could get a job working for an American family here?'

'What? Why?'

'I could earn money and send it home. Mother could stay here – it'll do her good to be in the place she was born, and I'll look after her.'

'Your father wouldn't allow it, would he?'

Michiko bit her lip. It was true: there was no way her father would let her stay here. But coming to Okinawa was an opportunity – the only one she might ever get. She had four weeks to figure something out. She had to find a way to escape.

Obā lived in a small traditional house on the outskirts of the city, where clusters of buildings gave way to fields. Encircled by a wooden verandah, the house crouched low behind a thick wall, fierce stone shīsā lions standing guard on the red kucha-tiled roof.

The benefits of the low-hanging eaves and thick walls became clear when the typhoon landed a day later. Water poured from the eaves and rushed under the raised house into Obā's garden. The wind shrieked and snatched at the house, flattening palm trees so savagely Michiko wondered how they didn't snap, but the high walls kept the worst of it away from the house. Once Obā closed the shutters, the three of them sat protected, though sweltering, inside. They ate their evening meal of cold soba noodles and vegetables, Obā and Michiko raising their voices against the howling wind, the rattling shutters and roar of the unrelenting downpour.

'We get a lot of these this time of year,' said Obā. 'We're used to it. The rain is good for the plants.'

Michiko couldn't sleep that night. She got up from her futon and stood on the verandah, listening to the storm. She felt an urge to step outside, to feel its power and become a part of it. She opened one of the shutters, just a crack, but a powerful gust blew them apart, soaking Michiko in an instant and pushing her back into the house as if in warning.

'What are you doing, dear?'

Michiko hadn't heard Obā come out. 'I'm sorry, I woke you.'

Obā pushed the shutters closed and dropped the latch. 'You're drenched.'

'I wanted to stand in your beautiful garden. We don't have one at home to soak up the rain anymore.'

Obā slid open a cupboard and took a towel and a folded cotton yukata from its shelves. 'Here, let's take these off,' she said, pulling the soaked pyjamas from Michiko's body. Unperturbed by her nakedness, Oba scrubbed Michiko dry. She unfolded the yukata and helped Michiko into it.

'Father had our house knocked down and built a modern building over it all, including our garden,' Michiko said. 'He used to be so obsessed with that garden. Now he says he makes more money from the tenants on the extra floors above the shop than he does selling tea. But when a typhoon passes, the rain just flows away on the pavements and into the sewers. I wanted to remind myself how it feels to stand in the rain, with my bare feet in the earth.'

Obā smiled. 'I know how good that feels. But it's dangerous out there. The wind hurls objects like a cannon. Besides, you need your sleep. Come along, back to bed, and quietly. We don't want to wake your mother.'

Within a few days the sun emerged bright from dark clouds, drying the mud of the streets back to dust, and Obā returned to work. The lush abundance of Obā's garden was the reward for so much rain. Fruit and vegetables Michiko had never seen before grew there: bitter, warty gōya gourds; sweet purple beni-imo yams; crunchy, slimy okra that sliced into green stars. Michiko loved the fragrance of passionfruit, plucking the wrinkled black globes off their vines and splitting them open with her nails to squeeze the seeds directly into her mouth. She learned how to slice mango flesh away from its giant seed and watched her mother's eyes light with pleasure as she fed her chunks of the golden fruit.

On Sundays Obā taught Michiko how to cook gōya champuru, rafute pork belly and fuchiba jushi with mugwort, food unlike anything Michiko made at home. The unfamiliarity of everything kept her feeling as if she was in a foreign country. She liked it.

Obā drove to work in Ginowan six days a week, leaving before dawn and coming home after dark. Michiko and Chiyo were often alone in the house. At first, Obā's daughters dropped by almost every day with their children to chat on the verandah over buku-buku tea and kunpen buns, but Michiko had little in common with them. She soon tired of their conversations, and their boisterous children annoyed her. Sensing her boredom and irritation, and unable to engage with Chiyo, they came by less and less until they stopped coming altogether.

Michiko grew restless. She took her mother for walks to the village shop, or down to the river that rang with the croaking of frogs. Everyone in Obā's village already knew who they were. The old women and men sitting outside their houses or the village shop would wave them over, smiling, wanting to talk. It was a community that shared stories, and they were eager to glean some from Michiko.

'Your mother is Uchinanchū, isn't she? How long are you staying? No husband or children yet? Is this your first time here? Are you going to the river? Watch out for habu snakes, there are lots of them about.'

They offered open invitations to drop by their houses and were warm and friendly, but Michiko yearned for the anonymity of the city, to be free to go unobserved wherever she chose.

She consulted a bus timetable and took her mother on an outing into Naha. Walking along Kokusai Dōri with Chiyo by her side, Michiko felt a thrill as she brushed by American servicemen, seeing how they turned to stare. She was wearing her best dress, a bright-blue striped poplin that came above her knees, showing off her calves and ankles. A GI called out to her – 'Hey, beautiful baby' – and when she smiled at him, he winked, making her heart pound.

They walked up the hill towards Shurijō, stopping on the way at a Blue Seal ice cream parlour for a scoop each – so sweet and delicious – and gazed at the ruins of Shuri Castle. The Imperial Japanese Army had requisitioned it as their headquarters during the war, and American shelling had destroyed it. The place bustled with students from the new university that had been built on its grounds, female students mingling with the men, books clutched to their chests. Michiko's father had strong opinions about women's education: not only did he think it unnecessary and a waste of time, he saw it as damaging a girl's prospects for marriage. 'Putting useless ideas into their heads, distracting them from domestic duties,' he'd said. 'They get notions they're above their station in life. What good is it for a housewife?' Michiko hadn't had the courage to fight him for the right to continue her education back then, and now she was too old to do anything about it. She would have to find other ways to carve out the future she wanted, and soon, before she lost her beauty and whatever youthfulness she had left.

With most of the food they ate coming from Obā's garden, and with Obā flatly refusing to take any money for their daily upkeep, Michiko still had most of the allowance her father had given her for their journey. Along with a replacement for the scarf she'd lost at sea, she'd wanted to use some of the money to buy a new dress for herself, but there was no need: Obā told her mistress that Chiyo and her daughter were staying with her, and the woman had passed along a dress she no longer wore. Michiko had never seen one like it. It was finely sewn, cut beautifully from red twill the colour of the ripe tomatoes in Obā's garden. She read aloud the name on the label: 'Halston'. Michiko loved the dress, though it was a little long. She borrowed a needle and thread from Obā and gave it a higher hem. It was a short-sleeved wrap dress, tightened at the waist with a sash, and a V-neckline scooped daringly low. She had never worn anything that showed her cleavage; her father would have called her a whore and beaten her for it. She wrapped the dress around her and tied it closed with the sash. It fit her body like a second skin. She leaned forward, reaching into her bra to push up her breasts, and looked down. Her eyes widened: she'd never seen them look this way. She put on the crimson lipstick she only wore out of sight of her father and smacked her lips, pouting like Marilyn Monroe. She looked at herself in the mirror and felt breathless. She was magnificent. She skipped a little dance, barely able to contain the bubbles of excitement rising. She couldn't wait to walk down Kokusai Dōri and turn all those GIs' heads.

Michiko got her chance the following Friday. Obā's mistress was attending a formal evening function at Kadena airbase. Obā was to stay in Ginowan that night and watch over the girls, and wouldn't be back until the following afternoon.

'You'll find some rafute in the fridge for your dinner,' Obā told Michiko. 'You just need to steam some rice. Help yourself to greens from the garden.'

'Thank you,' said Michiko. 'We'll be fine.'

It was early for an evening meal, but Chiyo ate the whole bowl of rafute and rice Michiko heated up for her. Michiko helped her bathe and get ready for bed, glad for once that her mother didn't understand enough to question why this was happening at four o'clock in the afternoon.

'I've laid out your futon, Okāsan. It's time for you to rest. I'm going into the city, but I'll be back in time for bed.'

She tucked the wallet her father had given her into her handbag, along with the red lipstick and a mirror. She caught a bus into the city, bare-lipped and wearing her mother's shawl around her shoulders, although the weather was warm. People in the village would see her, and she didn't want any gossip. 'I'm just nipping into the city to run some errands,' she explained, when she was asked where she was going.

She got off at the Makishi end of Kokusai Dōri, slipping into an empty shop doorway to put on her lipstick. She admired herself in the mirror and tucked the lipstick back in her bag. She took off her shawl and, standing tall, she strode out onto the pavement. It didn't take her long to notice that the shops at this end of the street catered more for locals; there were hardly any Americans. The people she passed gave her disapproving looks, and she regretted putting on her lipstick. An older woman bumped against her, deliberately, and muttered under her breath: 'whore'. Wrapping the shawl back around her shoulders and ducking her head, Michiko walked faster. When she saw a shop displaying clothes and jewellery, she slipped inside. She took a tissue from her bag and wiped her lips.

'How may I help you?' A young woman came out of a room at the back. Seeing Michiko's expression, she asked, 'Are you all right?'

'I'm fine,' said Michiko, holding the shawl closer. 'I'm not from Okinawa, and I ...' She looked around the shop. Maybe she'd find her new scarf here. She spotted the counter with its glass display. 'Oh, such beautiful jewellery.'

'My father makes it all,' the woman said, smiling. 'We've been silversmiths for generations.'

Michiko gazed at the array of earrings, necklaces, bracelets and rings with wide eyes.

'Would you like me to get anything out of the display for you?'

Relieved at the woman's friendliness, Michiko pointed to a ring that had caught her eye. 'May I?'

The body of the ring was made of two thick strands of silver that twisted up into a large knot, striking and simple. Michiko slid it onto her finger and grinned. It was a perfect fit.

'It looks like it was made for you,' said the woman. 'Maybe it's fated to be yours.'

Bit keen for a sale, thought Michiko, but when she looked up, she saw the young woman's expression was serious.

'It's an en-musubi ring,' she said. 'That knot, it's fate-binding. People buy them when they get married, sometimes, but it can be for any two people bound together. Two sisters, or a mother and daughter, for example. Do you have children?'

Michiko shook her head.

'Well, it can be a binding between two friends, or even a person bound in spirit to something in nature, like a place, or a tree, or a boulder. If you're a visitor here, then maybe it's binding you to our islands. It means you will return.'

'My mother was born here,' said Michiko. 'This is my first time in Okinawa, but ...' She stared at the ring on her finger. 'How much is it?'

'It's 3200 yen.'

131

Michiko gasped. That was almost half of the money she had in the wallet.

'I can let you have it for 3000,' said the woman. 'It's clearly meant to be yours. Look how good it looks on your hand. You know, sometimes I think women should buy rings for themselves. They shouldn't need to wait for a man to buy them one.' She blushed. 'If you don't mind me saying so.'

'I'll take it,' said Michiko. She took the money out of the wallet and laid it on the counter. 'Quickly, before I change my mind.'

She tried not to think about the money she'd just spent – it was more than a month's housekeeping allowance – and walked back onto the street with head held high, the ring on her finger. But up ahead there was some kind of commotion. As she drew near, she saw a pickup truck being driven slowly along the road. A mass of people shuffled along behind it, linking arms or holding banners high. The red painted slogans read 'OPPOSE THE VIETNAM WAR! MILITARY BASES OUT!' A voice blared through loudspeakers on the back of the truck, and the crowd shouted fervent responses. 'We want peace! No more war! American forces, out out out!'

Michiko tried to slip past unnoticed, but the crowd was too dense. Her bag caught on something or somebody as she squeezed through, and as she pulled it free her shawl fell from her shoulders onto the ground. She tried to retrieve it but it was already being trampled underfoot. A man grabbed hold of her arm. 'Hey, pan-pan girl,' he snarled, 'are you off to whore yourself to the Americans? Look at you, you traitor! No shame!'

'Don't touch me!' cried Michiko, pulling away, her heart racing. She yanked herself free and pushed through a gap in the crowds, escaping into an alleyway. She stood panting, back pressed up against a wall, waiting for her heart to settle. She shuddered, despite the heat, and crossed her arms. She'd have to let her mother's shawl go.

A sudden metallic clatter made Michiko jump, and a cat yowled in the shadows. It was getting dark. She had to keep moving. The alley opened onto a side street. She could bypass the protest if she walked more or less parallel to the main street. Turning one corner after another, zig-zagging through darkening alleyways, Michiko worked her way towards what she hoped was the other end of Kokusai Dōri. She wasn't sure what she'd do when she got there; her only thought was to get away from the protestors. Neon signs began lighting up, one by one, as dusk fell. Growing clusters of American soldiers signalled she was getting close. Some of the men smiled at her, others called out: 'Hey beautiful! Over here, *Onē-chan*!' She kept her eyes down.

She turned a corner and emerged, finally, into the din of Kokusai Dōri. She stood for a moment as the crowds flowed past her, blinking at the bright lights, wondering where to go next. Some men in uniform jostled past her, turning to stare. 'Woah, check out that rack, Johnny.' A low wolf-whistle; a palm on her buttocks. She recoiled. This was not how it was meant to be. What was she thinking? She should have been sitting with her mother on the verandah, feeding her mangoes. Folding her arms across her chest, head bowed, she turned back in the direction she'd come from. But in the distance, swelling above the hubbub of the street, she heard the blare of loudspeakers, the sound of angry chanting. Surely the protestors wouldn't come as far as this, where there were so many Americans? Fear prickled her throat – she didn't want to be in the street when they arrived. A neon sign pulsed above a large wooden door spelling out the words 'Paradise Bar' in pink. Of all the places nearby, it looked the least threatening. She took a deep breath, opened the door and stepped inside.

It took a while for her eyes to adjust to the dim, pink-lit room. Through the fog of cigarette smoke, a bar glittered with mirrored shelves laden with bottles; GIs sat on bar stools, animated, leaning into one another in shouted conversation. A double-bass player, drummer and pianist played slow jazz in the corner. Scantily clad Okinawan girls with bouffant hair piled high on their heads draped themselves around the men, their necks and red-taloned hands glittering with fake jewels. Sipping from champagne coupes, they smoked gold-tipped cigarettes in pastel colours, brushing the men's arms with their fingers, whispering into their ears. Michiko had never seen such a place; it was dreamlike, seductive, glamorous. The women seemed so self-assured, as if they were royalty. The men gazed at them with drunken, adoring eyes, as if they'd been bewitched. She was impressed. 'Oh,' said one of the women, noticing Michiko. 'Look what's just blown in with the rubbish.'

The men turned to follow her gaze and stared.

Michiko smoothed her sweating palms down her red dress. She was suddenly conscious of her unstyled hair, her modest jewellery. She twisted her new en-musubi ring around her finger.

Michiko searched the dingy corners of the bar and spotted a sign for the washroom. Locking herself into a cubicle, she sat on the toilet and closed her eyes, taking deep breaths to slow the pounding of her heart. I'm better than those women, I've got class, she thought. Any man would be lucky to have me. She stood up, drawing herself to her full height and strode out to wash her hands. Standing in front of the mirror, she patted her curls into place and tilted her face this way and that, trying on different expressions, different smiles. She examined her skin closely in the mirror; hardly any wrinkles. She was probably older than most of those women in the bar, but she knew she was more beautiful than any of them. It didn't matter that her perm had loosened, didn't matter that she wore no necklace or earrings. She put on her crimson lipstick, smacking her lips, and raised her chin to look down her nose at herself. In her red dress, she looked like an empress.

A man with a thin black moustache and slick, dark hair was waiting for her outside the toilet door. 'Hey, sweetheart, let me buy you a drink.' He gestured to the bar and, understanding what he meant, she followed. He nudged a man nursing a beer. 'Get off that stool, Buddy. Lady needs a seat.'

'Fast work, Marty,' said his friend, getting off the stool and pretending to dust it off. He was short, almost the same height as Michiko, with hair the colour of dirty dishwater. He gestured towards the stool with a bow. 'Here you go, ma'am.'

'What are you drinking?' Marty made a tipping gesture at Michiko with his glass.

Michiko had no idea. She skimmed over the mirrored shelves behind the bar, saw an elaborately carved glass bottle with amber-coloured liquid inside and pointed.

'You like the hard stuff, huh,' said Marty, slapping money on the bar for the bartender. 'Impressive.'

When the drink was pushed towards her, Michiko was taken aback by how little was in the glass. Was this right? Was the bartender, who was Okinawan and looking at her with a suspicious eye, mocking her? She tilted her head back in defiance and swallowed the contents of the glass in one gulp.

'Woah, lady,' said Marty. 'Now we're talkin'. Let's get you another.'

Michiko puffed out a breath, resisting the urge to cough. She felt as though she'd swallowed fire, and now it was blazing a path down her throat, past her heart, and into her belly. She'd never felt anything like this before. Her entire body was aglow.

'Very good,' she said. 'Thank you, mister.'

'You're quite the lady.' Marty laughed, winking at his mate. 'My name's Marty, and this here's Buddy,' he said, pointing first at his chest, then at Buddy's. 'What's your name, darlin'?'

'My name Michiko,' she said. She took a sip from the refilled glass.

'Going slow now, huh, Michiko?'

She didn't understand a word, but decided dignified silence would be better than stumbling over the few words of English she knew. She smiled. She liked how the drink made her feel strong, confident. She liked the way the men – and not just Buddy and Marty – kept looking at her. She smiled benevolently, gazing about with growing confidence.

She noticed some of the women glaring. She smirked and turned back to the men.

'You American GI?' she said, touching Marty's arm and leaning towards him.

'Proud and true, yes, ma'am.' He reached up and cupped her cheek. 'Damn, those lips of yours are just too kissable. Dontcha think, Buddy?'

'You gonna share this one too?' Buddy said to Marty. The men burst out laughing.

Michiko didn't know what they were laughing about, but she joined in, covering her mouth and giggling. 'More drink,' she said, pushing forward her emptied glass.

'Hot damn,' said Buddy.

Michiko felt his hand high up on her thigh. She crossed her legs, pushing it off.

'Who the hell do you think you are?' A woman wearing a tight pink satin dress pushed her way between the men and stood in front of Michiko. 'This is our patch.'

'I don't know what you mean,' said Michiko. 'I'm just visiting.'

'Ohhh! Oh! Listen to her! This little bitch is from Tokyo!' said the woman, looking around at the others. She pushed her face close to Michiko's. 'Why don't you just piss off?'

'There's no need to be so rude,' said Michiko, sitting tall. 'I'm just having a drink.'

'Acting all innocent,' the woman said, blowing smoke into Michiko's face. 'What do you think we are, stupid?'

A woman wearing a platinum blonde wig and green hotpants swaggered over to join her friend. 'Think you're better than us because you're some fancy Yamato bitch?'

Michiko's hands were trembling, but she got off the stool and drew herself to her full height. 'So much for Okinawan friendliness.'

'We're only friendly to people we like, and we don't like you.' The two women rounded on her.

'Cat fight!' Marty sniggered, rubbing his hands together. 'Looks like we're in for a show, Buddy-boy.'

Michiko leaned across them as casually as she could, took her glass from the counter, and emptied it, eyeing the women. 'Thank you, mister,' she said, turning to the men. She raised her empty glass. 'I go now.'

'Good fucking riddance,' said the woman with the blonde wig.

Michiko turned to her with a low-lidded gaze, arranging her face into a benevolent smile. 'I pity you,' she said, 'having to sell yourselves to men. I would never stoop so low. Only the very best man will get to keep me – and for that he'll need a lot of money, and he'll have to marry me. I'm not a cheap whore, like you.'

Michiko had already turned to walk out when the woman lunged at her.

'Come back and tell us we're cheap again!'

Michiko side-stepped; the woman stumbled. Michiko grabbed the blonde wig and threw it into the corner of the room, where it landed at the feet of the double-bass player. The woman screamed, clutching her stockinged head, and raced to retrieve it.

The woman in the pink dress stepped forward with an empty glass. 'You're dead, bitch!'

Michiko turned on her heel and left, the sound of the men's laughter ringing in her ears as the door slammed behind her.

Outside, the protestors had gone, and the garish neon street signs flashed like warnings against the black of the night sky. She had to find the bus stop, get back to her mother. She hoped Chiyo would be asleep by now. Michiko cut back through the side streets she remembered walking through earlier; there were fewer people milling about outside now.

'Hey, baby! Michiko!'

She turned and saw that Buddy and Marty had followed her. She turned back around without a word and continued walking.

'Hey! We wanna buy you another drink! Let's go someplace else!'

The hair prickled on the back of Michiko's neck. She walked faster.

'Hey!' they called. 'Where are you going? Wait for us!' She heard their footsteps quicken.

She reached down to take off her shoes and ran.

'We paid for your drinks, lady!' Marty shouted.

Michiko whipped down an alleyway and out the other side, turned a corner and sprinted down a long cobbled street, hardly registering the pain in her feet as she ran. At the other end of Kokusai Dōri there'd be fewer soldiers and more local people; she'd be safer there. But she'd lost all sense of direction and couldn't figure out where the main street was. She cut back down another alleyway aglow with red paper lanterns, and then another side street without slowing her pace. She kept going until she couldn't hear the men's footsteps anymore, and then further still. She paused, panting, at the base of a set of stairs rising up towards a ramshackle house. A sweet smell of honeysuckle pressed in from the dark. She was lost.

Michiko followed a path curving downhill. She couldn't remember walking any hills on her way into the city, so she knew she was going in the wrong direction, but the windows of the houses that now replaced the bars glowed reassurance and safety. She imagined families gathered around their tables, eating their evening meals. Night cicadas called out to her, and the warm air was fragrant with flowers. A streetlamp glowed white among the trees, burnishing their leaves so they glittered in the darkness. Her heartbeat settled and slowed. She kept walking, as if in a dream.

She turned a corner, and the path ascended again, growing steeper. Thick foliage shadowed its edges. Michiko panted her way upwards. She could hear the quiet shushing of waves somewhere down below.

A giant red torī gate loomed out of the darkness. In the moonlight, she could just make out the golden characters on the plaque hanging from the top. 'Naminouegū, Shrine Above the Waves'. She'd heard about it, a sacred Ryūkyū site that was turned into a Shinto shrine after Okinawa was absorbed into Yamato Japan. It was originally built to honour Nirai Kanai, the source of all life, the underwater realm of the Ryūkyū gods said to lie somewhere in the depths of the Pacific. Women had come here during the war to pray their men would escape conscription; for centuries, people had sought blessings here for good harvests and safe passage across the sea, for matchmaking or for marriage.

She bowed slightly, and walked through the torī towards the chōzubachi fountain. She went through the motions of the ritual as if hypnotised: taking up a ladle that lay on a bamboo rail across the fountain, she poured water first into her left hand, then her right, rinsing them clean. She poured another ladleful of water into her left hand and scooped it into her mouth, swilling it out into the pebbled drain below. She rinsed her left hand once more, then, filled with a final scoop, she raised the ladle vertically towards her so the water trickled down the handle. Purified, she walked to the left of the stone path towards the main hall. White paper shide folded into zigzags hung from the great pale twist of shimenawa rope that hung suspended above the offering box at its entrance. She bowed. She scrabbled in her wallet for coins; threw in two five-yen pieces. She bowed again, then clapped her hands, slowly, twice, and bowed her head, palms together, eyes closed. Moving her lips without a sound, she asked for a blessing, her wish.

She felt safe now. She wandered back down the hill and found a lamplit path that led down the beach and the ocean she'd heard earlier. Lit by the moon, the waves hushed a slow, gentle rhythm over pale sand. There was nobody there. She kicked off her shoes, leaving them at the edge of the beach, quickening her steps until she found herself running, slowly at first, each step sinking into soft sand, then faster when she reached the sea strand, where the wet had packed the sand flat. She tucked her handbag under her arm, hoisted her dress up high and splashed into the water, through the gentle waves until she stood thigh deep. The water was as warm as blood. She drew in a long, slow breath and closed her eyes, letting herself be rocked by the gentle push and pull of the current. She sank her feet further into the soft sand beneath the water, wriggling her toes, and felt small fish nibbling at her ankles. A wave broke unexpectedly high, soaking her underwear and making her gasp. She giggled. If she didn't have to get the bus home, if she wasn't wearing such a precious dress, she'd have let herself fall back into the ocean. She wanted to float, to be carried by the sea.

She looked out across the water, the twinkling lights of the port across the bay dancing in the waves. The soft sand of the ocean floor sucked at her feet as if it wanted her to stay. She turned around to look at the shrine behind her, perched high above on a bluff, peering at her through the trees. The beach below it was a bright brushstroke. At one side of it was the dark silhouette of a man, sitting in the sand, his hair glinting in the moonlight. An American. She froze.

He waved.

She was trapped. She turned to her right and began walking away from him in the water, parallel to the beach, but to retrieve her shoes she would have to walk past him. She wondered if she should scream for help. She clutched her handbag tight – she could buy herself time to get away if she hit him with it, hard, in the face. For a moment she wondered if she should make her escape without her shoes, but she had too far to walk. She'd have to grab them and make a run for it. As she drew closer she saw he was in civilian clothes – an open necked shirt and jeans – and he was barefoot. His golden hair was cropped short, and his face was turned towards her, though she couldn't see his expression.

She looked up at the shrine above her, called on it for protection, then sucked in a deep breath and straightened up. She would not show her fear. She strode across to her shoes and picked them up. The American didn't move, and when she looked across at him she saw he was smiling at her. He was handsome, like a movie star.

'Don't be afraid,' he said. 'This is where I come for some peace. Would you like to join me?' he said, patting the sand beside him.

Michiko stood, opened mouthed. He spoke perfect Japanese.

A Necklace with Gold Heart Padlock

The chain is made up of links so fine and delicate it appears smooth and seamless. It is slender and of dusky gold. On it is suspended a padlock in the shape of a heart, made of a paler gold than the chain. Of low carat, it is hard enough not to scratch easily, and the jeweller's tiny markings on its back, more than thirty years old, can still be seen: the initials WJS in a small rectangle, the maker's mark; below it a hallmark, with the 375 declaring it to be a gold of nine carats. Beside these are two symbols proclaiming the assay, miniscule and now somewhat too worn to be decipherable, even under a magnifying glass. The heart is roughly one-and-a-half centimetres wide by two centimetres high, with a thickness of a half-centimetre. Four make-believe screw heads are etched onto its face. The lock opens and closes on its tiny hinge without the aid of a key, although the keyhole in its front looks so real that one wonders if there was once a key; a key that might have kept the heart safely locked up.

Erika

They chase off hangovers the next morning with breakfast, washed down with Alka-Seltzers and several cups of black coffee. Marcus arrives early, ahead of the crowds. 'They've already closed Notting Hill Gate station,' he says. 'I made it through just in time.'

'Much easier if you'd stayed here last night,' says Sarah. 'Did you have a good time with Felix?'

'Yeah, we had a ball. It would have been a lot more fun if we'd all got together though.' Marcus glances at Erika, who's concentrating hard on buttering another slice of toast. 'Felix would have liked that. You could have brought Luca, Sarah.'

'Luca spent the day with Sarah's sister,' Erika says, giving him a look. 'Anyway, it's harder to get around with a big group, especially with kids. It's packed out there. You know what it's like.'

'I sure do,' says Marcus.

By the time they finish eating, the streets below are already heaving with people. The sound systems start rattling the windows again. Kei is wearing a bright-yellow tie-dyed sundress she bought from a stall the previous afternoon; her hair is untied and loose around her shoulders, her skin browned from the sun. Erika struggles to connect her with the pale, prim woman she picked up at the airport just over a week ago. The only reminder of that other cousin is the gold chain with the pearl pendant Kei's wearing.

They're dancing in front of a sound system when the pendant is snatched from Kei's neck. There's a vortex in the crowd around them, people shouting and pushing. At first it seems like another cluster of overexcited Carnival-goers, but it gains momentum, like a hurricane.

As it grows closer, Erika sees youths breaking free from the whirl, arms and hands snatching as they dodge and sprint. Watches are ripped from wrists, bags and jewellery grabbed. It all happens so fast that Kei doesn't notice at first; she's dancing, swaying, eyes closed. Feeling the quick tug at her neck she draws her hands there, but it's Erika – carrying nothing of value, not wearing any jewellery – who notices.

'Your necklace!'

Kei blinks, still unsure what's just happened.

'Oh, Kei,' cries Erika. 'They've taken your necklace!' A woman nearby has had earrings ripped from her earlobes; they're bleeding. 'Sarah! Are you okay?'

'I tucked my money in my jeans pocket but they didn't go there. I guess they didn't think my jewellery worth taking. What an insult.' Her grin is half-hearted.

Erika wonders if Kei understands she's just been robbed; she wears a perplexed expression and is rubbing the space at her clavicle where the pearl should be.

'Kei-chan, are you all right? Your necklace!' Repeating this is all Erika feels she can do. 'We have to report it stolen to the police.'

'It doesn't matter,' says Kei.

'But it's a gold chain! And a real pearl. Fucking bastards!'

'It doesn't matter.'

'I brought you here … now you've lost your precious necklace …'

'Eri-chan, stop shouting,' says Kei. 'It's just a necklace. Please.'

It doesn't take long for Met officers to arrive. A crowd clusters around them, gesticulating, giving descriptions, reporting what's been taken.

'Let's tell them about it. If they find it, they'll have a way to get it back to you.' Erika grabs her cousin's hand and pulls her towards the officers.

'Erika.' Kei stops and tugs back, forcing her cousin to face her. 'It's gone. Jun gave it to me. Maybe I was meant to lose it today.'

'You didn't lose it, Kei, it was stolen from you.'

'Maybe I'm meant to let it go. It's just a thing, Erika. Just a necklace. It's not my life, or yours. Let it go.'

'How can you? You've been violated! How can you let them get away with it?'

Marcus puts his arm around Erika. 'Look, Kei's fine. None of us got hurt. You didn't have anything taken, I didn't, neither did Sarah. Kei's the only one, and she's saying she's okay.'

'But her necklace. It was given to her by her husband.'

'Ex-husband,' says Sarah. 'Maybe it's good she's rid of something that reminds her of him.'

'Then why was she wearing it? It must still have meant something to her.'

'Let it go, Erika. She has.' Marcus rubs her arms. 'Come on. Let's go home.'

Although Kei seems unperturbed by the incident – Erika described the necklace to the police, just in case – the mood is noticeably subdued as they walk home.

'What a shitty end to Carnival,' says Sarah. 'Last year it was someone letting off tear gas canisters. We shouldn't be surprised.'

'It's still horrible when it happens,' says Erika.

'Your cousin's being amazingly cool about it though.' Sarah turns to Kei. 'Hey, are you okay?'

Kei smiles. 'Okay. No problem. This,' she says, waving a joint, 'helping.'

After a dinner of delivered pizza Sarah leaves to pick up Luca from her sister's. She leaves the bag of weed with them and Marcus rolls another. The three of them sit around the dining table, listening to music, smoking. Marcus suddenly sits upright and peers across to the alcove.

'Hey, the cabinet's all tidied up. Did you do that?' he asks Erika.

'Kei did it.'

'It looks good with the flowers. I can smell the incense,' Marcus says. 'Kei, you made the altar look nice.'

'For my aunt. She was special person.'

'I'd like to have met her,' says Marcus.

'I wonder what you'd have made of her,' murmurs Erika. 'She was special all right.'

'She was very beautiful,' says Kei. 'Also, very sick.'

'Erika told me. She died from diabetes, didn't she?'

'Diabetes?' Kei throws a quick look at her cousin. When Erika translates, Kei says in Japanese: 'You didn't tell him.'

'It's not an easy thing to tell,' says Erika. 'Please don't say anything.'

'It's a beautiful cabinet,' says Marcus. 'Now it's cleaned up it looks great. Is it antique?'

'It's a replica. An old one. It was my mother's. It's Korean,' says Erika.

'I always thought it was Japanese. I couldn't tell the difference,' says Marcus.

'Hard to describe, but there it is. It's subtle,' says Erika.

He pushes his chair back and wanders to the alcove, stooping to look at the lacquer tablet in its little case that sits on top. 'What does it say on here?'

'It's my mother's posthumous Buddhist name, a kaimyō. You can't use a dead person's earthly name when you pray to their spirit, because they say it calls them back instead of letting them rebirth into a new life. It's all superstition, of course.'

She goes to stand next to him. 'See? Written in gold on the front. The one written on the back in red is the name she had in life, Takigawa Michiko.' She takes a deep breath. 'And that's the date she died, in kanji. Twenty-second day of the sixth month of Heisei 3, in Imperial Japanese years. Which was 1991.'

Marcus stares at her. 'How come you've never told me any of this before? It's fascinating.'

Erika takes the tiny porcelain water cup from the altar and fills it with beer.

'Beer?' says Marcus, looking over at Kei.

'At Obon, when the spirits of the dead ancestors return, the graves are piled high with all the things the dead person loved – cigarettes, snacks, booze. Sweets and teddy bears for the poor kids. My mother loved her booze so much I should keep a bottle of vodka on the altar.' Erika lights two sticks of incense and stabs them into the ash of the burner. She taps the side of the bronze bell bowl too loudly with the wooden stick.

Kei gets up to join them; she puts her hands together, bows her head and closes her eyes. Erika looks at her for a second, then at Marcus, before doing the same. She opens her eyes and puffs out her cheeks. 'Okay, enough already.' She flops back into the chair and lights the joint up again.

Marcus runs his fingers across the cabinet. 'All these little panels and drawers.' He runs his hands down its sides. 'Hey. There's a bit coming loose here.'

He's pulling at one of the small panels on the front and it slides out sideways to reveal a tiny drawer.

'Have you seen this?'

Erika jumps up to look. 'Ha! How cool. I never knew.'

'There's something inside it too.'

Marcus is unwrapping something from its wrapping of tissue. It's a heavy and elaborate gold ring, set with a large blue stone.

Erika's eyes widen. 'What …?'

Marcus peers at it in the palm of his hand. 'There's an inscription around the stone. It's heavy – do you think it's real gold?'

'It looks pretty tacky to me,' says Erika, peering at it. '"West Point". And a date. 1959.'

'You think your mum put it there?'

'Who knows. It's not the kind of thing she'd have worn. Anyway, it's enormous. It looks like a man's ring.' She turns to Kei. 'Whose is this, do you think? Have you ever seen it before?'

Kei shakes her head. 'Maybe it was Julian's?'

'He hated rings,' says Erika. 'Never saw him wear one.'

Marcus is squinting at the engraving around the stone. 'Isn't West Point a military academy in America?'

'No idea,' says Erika, distracted. 'Maybe it was already in there when Michiko bought the cabinet. Can't think why she'd have kept something like that.'

Marcus bends down to take a closer look. 'I wonder if there are any other secret drawers.'

He crouches again to run his fingers across the cabinet and only takes a moment before he stands up and crows: 'I knew it! There's another on the other side.' He slides it out. 'Ha! There's something in here too.' He holds it out to Erika. Inside it is a silver ring, its two strands looped into a three-sided knot.

'Looks like a woman's ring.'

Erika picks it up to examine it, frowning.

'Surely your mother must have put these here,' says Marcus. 'It isn't that hard to spot the panels.'

'Well, I've had the thing for years and I didn't see them,' says Erika, trying the ring on. It fits perfectly. 'Wow, I actually really like this. I wonder if it was Michiko's? I never saw her wear it.' She spins the knot around her finger.

'A cabinet of secrets,' Marcus says, stepping back to appraise it. 'It's a beautiful piece of furniture; you should take better care of it. It's the first time I've seen it polished and tidy.' He looks over at Kei, then says to Erika in a quiet voice: 'So she forgave you?'

'It's complicated. But she's not as angry as I thought she was.'

'What did she say?'

'That I need to deal with it at some point. Look, can we talk about this another time? We're leaving her out.' She gestures at her cousin. Kei is looking at the gold ring with the blue stone, bemused, rubbing at the inscription.

'Definitely a man's ring,' she says. 'How strange.'

Two days before Kei's due to go back to Tokyo, it hits Erika that she might actually miss her cousin. She's relieved the visit went better than she'd feared. Despite the initial prickliness of their first week together and the theft of the necklace, the nightmare scenarios she envisaged haven't materialised.

After a day at Windsor Castle, they come home worn out. They decide to stay in for the evening, Kei insisting she'll cook.

'It won't be gourmet,' she says, 'just old-fashioned home-style tonkatsu.'

Erika thinks she'll enjoy eating the homely tonkatsu, cabbage, miso and rice more than the meal they're planning to have tomorrow to mark Kei's final night in London. Kei wants to eat at the restaurant where Erika works. She's booked a table for four – Marcus and Sarah, who's taken the night off, are coming. Frankie's being uncharacteristically nice and has promised to rustle up a 'genius dégustation your cousin won't forget, with extras'. A fine-dining feast, wine included; one of the best in London. But to Erika, the tonkatsu Kei's going to cook her tonight will mean so much more. She shivers, unexpectedly. Bewildered by the sudden wave of anxiety washing over her, Erika fetches her laptop and takes it to the dining table, where she occupies herself uploading the photos she took at the castle from her camera.

She knows she's shutting down to harden herself against the impending separation. Not long ago, she'd have given anything not to have to spend any time with Kei, but she feels so differently about it that she now doubts her stance about other things. Being back in the adrenaline-fuelled kitchen with André will keep her distracted, but she's shocked by the realisation that for the first time, perhaps ever, she feels reluctant to return to work. After Erika drops Kei off at the airport, she'll head straight to the restaurant to prep for service that same evening. If only she'd taken one more day's leave; she's clocked up so much overtime over the years that André would have given her the extra time off. But asking for it at this late stage is out of the question, even though she now feels a desperate need for time and space to process everything her cousin's visit has stirred up.

Kei comes out of the kitchen where she's been washing the rice, and sits across from Erika, taking a diary from the top of the pile. She flips it open at the bookmark and begins pencilling furigana with rapt concentration against the kanji in Michiko's diaries. Erika flicks through photos on her laptop, exclaiming now and then and flipping the screen around to show Kei, who has finished annotating the diary and has taken another off the pile. She flicks through its pages.

'Looks like this is another one from Obachan's time in Hong Kong,' says Kei. 'She and Julian were invited to so many parties! She hardly ever had a night at home.'

'I know. I remember,' says Erika.

Mostly, she remembers the apartment they used to live in half way up Victoria Peak. Erika was usually there alone, though the amah was usually just next door watching soaps on her kitchen TV. Michiko made a friend of that apartment, exploring its many nooks and corners. She remembers finding a doll in a box at the back of a shelf in her mother's wardrobe. It was so high up she'd had to tiptoe on a chair to reach it. She'd unwrapped it from its tissue and smoothed its golden hair and fluffed the petticoat under its red gingham dress. She lay on her mother's bed, clasping it to her chest, and that was where, hours later, her mother found her asleep, holding the doll in her arms.

The blow to her head had exploded her awake, making her ears ring. Her mother was standing over her, face red and distorted and raging. Erika recognised the familiar, heavy smell of alcohol. Michiko pulled off the fur coat Erika had wrapped herself in, and Erika rolled off the other side of the bed and scrambled underneath, taking the doll with her. She blocked her ears so she wouldn't have to hear the frightening sounds her mother was making, but when a red-nailed hand clawed blindly at her under the bed, Erika grabbed a tight hold of the doll again, as if saving it from a terrible fate. The hand caught one of the doll's legs and pulled.

'No,' Erika had shouted, 'Don't!'

But the hand wouldn't let go, jerking higher up the doll's leg to get a better grip. Erika pulled the doll back and tried to roll onto her stomach, using her body to anchor it. The doll's cloth leg stretched long and tight, painful against Erika's ribs. Then there was an ugly ripping sound; the tension against her side suddenly slackened. Cotton wadding trailed from the doll's body where its leg had been. From above the bed there came a howl that sounded almost inhuman. The hand flashed back under the bed, grabbing Erika's leg, and began to yank her out.

'I wish she'd put more detail into these diaries,' says Kei, jolting Erika back to the present. 'She just says where the parties were, what jewellery and clothes she wore and what they ate. I wish I knew more about what she was thinking.'

'She'll have left out anything that didn't fit in with her fantasies. I told you they'd be boring. Don't feel you have to transcribe all of them,' says Erika, eyeing the huge pile of diaries. 'Besides, we only have this one last evening alone together. Why don't we talk instead? Tell me more about Tokyo, about what you've been doing all these years.' She closes the laptop.

'There's not much to tell. My marriage only lasted a year. When I went back to my old apartment it was as if nothing had changed. I went back to working in the shop, back to looking after my nieces and nephews. Still the same house. Still the same shop. Still the same people. It's utterly dull. So no, I haven't changed my mind about this;

it'll give me something different to do. I can read about the exciting life you lived with Michiko Obachan.'

Erika contemplates her cousin for a moment. 'It's not the whole story, Kei.'

There's a silence, and then Kei shrugs. 'Well, I'm enjoying this. I'll take home any diaries I don't finish. You can come and get them back yourself. It's about time you came to see the family. We talk about you, you know, wondering what you're up to.' She slips the bookmark into the diary she's working on and closes it. 'So what about you? Do you have any plans for what you want to do next?'

'I haven't really thought about it,' says Erika. 'I'm happy to keep doing what I'm doing. I don't have the ambition or the personality to become a head chef. The job pays the bills, I get to cook, that's enough for me.'

'It must be tiring.'

'It's good. It stops me from thinking too much about things.'

'The hours are anti-social. No weekends, no evenings.'

'I see Sarah almost every day at work. There's Mrs Mac to look after. And I see Marcus often enough.' Erika sits back.

'Are you two going to get married?'

'God, no,' says Erika, laughing.

'Why laugh?' asks Kei. 'He obviously cares for you.'

'Yes, he does. And I care about him. But that's not enough reason for us to get married. He already has a son, and that's his number one focus. As it should be.'

'If you don't have children you'll end up lonely and alone.'

Erika frowns. 'You can have children and still end up lonely and alone.' She jumps up to get a couple of glasses and a bottle of red from the cupboard and pours, generously.

Kei takes a glass from her cousin and sips in silence for a few moments, as if mulling this over. Then she frowns. 'It must have been hard for Michiko Obachan, having to raise a child on her own –

especially a hāfu child.' She ignores the look Erika gives her. 'It was good she ended up with Julian.'

Erika snorts. 'Don't feel bad for her. She went straight from my father to Julian, and there were plenty of other men too. She probably worked her way through most of the American Club's male membership.' Erika drains her glass, pours again.

'Do you know what happened to your father? What was his name?' asks Kei.

'George. Michiko got angry whenever I asked about him. She told me he didn't want to have anything to do with me, but I didn't believe her, so when I was seventeen, I tracked him down.'

'That can't have been easy.'

'Actually, it wasn't that hard. I just wrote to the school in Tokyo where Michiko said she'd learned English, asked them if he still taught there. They said he was in England. Can you believe it?' Erika laughed drily. 'They wouldn't give me his address, but said if I wrote a letter they'd forward it to him. We were in London, so this letter of mine went from England to Japan and back to England again.'

'And?'

'I got a short reply, very polite, just a few lines. There was no suggestion to meet up, even though he knew I was in England. All he said was, he was sorry for my pain, but it wasn't his place to tell me the truth, and that I should ask my mother. Who, of course, wouldn't tell me anything. So it was a dead end. I had to let it go. But Michiko and I had a huge fight over it. She owed me an explanation, but wouldn't give me one. I was so furious I moved out.'

Kei looks at her with concern. 'Do you remember anything about him at all? You were so little.'

'I was a baby, so no. But I found a picture of him and me in one of Michiko's boxes of photos, so I know what he looks like. Hold on, I'll show you.' Erika heads over to the bookshelf and pulls out a box, rummages around.

'Here it is, look,' she says, handing a tattered photo to Kei. 'I thought about putting it in a frame, but it felt weird to display it. He's a stranger to me.'

'He has a kind face,' says Kei. 'He looks like a nice man.'

'The way he's holding me makes me think he'd have been a good father.' Erika trails off. 'I wish I knew what the hell happened.' Suddenly she snaps back, eyes blazing. 'Julian was the last person on earth who could be a good father figure. He was a nasty piece of work; arrogant, drunk, violent.' Erika suddenly feels drained. She inhales, eyes closed, holds her breath in. She counts to five, exhales. 'Forget it. Let's talk about something else. Actually – there's something I wanted to give you.' She goes to her bedroom and returns with something in her hand. She holds it out to Kei. 'It's to replace the one that was stolen. I found it in Michiko's old jewellery box. I don't know where she got it, but I like its symbolism.'

Kei lifts the fine gold chain out of Erika's palm. At its end dangles a golden heart-shaped pendant.

'A locket?'

'A padlock. A heart-shaped padlock, see, and there's no key. It means you're the keeper of your own heart, and nobody can take control of it and hurt you.'

Kei stares at the necklace without a word. When she looks up her eyes are shining. 'You can't give this to me, Eri-chan, it's your mother's.'

'I never wear it. Here, try it on.' She stands behind Kei to loop the chain around her neck and fastens it. 'Turn around. Let me see.'

The padlock is sitting slightly crooked in Kei's clavicle, and Erika is reaching forward to straighten it when it pops open with a tiny click. She gasps and jumps back.

'What? What is it?' Kei looks down at it, alarmed.

'I … I don't …' stammers Erika. 'I just thought …' She looks again. The padlock is closed, just as it was before. She opens her mouth, dumbfounded.

'Are you okay?' Kei is looking at her strangely.

'It's nothing. I ...' She manages to compose herself. 'I just remembered I was supposed to call André to confirm dinner tomorrow.' She reaches out to touch the necklace. The heart is locked, solid. She can't explain it.

'Well, I love it,' says Kei, smiling again. 'I'd much rather have this than the one Jun gave me. Thank you. It feels as though it was always meant to be mine.'

Kei heads for the kitchen, taking her glass and the bottle of wine with her, motioning for Erika to follow. She draws out a chair from under the yellow Formica-topped kitchen table and pats it, then pours them both another glass.

'Sit here. Talk to me while I cook, but don't help; you'll only get in my way,' says Kei. 'Let someone else cook for you for a change.'

Erika is still disoriented by what she's certain she saw. But watching Kei cook, and listening to her chatter about food and about their plans for tomorrow calms her nerves. She watches Kei dip thin slices of pork escalope in beaten egg, then flour, then panko breadcrumbs. She lays them in shimmering hot oil in a frying pan. The sound of frying is loud and comforting. Kei is proficient with the knife, finely shredding white cabbage with impressive speed. She mixes ketchup and brown sauce – 'Tastes just like Bulldog Sauce,' she says – and when the rice cooker pings she ladles a neat mound of steaming rice into Michiko's old blue-and-white rice bowl and another into Erika's red-and-blue striped one. She makes a bed of shredded cabbage on the white-rimmed, black-glazed, hand-thrown Setoguro plates she's picked out, the same ones Michiko used whenever she made tonkatsu. As Kei slices the crispy golden escalopes she puffs and blows at her fingers – 'Hot, hot!' – scoops them off the chopping board with the knife, keeping them neatly in the shape of the escalope, and arranges them on the bed of shredded cabbage. A flourish of her home-made Bulldog Sauce on top, the bowl of steaming rice on the side, and the meal is ready.

Erika wants to stay in the kitchen. Somehow it feels right to eat it here. She sets chopsticks, placemats, teacups and the pickle jar on the table while Kei boils the kettle for the hōji tea. She swaps wine glasses for oyunomi tea cups. Everything is laid out in the right order. Everything is under control. They tuck in.

'As delicious as the tonkatsu at Suzuki's,' says Erika, mouth full, blowing out steam as she chews. She realises this is the first time in years that both rice bowls have been filled and set out at the table. She feels something twist inside her.

Kei beams. 'Thank you!' She holds Michiko's old rice bowl and lifts a morsel of rice to her mouth. 'Michiko Obachan used to make the best tonkatsu. I think it was even better than at Suzuki's.'

They eat the rest of the meal in silence. Something about the choice of dish, about eating at the kitchen table, about the silence interspersed with occasional commentary on the food echoes inside her, prodding at memories of eating such a dish in such a way with someone she had both deeply hated and deeply loved; someone whose only way of connecting with her was by cooking for her, feeding her, by sharing a meal with her. But as soon as the thought arises, Erika shuts it down.

Erika and Kei argue over who's going to wash up.

'You cooked! Come on, I'm the one who should clear up.'

'I was offering the whole package, cooking and washing up too. The whole point is for you to have nothing to do except relax and enjoy the food.'

'It was delicious, and I'm happy. I'll be even happier if you let me wash up.' She stands in front of the sink, arms crossed, blocking Kei's way. Truth is, she feels oddly subdued. She's still shaken by the heart padlock; she was so sure she'd seen it opening. She needs a moment to herself.

Kei gives in. 'More transcribing, then. I've almost finished the diary I'm working on.' She empties her teacup. 'Looks like I'll be taking quite a few home with me. There's still a big pile of them left. So much more to discover.'

Kei disappears into the sitting room. Erika starts to feel herself again as she washes up. She hums, taking occasional swigs of tea. Once the teapot is empty she boils the kettle for more hot water. 'More tea?' she calls out.

'Yes, please.'

She takes it through to Kei, who slaps the diary closed with a flourish.

'Done! Right, next. This one's from 1972, the year she went to Okinawa with our grandmother.'

'Okinawa? My mother went to Okinawa?'

'See? Isn't it great? There's probably all kinds of stuff about your mother you don't know.'

Michiko

Michiko kept telling herself not all American men could be like the two GIs she'd met in the bar, but she couldn't shake her unease. On trips into the city she'd come across others who were perfectly civil, who tilted their caps at her and helped her mother onto buses – but who knew what monsters they might become at night after a few drinks.

The mismatch with her expectations slashed a rip in her silver-screen fantasies. The American she'd encountered as a child had grown in her mind to mythical proportions, a yardstick against which to measure all men. His appearance in the midst of her unhappiness had felt like a bright sun rising in a sky that, until that moment, had seemed eternally grey. It gave her hope. But the Americans in the Paradise Bar had been so incompatible with that fantasy that when she met Michael she felt an overwhelming urge to run away.

She stood there on the beach in the moonlight, and he'd told her his name. He asked for hers; she'd wavered, but decided there'd be no harm in telling him. He said he loved that beach and the beautiful shrine that watched over it and asked, did she love it too? It was strange to hear him speak such perfectly arranged Japanese sentences with an Okinawan lilt and American-softened vowels. She thought for a moment she might go to sit beside him, but fear flooded her once more. Clutching her shoes, she ran barefoot up the steps towards the shrine while he called after her, apologising for frightening her. She slowed down as she reached the top, sure he wouldn't follow her.

Michiko had started back down the hill when he appeared from the path that led to the opposite end of the beach. She let out a short scream that silenced the night crickets. Michael backed away, alarmed, raising his palms towards her and crooning reassurance as if he were trying to quieten a wild animal.

'Please,' he said, 'I won't hurt you. The men are making the most of the nightclubs before they're sent to Saigon next week. Some of them don't treat local women well. Let me accompany you until you're in a safe place. You don't need to tell me where you live. Here, I'll walk ahead of you.'

She mentioned her bus stop at Makishi and followed several paces behind him. As they walked, she examined the back of him: his broad shoulders, his narrow waist, the taut curve of his buttocks, his long legs. His neck gleamed in the light of the streetlamps, and when they reached Kokusai Dōri, which was overflowing with drunken GIs, she drew closer and saw his nape was golden with fine blond down. Her heart pounded. A soldier yelled, 'Hey sexy!' and another wolf-whistled; Michael barked words that made them draw up with a look of surprise and wobble a salute. He turned back now and then to make sure she was still there, and when the bus stop was in their sights, he bowed, bidding her farewell, and walked away. He never touched her.

She took the bus back to the house and found her mother asleep. Chiyo had eaten the food she'd left out for her, and Michiko felt her world right itself a little. She scrubbed herself until her skin was red; poured water over her body again and again until she imagined Buddy and Marty washing off onto the floor and disappearing down the drain along with the dirty suds. She soaked in the bath until she was dizzy, feeling the hot water purge the fear from her body. The night was so warm that when she emerged, sweat beaded her skin as quickly as she dried herself. She wandered naked to the verandah to seek out a cool breeze. The ringing of crickets surged like an altar bell reverberating inside her head; she closed her eyes and drew in the sweet scent of jasmine. The air was as warm as her body; she felt her edges melting, as if she no longer knew where she ended and the space around her began. She could stay like this forever, merged into ether between earth and sky, but then she thought of Michael, and wondered where he might be now.

When Obā came back from Ginowan the next day, Michiko asked where she might take Chiyo for an evening out, somewhere cheap with good food and drink. GIs made her nervous, she said, keeping what happened to herself. She wanted to know where locals went.

'Stay away from Kokusai Dōri at night and you'll be fine,' said Obā, who was too busy preparing lunch to notice Michiko's expression. 'Lots of good places to eat if you head south-east from there. Why don't we go out tonight? I know just the place. We can take the bus.'

That evening, the three of them wore cool cotton yukata and clattered along to the bus stop in their wooden geta, purses tucked into obi belts and clutching uchiwa fans. It was a humid night. They got off at Makishi but turned left instead of continuing on to Kokusai Dōri. It was quieter without the throng of bars and nightclubs; there wasn't a military uniform in sight. Families congregated outside open shopfronts, the cool white of fluorescent lights flooding out into the night. The smell of charcoal-grilled meat filled the air; young children played in the streets and adults fanned themselves while they drank bottles of Orion beer, the sound of murmured conversation intermingling with the thrumming of the night cicadas.

A few blocks further on, the shops gave way to houses and there were fewer streetlights. Nestled among them was a low wooden building, its doorway and windows aglow through a profusion of hibiscus bushes and flowering vines. Even before Obā slid open the door, Michiko could hear people inside whistling in syncopated rhythm to a woman singing along to a sanshin. She'd heard snatches of Okinawan music on TV before; its unique sound had always stirred something deep within her. Hearing it live made goosebumps rise on her arms. She took Chiyo's hand and led her in, ducking under the noren curtains.

A clamour of friendly voices greeted them. It seemed Obā was a regular. There was a small wooden bar crammed with glasses and bottles and condiments, with various pots bubbling on a stove behind and a charcoal grill sizzling with rows of little fish, the walls covered in faded posters of bikini-clad girls advertising beer. A sun-wizened man who looked to be about eighty sat at a corner table plucking the three-stringed snakeskin sanshin; next to him sat a woman who was coming to the end of her full-throated song, eyes closed, palms waving as everyone began to clap.

'Does your mother drink?' asked Obā.

'No, but I do,' said Michiko, as if she had been drinking all her life.

Obā called out to the landlord, and after a few minutes he came bearing a tray with a pot of tea, two bottles and some glasses filled with ice. 'Food's on its way,' he said.

'Have you tried awamori?' asked Obā. 'Our Okinawan spirit. It's strong. It's good.' She poured tea for Chiyo. 'I chose the food – I hope you don't mind,' she added. 'I know what's good here.' She poured Michiko a glass. The liquid looked benign, like water, but when Obā topped it up from the water bottle it swirled, a syrupy mist, turning the liquid opalescent white. She wanted to take a sip but knew from serving her father's guests that it was now her turn to pour for Obā.

'Ha! Such good manners,' Obā said. 'But you needn't bother with those here.' She raised her cup. '*Karī!*' she cried, and emptied the glass. '*Karī!*' came the response from the tables around them.

'*Kampai,*' said Michiko, raising her glass at Obā, then corrected herself. '*Karī!*' she echoed and followed suit, emptying the glass. It tasted surprisingly mellow, though it blazed that now familiar path down to her stomach. 'Oof!' she said, coughing. 'I like it.'

'Another?' Obā refilled the glass.

The landlord brought little dishes of strange food Michiko had never tried before: mimigā, a pickled salad of finely sliced cucumber and pig's ear; jīmami tofu, made with peanuts instead of soy beans and swimming in a pool of sweet soy sauce; a bowl of bitter gōya gourd fried with cubes of Spam, and a plate of tako rice.

'There's a lot of resistance against the American bases here, but at least they gave us the gift of Spam and tacos,' said Obā with a grin. 'Though we prefer our taco filling on rice. This bar has the best version,' she said, doling out portions onto their plates.

Chiyo put some of the jīmami tofu into her mouth. She paused, spoon held in the air, eyes widening.

'What's the matter, Okāsan?' Michiko asked. 'Are you alright?'

Chiyo beamed and spooned more into her mouth, spilling sauce down her chin.

'Do you like it?' Michiko took a napkin and wiped her mother's face.

'She must remember the taste from her childhood,' said Obā. 'I wish she could talk to us.'

Michiko poured them both more awamori. 'Mother hasn't spoken since the accident. She smiles sometimes, and makes noises, and I pretend she understands. The doctors say we should keep talking to her as if she does, but none of us think she'll get better. There hasn't been much improvement.'

Obā contemplated Chiyo for a moment. 'I wonder if we should take her to Kudakajima? There isn't anyone left from the family there, but seeing the place she was born might spark something. She could see the noro the Kudakas used to consult. She still lives on the island; she could pray for your mother's health.'

'Noro? I've heard stories about them, but I didn't realise they were still around.'

'I don't know of any in Naha, but on Kudakajima most of the women are still being ordained as noro. You know it's a sacred island, don't you?'

Michiko nods.

'The next izaiho initiation ceremony won't be until 1978. They have one every twelve years. They have to keep it going, otherwise there won't be enough young ones to continue the rites. If your mother had stayed on the island, she would have become a noro too.' The sanshin strikes up again. 'Ah! It's "Toshin Doi"! Come on, you have to dance!'

The upbeat tempo brought people to their feet, slapping out a syncopated rhythm on the wooden tables. Obā was laughing, dancing, palms waving aloft, and Michiko found herself joining in, loud whistles and cries of '*Haiya! Eya-sassa!*' swirling around the room. She felt a delicious turning under her breastbone, as if a creature was awakening. All this – Obā's company; the music; the awamori; this place – it felt right. She wished Sayuri were with her; they could have had such fun. I'll come back, she thought. I'll bring my friend to show her this place. It's where I belong.

'Look at your mother!'

Michiko turned and saw Chiyo. She was out of her chair and her arms were almost aloft. She was attempting to step in time to the music, and she was beaming.

Michiko's euphoria evaporated the next morning with a hangover and the dawning realisation that she would be leaving Obā and Okinawa in a fortnight's time. She wanted – needed – to stay longer, but didn't know how to make it happen. She knew she'd never be able to persuade her father, even if she explained that Chiyo seemed to be responding well, that if they stayed longer, they might see an improvement. Maybe her brother could talk to him for her. Even if her father refused, Kensuke was effectively the head of the family now he'd taken over the business. Ultimately it would be his decision. Surely he would see that staying in Okinawa was in their mother's best interests.

Obā had left early to visit a friend recuperating from surgery, and Chiyo seemed tired. Michiko decided to leave her to rest while she went into the city. She still had a little money left, thanks to Obā's generous hospitality, and Michiko still wanted to find a scarf to replace the one she'd lost to the sea. She was glad she'd bought the silver en-musubi ring, but worried about how much she'd spent on it. If her father noticed it and asked where it came from she'd tell him Obā had given it to her. The ring was her treasure: a talisman, and a reminder of the possibility of happiness. She felt that if she wore it, fate wouldn't forget that it had a brighter future in store for her.

At the last minute she decided to stay on the bus instead of getting off at Makishi; she wanted to see where the bus would take her. She felt expansive and adventurous. The bus followed Kokusai Dōri almost to its end, and when she got off she felt a thrill to see a sign with directions to Naminoue Shrine. I was led here, she thought. She recognised the hill path, thinking of the last time she walked it, and the man with the golden hair. The humidity and heat was as relentless as the deafening *shwaash shwaash* of cicadas, and there was no relief even in the shade of the shrine, where Michiko stood to clap her hands and pray, calling on the gods to answer her prayers.

Emerging into blazing sunlight, Michiko found herself hurrying down the stairs to the beach. She was surprised to find it almost empty apart from a couple swimming at the other end. She dropped her shoes and bag at the water's edge and waded in, lifting the hem of her dress. Such delicious relief. The cool water was so clear she could see each grain of white sand between her toes. She sighed and closed her eyes, wading deeper.

When the water reached her waist, she opened her eyes, and her vision was filled by the turquoise all around her. She fell back, letting the ocean take her body. She didn't care about her clothes – they'd dry quickly in the heat – but they felt restrictive. The couple were now back on the beach, too far away to notice what she was doing. She waded further until she was in the water to her neck, ducked her hand under the water and removed her underwear, unbuttoned her dress, unlatched her bra. Under the water she wrapped everything in the dress and rolled it into a package. Wading to the rocks beneath the cliff that the shrine was perched on, she tucked her clothes between two boulders and swam back out to the deep. She felt herself surrender. Her body, the water, her skin, merging. She reduced everything down to this moment, this acute pleasure. She did not want it to end.

'Hello again.'

She jolted upright, whipping her head around in shock.

The man with the golden hair was in the water a few metres away from her. He saw her expression. 'God, I'm sorry, I've frightened you again. We met the other night. Do you remember?'

She crossed her arms over her breasts, although he was far enough away not to see that she was naked beneath the water. 'Hello.'

'Erm, are those your things over there?' he said, pointing at her shoes and bag in the distance.

Squinting in the sun, she saw the waves had moved further up the beach and were now dangerously close to washing them away.

She gasped. 'Oh no!' She looked around wildly for the rocks where she'd left her clothes, but Michael was already on his way. She watched as he emerged from the shallows and strode out through the waves. His wet back glistened in the sun; he wore a small pair of swimming trunks. She had never seen so much of a man's body before, and felt a pulse low in her belly. He picked up her bag and shoes and rearranged them in the shade of the cliff further up the beach. When he turned back towards the shoreline, she saw the swirls of golden hair on his chest, saw how the hair narrowed into a line that ran down his torso and disappeared into his shorts. Her eye lingered there, then lower still. She felt reckless. She could have retrieved her dress in those moments but didn't move.

He was wading back. When he reached deeper water he started swimming, coming closer than he'd been before. She unwrapped her arms and released her breasts, feeling the ocean caress them. He stopped when he was still some distance away and stood up, rivulets running from the hair on his chest. He ran a hand through his wet hair, and she saw a golden ring on his finger, set with a large blue stone the same colour as the sea. The intimate sound of his breath, rapid with the exertion of the swim, reached her across the rippling water. It made him seem vulnerable. 'Thank you,' she said, 'you're very kind.' She wondered if he could see her body under the water, but his eyes were on her face. She moved closer. She wanted him to see. 'It's Michael, isn't it?'

'Yes. You're ... Michiko.'

Very close to him now, she ducked her chin below the water, opening her mouth to let salt water enter it. She bobbed up so her breasts briefly emerged from the water, then sank back, pursing her lips to spout the water out again. She smiled, fixing him with her gaze, and saw with a thrill that he was flustered. The pulse in her belly grew heavier, descended lower. It felt good, like an itch ready to be scratched. She saw the effect she had on him and spread her legs in the water, planting her feet in the sand, feeling the current between her thighs.

His gaze followed down to her body, and his face flushed. 'Oh ... ah ...'

'I love the ocean,' she said. 'I feel like a fish. Isn't it bliss?' She swam away from him, kicked up her feet and flipped forward to dive back into the sea. She felt her buttocks exposed to the air, knew he would see, knew he would look for the dark space between her legs. She sank deep to the ocean floor and pulled through the thick water, eyes open. His legs stood like pale and mottled pillars, their colour filtered green through the azure, and she held her breath until she had swum around to the back of him. She burst out of the water, laughing.

When he turned around she could see from his expression that he was aroused, but his laughter betrayed his embarrassment.

'I really should be getting back,' she said as he stood open-mouthed, and swam towards the boulders to find her dress and underwear. Treading water, she wrestled her clothes back on, then waded back to the beach. She sat in the sun, panting, and squeezed as much water as she could from her dress. Michael was still standing out in the ocean, watching her. She grinned and lay in the sand, not caring. She laid a forearm across her eyes to keep out the sun; the heat was beating down and she would be dry before long.

After a few moments, she felt a cool shadow fall on her body. Peering from beneath her arm, she saw Michael sit down beside her. She turned on her side to face him, head propped on her hand.

'Do you live in Naha?' he asked, dripping. The droplets were forming tiny bowls in the sand where they fell.

'I wish I did. I'm from Tokyo.'

'Ah, just visiting then.'

'It's my first time here. My mother and I have to go back soon. I wish I could stay.'

He contemplated this for a moment, squinting out at the horizon, and said, 'Would you happen to be free next Saturday? I have some leave, and planned to drive north. Have you been to the Motobu peninsula? It's beautiful up there.'

'No,' she said, 'but I'd love to.'

Michael drove her home and Michiko floated back into Obā's house, humming with excitement. She wandered into the garden and stripped off, grabbing a hose to rinse the salt from her clothes. She wrung them out and hung them to dry, then stood with her toes dug into the flower bed and rinsed the sea off her body. She closed her eyes, feeling the cold water flow over her breasts and her back, returning the heat of her skin to the earth. Her feet sank into the wet soil and she imagined herself growing out of it like a plant ripe with fruit. She held the hose over her head and combed her fingers through the tangles the wind had made in her hair as they drove in his open-topped car. She'd felt like a movie star, sitting beside him as they cruised along Kokusai Dōri. She felt the surge in her the pit of her belly again. She could hardly bear to wait through the week to see him. She reached between her legs with her fingers, and surrendered to the sun.

'I called the noro,' said Obā, while they ate their evening meal together. 'She remembers the Kudaka family, and she's agreed to see your mother next Saturday. I'm owed a few days off work, so I'll come home on Friday afternoon to get ready and we can leave just before dawn on Saturday to catch the first ferry. We can stay on the island for the night and catch the ferry back next afternoon.'

'Oh,' said Michiko, picking up her bowl of nakami jiru and slurping a mouthful to hide her dismay.

'I'm glad you'll see Kudakajima. It's where your mother's ancestors dwell, after all. It's a sacred island. Amamikyū descended there from heaven to create all the islands and all the creatures in them: the Ryūkyū kings, the noro, the farmers and the fishermen.'

Michiko nodded, remembering the childhood games she'd played during the war.

'It's where your mother belongs. You belong in the sacred groves too. You may have been born in Tokyo, but you still share your weka with the Kudakajima women.'

Obā and Chiyo continued to eat while Michiko's mind churned. She emptied her bowl of soup and was suddenly struck by a plan. 'Thank you, Obā,' she said after a while. 'That would be lovely. I'm looking forward to it.'

On Friday she stayed home with Chiyo and packed an overnight bag for them both. When Obā came home, Michiko politely refused her dinner, saying she didn't feel well. She lay listlessly on the verandah until she took herself to bed early.

'I'll be fine by the morning, I'm sure,' she said, waving away Obā's concern. She lay awake dreaming as the fan played warm breezes across her body, the sound of its spinning blades turning into a film reel spooling vivid projections in her mind: Michael proposing to her with a big diamond ring; Michiko excited to show the ring to Sayuri; the two friends shopping in Takashimaya department store for her dowry and honeymoon clothes. The final scene: the wedding, and Michiko escaping her awful life to live in Okinawa, bringing Chiyo with her. Maybe they would even move to America.

When Obā brought Chiyo into the room to help her change into her yukata after her bath, Michiko pretended to be asleep. But as Obā folded back the summer futon to get Chiyo into bed, Michiko rolled over and groaned, loudly.

'Oh dear. Are you still not well?'

Michiko groaned again. 'I feel terrible. Aching all over.'

Obā touched her palm to Michiko's forehead. 'Hmm. You don't feel like you have a fever. I'll bring you a herbal tonic and some water. See if you can get some sleep, you might feel better in the morning.'

'I'm sure I will, Obā. Thank you.'

Michiko was too electrified by desire to eat at first, but after they'd made love in the warm phosphorescence of the night ocean she was ravenous. When she emerged from the water she saw she was bleeding a little, but the pain had felt like rapture. Her body had convulsed, overwhelmed as if by shocks of electricity, and she had opened herself fully to receive him.

She sat naked and glowing on the silver-moonlit sand, watching Michael dry himself. She reached into the ice box she'd asked him to bring so the picnic she'd prepared for them would stay cool against the day's heat. There'd been just enough room for the bottle of awamori she'd also asked him to bring. She pulled its stopper out, poured a few centimetres into a glass and gulped back a mouthful, feeling the rush blaze down to meet the rising heat of her craving. She tapped the silver of her knot ring against the glass, clinking. Bind me to this place.

That morning Michiko had waved a lethargic goodbye to Obā and her mother as they drove off for the ferry. She'd had to persuade Obā not to cancel the trip, telling her she'd be fine on her own, that she was sure the sickness would pass, that she just needed to rest. She was sorry, she said, for missing the chance to visit the sacred island of her ancestors. All of that felt as if it had happened long ago, as if that had happened in another world. If she had let her mind travel even further back to Tokyo, it would have seemed as grey and distant as her mother's faded photographs from before the war. Here, on these shimmering islands, there was warmth, and colour, and life, and there was Michael.

They had driven that morning along the western coastal road, past Camp Kinser where Michael was stationed, and through Ginowan, where Obā worked. They stopped for coffee and a doughnut at an American-style diner, and in the shop next to it she spotted a scarf she liked. He bought it for her. 'For your hair when we're in the car,' he said. 'So it doesn't get messed up in the wind.'

As they went further north, the hills grew into mountains, thick forest hemming them in between the mountains and the sea. They drove past a small village, stopping for a lunch of Okinawa soba. As they left the village, a cluster of strange oval-shaped stone structures appeared dug into the hillside, small doors carved into their flat facades. 'Kamebaka,' Michael told her. 'They're called that because the graves are shaped like turtle shells.' Michiko turned to him, amazed. 'Why do you know so much about these things?'

As she looked at him, she thought she saw something desperate and sad in his expression, but when he started talking he seemed lively again. He was born at Kadena where his father had been stationed, and made friends with an Okinawan boy. At weekends he often went to the Motobu mountains with the boy's family, or to the smaller islands scattered along the coastline, he said. He'd dive on the coral reefs with his friend, holding his breath. He grew to love the islands. But when he was thirteen, his father was killed in the Korean war, and his mother had taken him back to Tennessee. He didn't fit in with the other kids in his school, and was homesick for Okinawa. His mother wasn't happy when he decided to follow his father into the military and got himself stationed back there. He wasn't sure when he'd be called to Saigon, he said. Michiko wondered if the thought of going to Vietnam was what was troubling him.

She felt touched that he was drawing her further into his life with these stories. Now that he was laying out his past for her, she hoped this was a sign he'd invite her into his future. She twisted her silver knot ring and gazed at the sea as it flashed past. Everything felt so right. Maybe fate meant for her to end up here after all. She laid her palm on Michael's thigh and felt its firmness, its warmth. After a while he took his hand from the gear stick and covered her hand with his, and she watched the blue stone in his golden ring flicker with the colour of the ocean.

In the afternoon they drove to a gusuku, the ruins of Nakajin castle that had stood on the north-eastern corner of the island for six hundred years. It was there they saw a woman in a white robe kneeling at the foot of a wind-gnarled tree. She wore her hair in a topknot, a white band around her forehead. She'd placed a tray among the tree roots with an arrangement of a branch of green leaves, a burner of incense, a small white cup, a mound of raw grains of rice and an orange with its leaf attached. They watched as she poured awamori into the cup and raised her palms heavenwards, eyes closed. Lowering them, hands together at her breast, she bowed her head, rocking gently back and forth, muttering in a low singsong. As Michiko listened to the soft hum of the woman's incantations, the hair rose on her neck and a prickle ran down her spine.

Michael leaned towards her and whispered: 'That woman is a noro.'

Michiko nodded, trying not to think of her mother and Obā on Kudakajima at that same moment. Though they were a hundred kilometres away at the other end of Okinawa, she had an uncomfortable feeling someone might sense her deception. She shook her head as if to clear it of a spell. 'Can we go back to Nakijin town now? I'm thirsty,' she said, taking his arm and leading him away. 'Do you think we might find a bar somewhere?'

Over a drink she told Michael that her relatives were away for the weekend, that there was no need to go back to Naha in a hurry. She'd smiled at him, crossing her legs as she sipped from a cocktail through a straw. He looked at the bar menu and she reminded him they still had the picnic she'd brought in the cooler. 'Why don't we go to one of these beautiful beaches after dark?' she said. 'We can swim, and have our picnic under the stars.'

Now, on the beach, she was soaring high, so high she could look down on the life she'd lived until this moment. It felt like it belonged to someone else. She wanted to eat, she wanted to make love again. In the ice box was the plastic wicker basket she'd brought from Tokyo and filled with salted salmon and umeboshi onigiri she'd made that morning; there was a salad of tomatoes; a bowlful of papaya and passionfruit from Obā's garden; a box of sweet sata andāgi from the local bakery; and two bars of chocolate. She ate her fill, watching Michael devour everything with obvious pleasure.

'Kiss me,' she whispered, using American words she'd learned from the movies, and nuzzled his neck with her lips, moving to the side of his mouth, until, breathing hard, he turned to drink from her.

She felt they were the only two people in the world. Nothing mattered; they were merged, moving against one another again. The white sands glowed luminous and the ocean hushed onto the shore in tiny sighs. As he moved over her, she closed her eyes to feel him, scooping her hand through the tiny grains of dead coral and the ground-up shells of sea creatures and scattering them over his back. The heat and the thrill of their sex slickened their skin with sweat; she felt a bubble of heat rise to her throat as a bright ray pierced the crown of her head and rushed through every cell of her body. She cried out, felt as if she were turned to mist, mingling with the air, the sea below, the sky above, the sand that held her body, the island itself.

Michael cradled her face in his hand and kissed it everywhere, and where his soft lips touched her skin, her nerve-endings prickled bright, like sparklers. She looked at his face, and was deeply moved to see it wet with tears.

'Don't be sad,' she whispered. 'We'll be together again. I promise I'll come back.'

She traced his fingers with her lips, kissed the golden ring he wore on his finger, feeling the smoothness of its blue stone, the roughness of the words engraved around it with the tip of her tongue.

She took up her glass, asked him to fill it. She was drunk with pleasure, her head spinning from the intensity of this moment, from the awamori. His hair glowed pale in the moonlight and his skin shimmered, as if lit by some unearthly inner luminescence. He looked like a god she could take refuge in. A memory from long ago rippled across her mind. She felt whole. She felt safe.

A Birth Certificate

The paper is official, a long, slightly yellowed rectangle, with black letters running across its top: 'BIRTH within the district of the British CONSUL at TOKYO'. Below it is a table split into ten columns: Number; When and where born; Name; Sex; Name and surname of father; Name and maiden surname of mother; Rank, profession or occupation of father and claim to citizenship of the United Kingdom and Colonies; Signature, description and residence of informant; When registered; Signature of consular officer. A green stamp is pasted on the bottom right-hand corner, bearing the Queen's head and the words 'Five Shillings', and ring-stamped with the words 'British Embassy Consular Section of Tokyo, February 1966'. Hidden within this official document, embedded within the table, is a lie.

Erika

The meal at André's is as magnificent as Frankie promised. Kei seems impressed that Erika works at such a fancy restaurant. Frankie brings out their amuses-bouches himself before the meal gets underway.

'Alright, you lot?' he says, his face red and sweating. 'Thought I'd come out now before we get slammed. Wanted to check out your cousin. Hello, how are you?' He shakes Kei's hand.

'You don't have to look so impressed,' Erika says to Kei, 'that's only Frankie. André will probably be out in a bit.'

Over the course of the evening, dish after dish is brought to their table – 'Something extra, compliments of the kitchen' – and their glasses are never empty. André comes out at the end of their meal and asks Kei if she's enjoyed it, then kisses her hand in response to her enthusiastic appreciation of everything she's eaten.

'Ugh, he's flirting with her,' Erika whispers out of the corner of her mouth at Sarah. 'Do something. It's embarrassing.'

'Bless. I've never seen him so charming,' says Sarah, fascinated. He's bent over Kei's chair, keeping her hand in one of his while gesturing expansively with the other. She seems flattered to be given all this attention by the famous chef on a busy night.

'You two leave him alone,' whispers Marcus. 'Look, he's in his element.'

'Very delicious,' Kei is saying, beaming and bobbing her head. 'Very nice meal. Very nice restaurant.'

When André leaves, Erika sees the smile drop from her cousin's face so completely that she almost asks there and then what's wrong. Throughout the evening Kei has behaved as if she were relaxed and happy, loudly appreciating every dish that appeared on their table; she's joined in the conversation with her faltering English, has laughed along at the jokes with everyone else. But in between moments, when everyone else was absorbed in conversation, Erika would glance at her cousin and notice a look of apprehension. She is sure she wasn't imagining it.

'Does Kei seem upset to you?' Erika asks the others when Kei goes to the bathroom.

'No, why?' says Marcus.

'I don't know; she seems a bit … down.'

'She seems fine to me.'

'I didn't notice anything either,' says Sarah. 'But then again, you know her best. Maybe she's sad that this is her last night in London.'

'Maybe.' Their coffees arrive with a plate of glistening jewel-like petit-fours.

'I'm pleased it turned out so well, babe,' says Marcus, spooning cream into his espresso. 'Considering how much you dreaded her coming.'

'I like her,' says Sarah. 'She's not how you made her out to be at all.'

'I feel guilty about some of the things I said about her now. She was different last time I saw her.' Erika downs her espresso in one. 'As much of a pain in the arse as she can be sometimes, I think I might even miss her. Shh, here she comes.'

Erika asks the cab driver to take the scenic route through London on their way back home, a final tour for Kei. She pulls the windows down; the balmy air of the late summer evening helps her forget autumn is near. They gaze out at the glittering jewellery box of the city night. As they drive across Waterloo Bridge, St Paul's Cathedral glowing iridescent in the distance, Erika sticks her head out of the window and whoops. She pulls back inside and turns to Kei.

'I love crossing the Thames at night. London's so beautiful when it's all lit up like this, don't you think?'

Kei has a distant expression on her face. 'Mm.'

'Are you all right? You seem ...'

Kei shakes her head, as if she's trying to wipe away her thoughts. 'I'm fine.'

They're driving along the Embankment.

'The lights strung along the river – they look like diamond necklaces,' says Erika. She's drunk. She puts her arm around Kei's shoulder, grinning at Marcus and Sarah sitting opposite them on the cab's flip-down seats. 'Gorgeous, don't y'all think?'

Kei stiffens a little, then relaxes. 'Erika, I've enjoyed visiting you so much. Thank you for looking after me. Tonight was wonderful.'

'It's been my pleasure,' says Erika, meaning it. 'You should come to visit more often.' She turns to the others. 'Wouldn't it be great if Kei came to visit again?'

'And you must come to Tokyo.' Kei nods at Sarah and Marcus. 'You too, please come and be my guests in Tokyo.'

'You bet,' says Sarah.

They're in Chelsea now.

'Albert Bridge, miss?' asks the driver.

'Yes, please! Look, Kei, the most beautiful bridge in the whole of London. Do you see the lights? And over there in Battersea Park, do you see that? That's the Peace Pagoda. It's a Buddhist one.'

Kei nods. She still seems troubled. Maybe she *is* just sad to be leaving. Erika isn't particularly looking forward to their parting tomorrow either. She gazes at her cousin, the closest thing she has to family, and she marvels again at how, in just two weeks, so much has changed.

At the airport, Erika and Kei embrace before Kei heads to departures. The awkwardness with which they greeted each other only two weeks ago between them is gone, and they smile and promise one another that they won't leave it so long before they meet again. Kei's flight isn't due to take off for over two hours – they arrived early, leaving the house with plenty of time to spare in case of delays on the Tube, but the journey has gone smoothly. Kei tells Erika she hates lingering goodbyes, and hopes she won't mind if she goes through the security checks straight away. She promises to call as soon as she arrives back in Tokyo, and joins the queue. Kei seems cheery, but Erika sees her dab her eyes with a tissue once she turns away. She doesn't turn back. Erika watches until her cousin is swallowed up behind the barriers.

She sheds a few tears of her own on the Tube journey home. She's tired. Maybe she should go home for a quick nap before she heads to the restaurant in the afternoon. Maybe it's just as well she didn't take that extra day off. Better keep herself distracted with work. Marcus is with Felix for the fortnight, and she's not looking forward to going home to an empty flat. She's sure once she's back in the rhythm of work, everything will be all right again.

She's been asleep for less than half an hour when the phone rings. She's been dreaming; wrenched from deep sleep, she groans and rolls over, putting a pillow over her head. The phone rings on until she hears the answering machine click into action.

'Erika?' It's Kei.

Erika almost falls out of bed in her haste to get to the phone. She grabs the receiver. 'Kei! I'm here.'

'I thought maybe you'd gone somewhere on your way home. You sound fuzzy. I'm sorry, were you asleep?' She sounds anxious.

'What's happened? Is your flight delayed?'

'No, we're boarding in a few minutes.' She falls silent. Erika hears her breathing on the end of the line, the soft buzz of the airport's ambient noise in the background.

'Kei, are you okay? What's the matter?'

'Erika, I have to tell you something.'

'What about?'

'I was just sitting here at the gate waiting and had a thought, you know, about what would happen if there should be an accident.'

Erika laughs. 'Oh, Kei, don't worry. You know how rare it is for anything to happen, it's so much safer to fly than —'

'I'm not afraid to fly.'

Erika rubs her head in frustration. What is Kei getting at?

'I was going to wait until I got back to Tokyo to tell you,' says Kei.

'Tell me what?'

'But just now I thought, as I sat here, that if there should be an accident during the flight, and I never make it home, say, then there's some important information I needed to tell you, that I didn't tell you. And I saw a payphone here so I decided to use up my English change and call you. To tell you.'

'Tell me *what*, Kei?'

'Yesterday afternoon, I transcribed the next one from the pile of Michiko Obachan's diaries. The one from when she went to Okinawa. I would have told you yesterday but I just didn't know how to. It was a lot to take in. I'm sorry I didn't tell you straight away.' She pauses.

'*Tell* me, Kei.'

'Eri-chan.' Erika hears Kei draw a deep breath. 'George isn't your father.'

Michiko

If Michiko had known as she stood on the ferry, waving at the receding figure of Obā, that she would never return to Okinawa, she'd have jumped overboard and swum back to shore. But despite her sorrow at parting with Obā, the island, and most of all with Michael, she was still filled with hope.

She'd slipped out of the house the night before and met Michael by the river. They'd walked hand in hand along the dark river path to the fields, lying down between tall green rows of sugar cane that whispered at them in the breeze, and made love one final time. She ached with grief, then, and could not stop weeping. He had given her his ring. 'To remember me by,' he'd said.

She stood on the deck holding Chiyo's hand until she could no longer make out the dark dash of land on the horizon. She wore the scarf Michael had bought her tightly knotted under her chin, though the wind was kinder on this return journey. Against her belly, she felt the solidity of his ring, strung onto a long loop of ribbon around her neck.

The sea was calm and the rocking of the ship gentle, but after a few hours Michiko was dismayed to start feeling the seasickness she'd escaped on their outwards journey. Chiyo seemed fine; Michiko left her in the cafeteria and crept to the toilets. She sat in a toilet cubicle in a cold sweat, the turmoil of her thoughts at the reality of returning home mirroring the tumult in her stomach. She tried to make herself sick, but could not, and sat with her head between her legs, praying for the nausea to ease. As she fought the seasickness, she also fought the fear and doubt that rose up with it. She told herself Michael and she would be reunited, that he would write to her asking her to marry him, that she would return to him to act out her final scene, the happy ending. *My fate is to be extraordinary*, she repeated silently to herself, twisting the en-musubi ring on her finger. The thoughts reduced the intensity of the nausea, and she repeated them again and again, as if in meditation.

The seasickness stayed with her the entire journey. At times it had felt unendurable, like her grief; she was overcome by fits of sobbing, and she did not sleep. Even Chiyo seemed to notice her unhappiness, reaching for her hand whenever Michiko returned from the bathroom. When they finally reached Kagoshima, Michiko was exhausted, and for a few hours the ground beneath her continued to pitch and fall as if she were still on the ship, giving her little relief. But by the time they boarded the train, the nausea receded, and she turned her mind to home. She was looking forward to telling Sayuri about Michael, knowing that sharing it would lighten her burden. Her friend would help nurture her hope.

They didn't stop anywhere on their homeward journey; she was needed home quickly to help prepare the shop and the family for the autumn equinox holidays. Michiko didn't mind; it was best she kept busy. She would write a letter to Michael as soon as she arrived home, and then she would have the anticipation of his reply. She surrendered to her fatigue, her head rocking on her mother's shoulder, and slept for hours, lost in feverish dreams.

They arrived back at Tokyo station on a Sunday, and the entire family came to meet them. Fusae had taken leave of her husband and come with her children, who held up a 'welcome home' sign they'd crayoned onto a large piece of paper. Everyone seemed excited to see them – even Michiko's father was smiling – and they were full of questions. Michiko felt herself split, half of her left behind in Okinawa with Michael, the other half glad to be home. She'd missed her siblings.

Fusae and their sister-in-law had prepared a feast. They sat around the table to eat as Michiko told them about Obā, about the night Chiyo got up to dance the eisa, about the strange food, about Obā's garden and Shuri Castle and the flowers and the beautiful sea. She didn't mention the constant reminders of the US military presence for fear her father would launch into one of his anti-American tirades, saying only that Obā's employers treated her well.

She took care not to mention that she'd been to the Motobu peninsula and seen Nakijin Castle, and certainly not that she'd had a moonlit picnic on an isolated northern beach and lost her virginity to an American man. She would save all that for Sayuri. Instead she told the family how Chiyo and Obā had gone to Kudakajima; that she had been too sick to go, but that Obā had said old neighbours remembered Chiyo as a little girl, though Chiyo could not remember them; that Chiyo had seen the noro and slept for twelve hours afterwards, waking to wander beside the island's ancient square-hewn rock walls, humming as she walked the sandy paths. That Obā had found her lying in one of the sacred groves, eyes closed and smiling. There hadn't been much sign of improvement in her comprehension, but they all agreed that Chiyo seemed more peaceful.

After she and Fusae had cleared up the dishes and everyone had bathed and gone to bed, Michiko sat at the table to write her letter to Michael. She told him how sick she had been on the ferry home and how glad she had been to reach dry land; she wrote about how much she missed him, how much she missed the island, and that she couldn't wait until they were together again. She found a stamp and put her shoes on so she could go out and post it, but her father suddenly appeared in the corridor on the way to the bathroom and she jumped, clasping the envelope to her chest.

She hoped she hadn't woken him, she said, and apologised, saying she needed to get something from the pharmacy urgently, that she was going to post a letter she'd written to Obā on the way. She hoped her terror didn't show; if he'd asked to see the envelope that would have been the end of everything. But the implication of that emphatic 'something' worked; he harrumphed and continued on his way. She breathed a sigh of relief, but just before he slid open the door to the bathroom he turned back.

'You've done well, Michiko,' he said. 'Your mother seems healthier and happier than before. This trip has shown you can be a responsible adult. Even though you're well past the normal age, perhaps it isn't too late to find you a husband. An older man – a widower, perhaps. Someone who needs to be cared for.'

She walked to the post box with her head bowed. She kissed the envelope before she dropped it through the slot, and whispered her wish that she would not have to wait too long before she could begin a new life with Michael.

Instead of returning home she walked on to the next neighbourhood, past the Imperial Palace, and then beyond, to where nobody would know her. She found a sakaya shop still open. She wandered inside and, pulling out the rest of the money left over from her trip, asked the man behind the counter if he sold awamori. He gave her a strange look and said he didn't, but the shochū they had was similar.

He pulled a bottle off a shelf. 'This is thirty-two per cent alcohol and it won't be as strong, but it's far superior to anything they could make in Okinawa,' he said. He looked her up and down. 'Explain this to your husband; I'm sure he won't mind.'

Her old life resumed its relentless grind, and as she donned her white headscarf and apron at the start of the week to open up the tea shop with Kensuke, her heart was heavy. She wished now that she'd sent her brother the letter she'd written at Obā's after all. She'd lost her nerve at the last minute. She decided to wait until she heard from Michael; it would be easier to explain everything properly to her father once the engagement was official. Her father had already gone back to his abrasive ways; Fusae had gone home to her husband and for now, Michiko could not confide in her brother. Chiyo remained her usual enigmatic self. Michiko found comfort in imagining the journey her letter would make to reach Michael; she imagined the postman collecting it from the red post box to be sorted and put into a mailbag, imagined the mailbag being loaded onto a ship to make its journey south, imagined the letters sorted in Naha and dispatched to Camp Kinser. She counted out the days it might take to get there. Michael would be overjoyed to hear from her; he would surely write back straight away. She estimated she'd have to endure another two weeks before his letter arrived in Tokyo, allowing for unforeseen delays. Of course, it was unlikely he'd propose marriage in that first letter, but after waiting a week or two for her reply, it would be long enough for him to really start missing her. He'd probably ask her to join him in Okinawa in the next letter. She wasn't sure yet how she could make this work, but she'd think of something.

At least she could look forward to telling Sayuri about him on Sunday. Michiko had arranged to meet her friend at a new restaurant at the top floor of Takashimaya department store. Sayuri had suggested they meet in their favourite soba shop as usual, but Michiko had scoffed.

'It's old-fashioned to eat out at a Japanese restaurant these days,' she said. 'This new place serves French-style food and wine,' she said. 'It's much more my style.'

Michiko was early, and had already started on a bottle of wine when Sayuri arrived. Sayuri widened her eyes. 'Wine? At lunchtime? I didn't even know you drank.'

'I've changed, Sayu-chan,' said Michiko. 'Going to Okinawa really opened my eyes to a different life.' She proffered the bottle. 'Any wine? I've already ordered food for us, by the way.'

Sayuri frowned, shaking her head. 'No! No wine, thank you. I'm picking up the kids later.' She watched Michiko pour herself a glass.

'Isn't Okinawa all just sugar cane and farmers?' said Sayuri.

Michiko leaned forward conspiratorially. 'What if I told you I met a handsome American there? A kind one, who owns a car. A red Dodge convertible.'

'No!' said Sayuri, excited. 'I thought you were staying with relatives? How did you manage to meet an American? Was he a GI? Did you actually see his car?'

'I did more than *see* the car, Sayu-chan,' said Michiko, sitting back, swirling the wine in her glass. 'He drove me across Okinawa in it. I did more than just "meet" him too.'

'What do you mean?'

Michiko curled up one side of her mouth in an impish smile.

'You didn't!' Sayuri sat staring.

'Oh yes, I did.' Michiko grinned at her friend, but when Sayuri said nothing, her look of shock unchanged, she added, 'He's going to ask to marry me.'

'Has he given you an engagement ring?'

Michiko reached into her blouse and pulled out the ribbon to show Sayuri Michael's ring.

'That's a funny-looking engagement ring. It's too big for you.'

Michiko scowled at her friend. 'Why are you being so negative? Aren't you happy for me?'

'He hasn't actually asked you to marry him yet, has he?'

'No, but I know he will.'

'How can you know?'

'I just know, all right? You weren't there. You didn't see how much love he had in his eyes when he looked at me.'

Sayuri muttered something under her breath.

'What did you say?'

'I said maybe you mistook his lust for love.'

Michiko sat back with a theatrical gasp. 'You're supposed to be my friend, Sayuri.'

'I *am* your friend, Michi. I'm worried for you.' She lowered her voice. 'Did he use condoms?'

'He didn't need to. The times we slept together, it wasn't on my fertile days.'

'You slept with him more than once? Without condoms? Are you crazy? What if you got pregnant? What if he gave you some awful disease? I've heard about those GIs in Okinawa, they sleep with whores, they don't care who they have sex with.'

'Michael's not like that!' Michiko blazed. 'He was a gentleman.'

'Really! A gentleman that has sex with someone he's only just met? A Japanese woman who lives thousands of miles away, who he presumably knows will be leaving the island soon? A Japanese woman he hasn't asked to become his wife?'

Michiko's voice quaked with rage. 'You know what? You're just jealous because you're married to a man you can't stand.'

Sayuri stood up. 'I'm not hungry any more. You're right, you really have changed, Michiko.' She put a handful of notes down on the table. 'Here, for whatever you ordered for me. It's too late to cancel it now.'

Michiko shook with rage. 'Some friend you are, Sayuri.'

'You know, I always thought you were quite selfish,' Sayuri said, picking up her bag, 'but it was always fun spending time with you. This,' she said, gesturing at the table, 'This was not fun. You haven't even asked how I am. Do you know how hard it was to persuade my mother-in-law to look after the kids today so I could come to see you? And here you are, all high and mighty, telling me you slept with an American – several times, without protection – as if that was some glamorous thing. It's not. He hasn't promised to marry you and he's thousands of miles away, and out of your life.'

'He *is* in my life, Sayuri. You'll regret saying these things when you meet him and see how wonderful he is.'

'I'm worried for you, Michiko,' Sayuri said.

Michiko watched her walk out of the restaurant. She was so angry she wanted to scream. She closed her eyes, taking deep breaths, trying to empty her mind. Once her hands had stopped shaking, she took the money Sayuri had left on the table and waved the waitress over. 'I'm sorry, my friend was feeling unwell and had to leave. May I cancel her food order, if it's not too late?'

'I'll go and check.'

Michiko emptied her glass and prodded listlessly at a dish of olives with a toothpick. The waitress returned.

'It seems they hadn't begun the food orders, so yes, we can cancel it.'

'In that case,' said Michiko, 'you may as well cancel my food order too. I'll just have these olives, if you don't mind, and perhaps you could bring me some more bread. Oh, and another bottle of wine. I'll have the same again, thanks.'

Two weeks, then three passed, and no letter arrived. Michiko was sick; lovesick, sick with worry, sick with stress. Her father had grown suspicious of her frantic riffling through the mail. One morning, after she'd asked him a third time if he was sure this was all the post there was, he asked her what, exactly, was causing her to behave like a frenzied cockroach in a trap.

'Oh, ah … a letter. A letter from …' She played for time.

'Letter from who?'

The words just formed as she said them. Panic channelled inspiration directly to her mouth. 'It's a letter from an English-language school, to tell me if I've been accepted into their class.'

'English-language school!? What on earth do you want with an English-language class?'

'Ah … well, father, you've probably noticed recently that we've had one or two foreigners come into our shop. I think that's only going to become a more frequent occurrence. I thought it would be good for business if at least one of us could speak English. The gaijin-san who live here will know they can come to our shop and be served by someone who speaks their language, and they'll tell all their friends.'

'This tea shop is not for foreigners. The subtleties of our different teas are wasted on them.'

'Then surely it's a good thing if I learn English so I can explain the differences to them.'

It was enough to get him off her back. He grunted and walked back into his study.

Checking the post every day and finding nothing from Michael was torture. Michiko was so distressed she struggled to eat. She stopped drinking the shōchū she had each night, but her agony continued to make her feel unwell, especially since she wasn't sleeping. Sayuri still wasn't speaking to her, and without anyone to share her burden, and without the shōchū each night to help her sleep, Michiko couldn't stop her thoughts from corroding her like acid. What if he'd been called up to Saigon? But he would have known in advance he was leaving, and he would have written to tell her. What if he'd had an accident? What if he'd written back, but his letter had been lost? It had been known to happen. She was struck with horror at the thought that he might be waiting for her reply, wondering if she had forgotten him. Better to write him another letter, just in case.

She wrote. She waited.

Michiko finally gave in and decided to call Obā.

'Ah! Wonderful girl! How are you? The house is so quiet without you and Chiyo. When will you be coming back?'

'Soon, I hope, Obā. I miss you; it's good to hear your voice. But I'm phoning to ask you a favour, I hope you don't mind. Is there a way you can get a message to someone at one of the US bases?'

Obā sounded intrigued. 'Go on.'

'He's at Camp Kinser. Mother and I met him one day in Naha, we were lost, and he helped us. He was very kind, and when we got talking he told me he had a position for a housemaid, and asked if I was interested, but of course I told him I lived in Tokyo. I didn't tell you about it at the time, Obā, because I just dismissed the idea straight away. But I told Father about it, and can you believe it? He seems to be coming around to the idea. I was hoping you might help me find …'

'You don't need to pretend to me, dear girl, I can hear it in your voice. You met him here, and you fell in love with him, didn't you?'

Michiko said nothing.

'Don't worry, I'm not judging you. I've been in love myself. I understand. You have to take your chances for happiness. Wait for a second, I'll find a pen and a piece of paper so I can write his name down. I'll ask my employer when I'm at work tomorrow, see if she can make enquiries.'

It struck Michiko that since her father had not banned her outright from attending English classes, and since she'd already told him she was going to sign up for some, she may as well go ahead and actually do it. Even if Michael did speak fluent Japanese, if she was to become his wife, it made sense for her to learn English. It would be a good way to make an impression on his American friends and family. Besides, she needed something to occupy her mind after preparing and clearing away the family dinner, and at weekends, when she had some time off. Anything to distract her from the agony of waiting. She imagined herself writing Michael a letter in English, how impressed he'd be.

She found an English-language school in Roppongi that held classes in the evenings and on weekends. It was safer to get the fees for her classes from Kensuke. He was taking over more and more of the business anyway, and Michiko told him that she'd already spoken to their father about how useful it would be for someone in the shop to speak English, and that he hadn't objected. Her brother was busy and tired, and he handed over the cash without asking too many questions.

It was a typical typhoon season day, windy, with torrential rain. Michiko started walking from Roppongi station and was nearing the address she'd written down when a savage gust of wind blew her umbrella inside out. As she struggled to fix it, the downpour continued, soaking her to her underclothes. It was no use; her umbrella was broken. She threw it in a nearby rubbish bin and ran the rest of the way to the school.

As she ran into the building she nearly collided with a foreign man in a brown tweed jacket.

'Woah! You're in a hurry,' he said, in Japanese. He looked at her again. 'You poor thing, you're soaked.'

'My umbrella broke,' said Michiko.

'Come upstairs and we'll get you dry,' he said. 'I'm sure we can find a towel somewhere. Are you here for English class?'

'Yes. I mean, no. I mean, I came here to make enquiries. I'd like to start learning English.'

'You bumped into the right man then. My name's George. I'm one of the English teachers here.'

She liked George straight away. He was good-looking, in a bumbling sort of way, and though he was nothing like Michael, he was kind, finding her a hand towel from the caretaker's cupboard to dry herself with and making her a cup of tea. They sat in the office together while he explained the course structure and the class schedule, and although she hadn't brought enough money with her, he registered her anyway, telling her to bring the cash with her when she came for her first class. It wasn't usually allowed, he said, so she wasn't to tell anyone. She thanked him several times, smiling and touching his arm, telling him what a gentleman he was, and he seemed flattered.

After she finished filling in her registration forms they'd carried on talking; he seemed impressed when she told him her reason for learning English was to help her beloved father, now getting old, with the family business. She asked him questions, and was attentive to his replies, and when he made a joke she tossed her head back and laughed. She sat back in her chair opposite him, crossing and uncrossing her legs in her minidress and watching the effect it had on him. It felt good after the feeling of powerlessness that had overwhelmed her the past few weeks.

She was glad she was the one to pick up the phone. 'Obā! Do you have news for me?'

There was a pause.

'Hello? Obā? Are you there?'

As soon as Obā started speaking, she knew. Somehow she managed to stay standing as Obā told her everything. That she'd spoken to her employer, who'd managed to track Michael down at Camp Kinser. He was still in Okinawa, and wasn't due to go to Saigon for some time. He'd been allocated duties that allowed him stay on the island. His superiors felt it was the compassionate thing to do, since he needed to stay on the island to take care of his wife, who was Okinawan. When Michiko and Chiyo were with Obā, Michael's wife had been in Naha hospital, recovering from severe complications after giving birth to their first child. It had been a boy, and he had been stillborn.

A Military Ring

Weighty in the hand, it is a chunky gold-plated ring designed for a man's finger. It has an oval of blue stone set in its centre – glass, perhaps, or semi-precious stone, it is hard to tell – measuring one and a half centimetres high by a centimetre wide. The words 'West Point' are inscribed in a semicircle above the stone, and a date, 1959, is similarly curled beneath. Swirling and curving black filigree, contrasting with the gold, covers the remaining surfaces of the ring. It is ostentatious and serious at the same time, a bold ring that denotes belonging and pride.

Erika

Erika sits propped against a pillow, watching the ebb and flow of the emergency department past her cubicle curtains. The hospital is chaotic with the usual human detritus of a Friday night. From a few doors down she hears shrieks of pain. A voice, wearily patient, says: 'Come now, Mrs Harris, please try to keep still.' Grim-faced nurses stride to and fro. A tattered man – drunk or sick – is staggering about, slurring: 'Oi, 'scuse me, nurse.' Erika has been waiting for over two hours and she just wants to get home, but then again, given the circumstances, she isn't in a position to complain.

Her phone rings. She fumbles as she answers it with her free hand and tucks it between her ear and shoulder. 'Marcus, hi.'

'You still at the restaurant? I dropped Felix off at Mel's earlier. Do you want me to come 'round when you're finished?'

'I left a while ago. At the moment I'm just … I've just got to hang around here for a bit.'

'Where are you? What's that beeping?'

'St Mary's A&E.'

He shoots back immediately: 'What happened?'

'Nothing major. I cut my hand at work. I'm waiting to get stitches.'

'Shit. I'll come over. I can be there in twenty.'

Erika laughs. 'Honestly, don't worry. I'm fine.'

'If you're in A&E you're not fine.'

'It's a clean cut, it'll probably only be a couple of stitches. I'll call you when I get home. It'll be a nightmare parking around here, anyway.'

She looks down. Blood seeps between the fingers of her left hand, wrapped in a sopping bandage. She raises her arm. A drop falls onto the sheet and blooms into a crimson flower.

'I'm coming now. You're not getting the Tube home by yourself. Okay? I'll come and pick you up. Leave me to worry about parking. Don't leave before I get there.'

'I don't think I'll be leaving for a while. They're too busy treating gunshot wounds and stabbings.'

After she hangs up, Erika's tired enough to drift off, despite the pain and surrounding chaos. She hasn't been sleeping all that well since Kei left. The sound of her phone wakes her. It's Sarah. Erika leaves smears of blood on the answer button as she picks up. The blossom has grown into a scarlet bouquet on the sheet.

'Are you all right? I'm sorry, I'd have come with you, it looked pretty bad, but they couldn't spare me – it was a full house tonight. I'd come now but I've got to get back for the babysitter. What's the doctor say?'

'Haven't seen one yet. The nurse says I'll need stitches. Marcus will be here soon. Cab got me here quickly.' Erika laughs. 'The driver freaked out at the blood. I had to promise I'd pay for cleaning if I got any on the seats. You should have seen his face. It was pretty funny.'

Sarah doesn't sound amused. 'Listen, Erika, what happened tonight, exactly?'

'I cut myself.'

'Yeah, obviously, but how?'

'With my knife.'

'But it's not like you're a novice, is it? It wasn't just a little cut, either.'

The throbbing in Erika's left hand is intense; she feels her body rocking in time with its pulsing. The pain is radiating up her arm. Maybe she should ask for more painkillers.

'Hey. Are you there?'

'I'll call you tomorrow. I don't feel up to talking right now.'

'Erika?'

'Yeah?'

'We were talking about it after service, and Frankie said ...'

'Said what?'

'Never mind. I'll talk to you later. Marcus is definitely coming, right?'

'Yep.'

'Okay then. Take care of yourself. I'm worried about you.'

'No need.'

'Mmm.'

'Kiss kiss. Talk tomorrow.' She hangs up.

Erika's head lolls against the car seat as they take off along Praed Street. Her hand is wrapped tightly in a fresh bandage and the Tramadol has seen to the pain, for now. She closes her eyes.

'Thanks for picking me up. It was a good idea after all,' she murmurs.

'The nurses said they wouldn't have let you go home on your own anyway, with those painkillers and all the blood you've lost,' says Marcus. 'All you're good for is a cup of tea and bed. I guess I'll have to drink this bottle of wine by myself.'

The car feeds into the traffic flowing past Paddington Station, and the stopping and starting makes her nauseous. She opens her eyes again, fixes them on the road ahead. It's started to rain, and the shining black of the road reflects the lights from Queensway and Westbourne Grove, the bus in front of them marking their way with ruby smears.

'Sarah rang me earlier. She says she thinks you cut yourself on purpose.'

She rests her head against the window, fogging the glass with her breath.

'Did you, Erika?'

She carries on staring at the road. Her head is empty.

'Erika?'

She clears her throat. 'My head's foggy, sorry.' She wants to lift her head, but can't.

'Just tell me, yes or no.'

'I don't know.'

'Of course you know. How can you not?'

Erika stays silent.

Marcus shoots through an amber light just as it turns red. A car horn blares.

'Don't be angry,' she says.

'I care about you, Erika.'

'I know. I'm sorry.'

'Jesus Christ. What's going on?'

'I don't think I can do this now. I don't feel great. We'll talk tomorrow. Promise.'

As soon as she finishes the tea Marcus made her, Erika goes to bed and falls into a deep, dreamless sleep. The painkillers knock her out for a solid nine hours. When she wakes, Marcus is spread-eagled across most of the bed. She slips out from under the sheets so as not to wake him.

She's in the kitchen breaking eggs into a bowl with one hand when Marcus appears in the doorway, rubbing the stubble on his face.

'Morning.' He kisses her. 'Breakfast prep with Captain Hook, aye aye. Here, let me help.' He tries to take the bowl from her, but she holds it tight.

'It's okay. I'm doing it,' she says.

'Your hand. I should be making breakfast.'

'Put the coffee on, then.'

Marcus fills the coffee machine. 'I need you to tell me what's going on.'

'There's nothing to tell, honestly.' She passes him the chopping board and knife. 'Could you chop the herbs up when you've finished that? I can't quite manage …' She whisks the eggs, cuts a lump of butter into the pan and waits until it begins to fizz. Marcus switches on the coffee grinder and she's grateful for the gritty whine that fills the silence. When it stops, the kitchen seems quieter than before, as if it's holding its breath.

'Well?' says Marcus, tipping the grinder's contents into the filter and flicking on the switch. He takes the knife and chops herbs, frowning.

Erika pours the egg into the pan, swirling it with a spatula. 'I'll need those in a second.'

'Erika.' He puts down the knife, turning to her. 'Would you please stop acting as though nothing's happened? I need you to talk to me.'

She takes the board from him and sweeps the herbs into the eggs. She stirs hard, adds another knob of butter. 'The toast – please could you put on a couple of slices?' she asks.

'Okay, you're starting to piss me off now.'

Erika turns off the gas and looks at him. She wants to go back to bed but his expression keeps her standing there. She takes his hand. 'I'll do my best to talk to you about it, but let's have breakfast first. I'm not sure what's going on myself.'

'So you did cut yourself on purpose.'

'Please. Breakfast and coffee first, and then we'll talk about it. Let me figure things out.'

The rain has cleared up overnight and the autumn sunlight sets the colours in the room alight. There's a glint from the alcove. The sun is lighting up the gold leaf on Michiko's lacquer tablet with its low sweep. Erika contemplates this for a moment before pushing piles of newspapers and books out of the way on the dining table with her elbow and plonking the saucepan of scrambled eggs on a magazine. Marcus butters Erika's toast for her and she scoops creamy golden scrambled eggs onto each of their plates.

They eat in silence, a comforting cocoon Erika knows she'll have to emerge from soon. Toast and eggs finished, Marcus sits back, cup of coffee in hand, and waits. She keeps eating, head down, cradling her injured hand in her lap under the table.

'How's it feeling?' he asks, at last.

'It hurts a bit,' she mumbles. 'I might need another painkiller.'

'More coffee?'

'Yes, please.'

He disappears into the kitchen. When he returns with filled cups he gestures at Erika with his head to follow him to the sofa. 'Come and sit,' he says, softly, in a way that makes her eyes sting.

She swallows hard. 'Right,' she says, dropping onto the sofa beside him. She sips coffee, hiding her face behind the mug. 'Okay. So it wasn't an accident. Not exactly.'

'Go on.'

'I honestly didn't mean to do it; I just felt like I had to, really suddenly, right before I did it.'

Marcus waits, frowning, looking at her.

'I was boning quail. I was looking at these little birds, all tiny and naked and plucked, you know, and it got to me, seeing them there. I don't know, I wasn't thinking anything when I did it. I don't think when I'm cooking, everything's automatic. My hands just do what they're supposed to do.'

'Just tell me exactly what happened. Try to remember what you were thinking before you did it.'

She cradles the cup in her hands, the bandaged one oversized and cumbersome. She breathes long and steady.

'I was boning the quail, about twenty birds. There was a pile of them to my left, ready for deboning. I'd just finished one and put it in the tray with the ones I'd done already. And when I reached over to get another from the pile, when I put it down on the chopping board, I suddenly felt awful. And somehow my hand looked like one of the deboned quails. Maybe I thought about how a dead quail doesn't feel anything anymore. Maybe I was wondering what it would feel like to cut into my hand. I don't know. It was all over in a split second. I had my hand flat on the chopping board and before I knew what I was doing I'd done it, just like that.'

'Show me where you cut it,' says Marcus.

She draws a long diagonal line along the flesh between the thumb and forefinger of her other hand.

'Fucking hell, Erika, there's ligaments and arteries in there! What did the doctor say?'

'That I'd be fine. I lost a lot of blood. I've cut through some nerves … They've stitched it up nicely. It's fixed. So I've lost a bit of sensation but some of it should come back. It just needs time to heal and then they'll give me exercises to strengthen it again. It'll be all right.'

'What about work?'

'Oh, I'll go back on Monday. Honestly, it'll be fine.'

'You just said they told you it needs time to heal.'

'But it's in a splint, so my thumb stays steady.'

'Erika, you're dreaming. How are you going to cook? No way is André going to let you prep food with that massive bandage on your hand!' He jumps up off the sofa. Her heart leaps.

'Please, Marcus, I understand why you're angry. I … I need to think about all of this.'

'Yeah. Me too,' he says.

'It's not like I've got issues or anything, it was just a weird impulse. It's not like it's self-harming.'

Marcus sits back down again. 'Erika, that's exactly what you're doing. Cutting yourself is self-harm. You need to talk to someone. Frankie saw you do it and told everyone. André knows. Sarah said to tell you he wants you to call him on Monday morning. He's not expecting you to go in. He just wants to talk to you.'

'Shit.'

'At the hospital they asked me if I thought it was an accident,' said Marcus. 'They said it was an unusual place for a chef to cut by mistake. I told them I was sure you did it accidentally, that I've never known you to do anything self-destructive before.'

Erika holds her breath, says nothing.

'Help me understand here. Things went so well with Kei. I know you haven't been sleeping well, but you've seemed okay these last weeks. What happened?'

Erika coils herself deeper into the sofa. 'There is something.'

'What, with Kei?'

'She phoned me from the airport just before she got on the plane. She said she needed to tell me about something she'd read in Michiko's diaries. It really shook me up.'

Marcus is as shocked as Erika was. He's cleared up the breakfast things and they are sitting on the sofa.

'Did you have any idea? Any at all?'

'Nope. I always thought George was my father. I even tracked him down when I was about seventeen. I wrote to him, and when I got this weird letter back from him I asked my mother about it and she went ballistic. She still didn't tell me the truth. I moved out after that. I can't believe she lied to me about this.'

'People have their reasons. Maybe she just never got around to telling you before she died.'

'She was selfish to the end.' She sniffs, gets up to take her coffee cup to the kitchen. 'She was so messed up, if I told you some of the things she did you'd think I was exaggerating.'

'You told me about how she forgot you in a department store once. And how she drank a lot.'

Erika snorts. 'Yeah, a lot. She was a full-blown alcoholic; Julian was too. They had terrible, physical, violent fights – smashing stuff. I remember Michiko hitting him with a bottle once. There was blood all over the floor. I'd hide in my wardrobe waiting for it to be over, terrified they were going to kill each other.'

'Jesus,' says Marcus. 'I didn't realise ...'

'When Julian left her for someone else he moved to London, and we moved here too. She went crazy. She stalked him and his new girlfriend and made threats against them until he took out a restraining order. And then she took her rage out on me. She said she hated me for giving her diabetes.'

'What? How could you have given her diabetes?'

'She got gestational diabetes and it didn't go away after I was born.'

'But that's not—'

'She didn't care if she destroyed herself. She drank and drank ...' Erika trails off. It makes her exhausted to talk like this, but she knows she owes it to Marcus. 'I kept trying to fix things. I had to keep cleaning up the messes she made – vomit, blood, stuff she'd smashed during her rages. I took her to the doctor and he warned her that she'd lose her sight unless she controlled her drinking. Her circulation was terrible and her legs were always this awful mottled colour, and he said if she wasn't careful she'd get gangrene and lose her feet. But she carried on drinking anyway, and complaining, and taking everything out on me.'

'Why've you never told me this?' says Marcus, his face stricken.

'Too hard to talk about. It's easier to forget about it,' says Erika, picking at the bandage on her hand.

'You don't forget about stuff like that, Erika.'

'She'd been so horrible to me when I was a kid that I thought, why the hell should I have to look after her? But I still loved her. I loved her so much but I was cruel to her. And I didn't save her.' Erika swallows hard.

'Oh, babe,' says Marcus. 'It wasn't your responsibility to save her. You were pushed to your limits.'

'It gets worse. You only know the half of it.' Erika closes her eyes and takes a deep breath. 'Sorry, I feel a bit sick. It's probably the Tramadol.'

She gets up and moves into the kitchen. Marcus follows, leaning in the doorway as she pours water into her cup. 'I think you should see someone. A psych or something. The GP could get you a referral.'

'Really, no. Talking about it just makes me feel worse.'

'Well, if you won't see someone then maybe you should take a break from things.'

'I've just had one.'

'A proper one. A holiday. I could come with you. Thailand, maybe. I could do with lying on a beach somewhere, doing nothing except eating and swimming and sleeping. You're not going to be able to do much with that hand. Why don't you talk about it to André on Monday?'

She looks at him, raises her bandaged hand. 'Apart from not being allowed to get this wet – beach holiday? You know how much I hate the sea.'

'That's another thing. Why are you so afraid of water?'

Erika doesn't answer. She pushes past him out of the kitchen, ignoring the look he's giving her, and wanders into the sitting room. She stands for a moment, transfixed. The room has turned golden. The late September sun gleams through the windows, high in the sky now, filling the room. It's rising later each morning; it will soon be time to turn back the clocks. Its rays are slanting into the alcove now, and Michiko's altar is aglow, everything on top of it glittering as if under a spotlight. She hears Marcus behind her, quiet. Despite the radiant light, the room is chilly; Erika shivers and reaches for a jumper from the back of a chair. Shrugging it on, she walks to the cabinet, slides open the secret drawer and takes out the military ring.

She turns it in her good hand, struck by the way the light penetrates through the facets of the blue stone, revealing its depths as if it were a miniature ocean. She puts it on the ring finger that's exposed above the bandage, holding it in place to keep the weight of the stone from turning its face from her. This ring has been on the hand of the stranger who made her, she thinks. She wonders if it carries traces of her father's DNA, random cells of his dead skin stuck in its tiny crevices, containing microscopic codes echoing her own. She is touching him, her father. She wonders if it's reverberating out to wherever he is now so that he feels it, a ripple in the fabric that connects everything. The blue stone rises up to meet her, liquefying, opening up, a limpid pool. She begins to sink, drifting down, fathom after fathom; she is floating in clear cobalt, weightless, her hair and her robe drifting like sea wrack, and she is unafraid.

'Hey.'

Erika jolts back to the room, gasps.

'Are you okay?' Marcus has his arm around her. 'I thought you were about to faint.'

She sits on a chair, breathes, nods. Takes off the ring and places it on top of the altar. There's no way she's ready to work in the kitchen again; Marcus is right. She'll talk to André, tell him she'll go back once her hand has healed.

She feels a strange force building, like a tightness rising into her head. And then, in an instant, she knows what she must do. She has to go to Okinawa. She's accumulated enough leave and a decent amount of money in her savings account. She'll book herself onto a flight, as soon as next week, even. The discomfort that's been creeping into her core ever since Kei left is becoming more intrusive; Erika can't stay as she is any longer, treading water. She has to keep moving, or she'll drown.

Michiko

They were polite to him, face to face. It was a Sunday evening and everyone had gathered in the large tatami room above the shop. Fusae had joined them with the boys, leaving her husband at home. Curiosity had drawn some of the neighbours out into the street as George Underwood arrived at the Takigawa household. Michiko let him in.

'Line your shoes up neatly when you take them off,' she whispered. 'They'll be checking for anything that confirms you're a gaijin that doesn't know our ways.'

They went upstairs. Michiko slid open the door and there they all were, gathered around the table: her father at the head; Fusae seated to his right. The children stared goggle-eyed at George as he sat down, giggling at the sight of him plopping awkwardly onto the tatami and using his hands to cross his legs. Michiko's sister-in-law, Mayumi, had made fresh red bean paste daifuku dumplings and arranged them in a pile on an enormous plate in the middle of the table. Heavily pregnant, Mayumi struggled up off the floor and went into the kitchen to boil water for the tea.

'*Hajimemashite*,' said George to Michiko's father and mother, bowing deeply. *I am honoured to meet you.*

Michiko's father grunted. Inclined his head a little.

Michiko hadn't known what to expect. It was awkward, certainly, but she was incredulous when her father engaged George in conversation, asking him about his teaching job, about his family in England, asking him how long he'd been in Japan and what he thought of it. George's forehead shone with sweat. Michiko had grown impatient with all the nervous questions he'd been asking over the past week: what should he wear to impress her father, what should he talk about, will her father

203

like him, how could he make up for being a gaijin with no matchmaker to act as a go-between for the wedding arrangements.

'Figure it out for yourself,' she'd snapped. 'We'll find a go-between. Isn't there someone at the school who would do the job?'

He'd put on a tie and his tweed jacket with the patched elbows, and slicked his hair across the top of his head with Brylcream. Despite Michiko's protestations, he hadn't bought a suit for the occasion. 'I'd only be buying it for this one time, Michiko, and I'd never wear it again,' he'd said.

'What about when we get married?'

'I'll hire one.'

'I can't believe I'm marrying a man who doesn't have a suit,' said Michiko.

George protested. 'I don't need them, working at the school. Better we save the money. When the baby comes we'll need every penny.'

'Don't say it!'

'What?'

'Don't talk about the baby!'

'Of course I won't talk about the baby. It's the last thing I want your father to know.'

'I mean at any time. I don't want to talk about the baby at all!' And she had fled the room, slamming the door.

In the Takigawa home, Chiyo sat to the left of her husband at the table, a blank smile on her face. An awkward silence filled the room. Mayumi came back in, passed Michiko the teapot to pour and handed the plate of daifuku to George. 'Please, help yourself.'

He took one and nibbled at its corner. The children sniggered.

Michiko took the teapot around the table to her mother and poured her another cup. 'Here you go, Mother, drink it while it's hot.' She took Chiyo's hands in hers, and peered into her face, stroked her hair, her cheeks. 'Mother,' she said. 'Mother, dear, this is George. He's come here to meet you.'

'Hnn,' Chiyo said, nodding, smiling.

'So. You are Michiko's English teacher,' said Michiko's father.

'Actually, she is now being taught by another teacher, since it wasn't appropriate for her to be in my class any longer once we ... once we ...' He searched for somewhere to put the daifuku.

'Do you not like the cakes, Underwood-san?' asked Mayumi.

George flushed. 'Yes, yes, of course, they're very nice, thank you,' he said, then stuffed it into his mouth, whole, and gagged. Michiko glared at him. The children laughed out loud.

'Quiet!' shouted her father, and they fell silent. 'I do not approve of her learning English,' he said.

'Oh ... I ...' stammered George. 'I thought ...'

'She has no need for it,' Michiko's father continued. 'It is ridiculous. She says she will need it in the shop, but how often do we get foreigners coming to buy tea? She will not need it to take care of her nieces and nephews, she will not need it to take care of her poor mother. But ever since she returned from a visit to her mother's family home in Okinawa she has insisted on English lessons. A waste of money.'

'Her English will come in useful when we are married,' said George, in quiet, faltering Japanese.

Michiko's father glared at him a long moment. The silence grew painful. Then he slurped noisily at his tea. 'Well,' he said, putting down his teacup. 'You have been welcome in our home.'

'Th-thank you,' said George. More silence. He sipped his tea.

Nobody said anything. Michiko leaped up from beside her mother and took George's arm. 'You needed to go and meet someone about work, didn't you?'

'Er ...'

'Come along, George, you don't want to be late,' she said, ushering him out of the room and sliding the door closed behind them.

'That meant it was time for us to leave,' she whispered as they went down the stairs.

'What was?'

'My father saying you were welcome in our home.'

'Oh. Right.' He nearly tripped down the steps.

'What were you thinking, talking about us getting married?'

'But we are. We have to,' he said, reaching out for her belly. 'N-not that that's a problem, my darling, of course,' he added.

She slapped his hand away, furious. 'I told you not to mention marriage to my father until the next meeting!' she hissed. 'It wasn't the right time. You've gone and spoiled it now.' Her eyes welled with tears.

'My darling … it's just the way the conversation went. I'm sorry …'

'You can leave now. I have to stay here,' said Michiko. 'Pick me up tomorrow after I finish at the shop.'

He bent down to tie his shoelaces, red in the face. They could already hear the neighbourhood children gathering outside the opaque glass of the sliding door, whispering – 'It's the gaijin Michiko Onē-chan's dating! Come and look!'

Michiko had not expected her father even to talk to George, so she had some hope as she climbed back up the stairs. But there would be no next meeting. The intensity of her father's rage stunned all of them.

'No daughter of mine is going to marry a foreigner,' he shouted. 'What cheek did that gaijin have, talking as if it were already decided? Who did he think he was? How dare he presume he could marry into a family like this, as a foreigner? And to think: my daughter consorting with the old enemy as if she were some cheap pan-pan girl in a GI brothel!' He slammed his fist on the table, making the teacups and everyone sitting around it jump. 'A disgrace!' he cried. 'A good thing your mother is out of her mind. She would die of shame if she understood what you were up to.'

The children crept away but the others remained trapped around the table, Fusae looking down at her hands. 'Father …' she whispered. 'Perhaps you are being a little harsh …'

'Shut up!' he thundered. 'Michiko. You are not marrying that foreigner. That is final. You are needed in this house. If you are lucky enough to marry at your advanced age it will be to a Japanese man from a family of which I approve. Do you understand?'

Michiko rose up from the tatami.

'Sit down while I am talking to you!'

'No.'

Fusae and Mayumi gasped. 'Michiko …' her sister pleaded.

'I will *not* sit down!'

Her father stood up. A vein on his forehead bulged. 'Sit down this instant!'

'No!' She turned her back and made to leave the room.

'If you go through that door now you are never to come back.'

'Fine.'

'Michiko …' said Fusae.

'You will not come back to this house. Do you understand? You will pack your things and leave. If you leave this room you are no longer a part of this family.'

Michiko slid the door closed behind her.

'Never come back!' she heard her father shout. 'You are dead to me! Do you hear me?'

Fusae came into the room to find Michiko hunched over a suitcase in their old room, weeping as she packed. 'Oh, Michi, why do you do these things?' she asked. 'Why do you always have to make father so angry?'

Fat tears dropped onto the clothes Michiko was packing. She picked up a small cloth doll wearing a red-and-white gingham dress and blue shoes. She smoothed its golden hair and placed it carefully on top of her clothes. 'You have no idea how awful things have become for me. I don't know what to do, Onē-chan.'

'Just stay for a little while. Father will calm down. Then go and apologise. You know how he says things he doesn't mean when he's angry. He'll change his mind if you say you're sorry.'

Michiko wiped her face. 'I won't apologise! I'm not sorry!'

'Michiko … they're just words. Just say you're sorry. For Mother's sake, more than anything.'

'Oh come on, Fusae, Mother doesn't know what's happening. It won't make any difference to her whether I'm here or not.' She broke down again in tears. 'But I'll miss her. Even the way she is, I'll miss her.'

'Well then, stay. And stay for me. It makes a difference to me.'

'You don't even live here anymore. You have Haruo-san and you have the boys. You don't need me. Kensuke hardly talks to me these days; he doesn't even stick up for me anymore.'

'He's busy, Michi. He's taking over the business, and the baby will be born soon. So yes, we need you. We need you to take care of Mother. And when Ken and Mayumi-chan's baby arrives, we'll need you even more than before.'

'My life was meant for more than that, Onē-chan. I wasn't born just to be a slave to everyone.'

'We all have to accept our lot in life, Michiko. It's the only way to be content. If you fight everything, you'll never be happy.'

'I need to try for the best. If I don't leave, I'll never know what I missed. George will take me to England so we can be married. On an airplane! Then we'll come back to Tokyo. I'll bring you presents. Besides, George is hoping to get a promotion at the school. We'll still see each other, you and I and Kensuke; you can bring Mother to see me. I'll be an Englishman's wife, dressed in nice clothes. I have to look for my happiness, Fusae. I can't wait and hope it'll find me. Besides …' she said, and placed her hand on her stomach.

'Besides, what?' asked Fusae.

Michiko wiped her eyes with the back of her hand and looked at her sister. Over the silence that yawned between them their eyes met, and held. Under the veil of fatigue cast by motherhood and wifehood, frayed with the beginnings of fine lines, Fusae's eyes were the same as Michiko had always remembered. Unable to bear looking at her any longer, Michiko cast her eyes about the room, lingering on the damp-stained walls, the worn tatami mats, her calendar on the wall with pictures of the Hollywood greats. She would never see any of this again. She wished she could tell Fusae everything, but could hardly bear to put her sadness into words.

'Michi,' Fusae pleaded, 'what do you mean, "besides"?'

Michiko said nothing, and carried on packing.

Although she sobbed for hours after her father first cast her out, Michiko was surprised by how quickly she stopped feeling sad. Maybe I've already used up my lifetime's supply of sadness, she thought. If anything, she became euphoric at having defied her father. And then there was the excitement of the first few months with George, and her first international flight – to England, where they would be married. She bought two red suitcases with chrome clasps for the journey, and a new coat. Before Michiko left, she phoned Sayuri to tell her George had proposed, and they made up. They met in the cocktail bar at the New Otani Hotel, and Michiko showed Sayuri her passport, the first she'd ever owned, and her emerald-set engagement ring. Michiko was gratified to see that her friend was impressed, and thankful she didn't mention Michael, or ask too many questions. Michiko sat back on the leather banquette, legs crossed, a cocktail in her hand, looking perfectly at home.

'Look at you, in your fancy new clothes,' Sayuri said. 'Like a movie star.'

Michiko and George were married in a small civil ceremony in Hampshire, where George's elderly parents lived. There was only a handful of guests, and the wedding reception afterwards in her in-laws' home was modest, but Michiko didn't mind; she loved the quaint Englishness of their village, with its thatched-roof cottages and rose-and-honeysuckle-filled gardens, its bright-red telephone box and its village green. She was in a whirl of excitement.

Things began to change when they returned to Japan. Their apartment was small and in a distant suburb an hour's train ride from central Tokyo. Michiko had never lived anywhere except in the middle of the city. George didn't seem to understand how much smaller the apartment would seem when the baby came. He told her they would move as soon as he got his promotion, but this never seemed to come.

With the flights, the suitcases, the new coat, the engagement and wedding rings, the wedding outfits and the wedding itself, George's savings were almost gone. Their first arguments were about money. Michiko had spent more than his month's salary on a 22-piece Wild Strawberry Wedgwood tea set from Mitsukoshi department store. It would have cost far less if she'd bought it in England, but that was beside the point. The money for such things simply wasn't there. The conversation did not go well. Michiko panicked whenever he talked to her about budgets. She would cry and tell him that she'd left her family to be with him, that she needed to feel safe, that she didn't want to be worrying about money when she was so tired from the pregnancy.

'Can't you find a job with a bigger salary?' she'd pleaded.

Michiko's drinking also caused arguments. Once she'd stopped suffering morning sickness, her taste for alcohol had returned. George was adamant she shouldn't drink until the baby was born. She smuggled bottles into the house, but George soon learned her secret hiding places and would regularly check them and throw out whatever he found there. Then they would fight. She needed it, she said, because she was bored and depressed. If she had a more active social life then she wouldn't feel the need. She persuaded George to sign up for an expensive membership at the American Club. She'd benefit from swimming in the pool, or playing tennis, and they could meet people at the club for dinner or drinks. 'It'll be cheaper than inviting people to dinner at home,' she said, knowing this would help get him over the line. 'They'd be paying for their own food and drink. There's no room in the apartment for entertaining anyway.'

Wearing a low cut ruched turquoise swimsuit with extra stretch to accommodate her bump and growing breasts, she started going to the club swimming pool most days of the week, meeting regularly with some of the wives of George's friends. She was fully aware, as she stretched out on a lounger beside the pool, how men looked at her, though she pretended not to notice.

But at six months pregnant, she grew too tired and stopped swimming. Another week later, she felt so leaden with fatigue she struggled to get out of bed at all. Seeing her pale cheeks and alarmed at her constant trips to the toilet, George booked her in to see her obstetrician, who diagnosed her with gestational diabetes.

'It will probably go away once you've had the baby,' the doctor told her. 'But until then you'll need to inject insulin.'

She cried, telling George that she couldn't possibly inject herself every day with those needles, but in time she learned how to monitor her blood glucose levels, pricking drops of blood from her finger, pinching the flesh on her thighs to push in the syringe. It's only until the baby comes, she reminded herself.

The baby came on a cold April night after a protracted and painful labour. The obstetrician had to use forceps, and Michiko tore badly. George had paced the hospital corridors for hours, listening to his wife's screams; he'd asked the midwives and the obstetrician again and again for reassurance, worried that the baby had come early, but they seemed distracted, and nothing they said reassured him. So he was relieved – and surprised – when the little girl arrived healthy, with a head of thick black hair and weighing only a little less than average.

They'd already agreed to call her Erika, a name that was both English and Japanese. Michiko cried when the midwife brought the baby to her, cleaned up and wrapped in a blanket. She felt as if her life had ended. The baby felt so heavy. She found it hard to look at its face. It wouldn't latch onto her breast, and Michiko grew tired of trying. Formula milk was thought to be best for a baby these days anyway, and it meant George could take over feeding duties.

The diabetes did not go away. It was likely Michiko already had the early stages of it before the pregnancy, the doctor told them. She was going to have to monitor her diet, and would have to be especially careful, he said, around refined carbohydrates such as white rice, sugar, or alcohol. She'd need regular checkups. And she would need to inject insulin for the rest of her life. The doctor said plenty of people managed their diabetes just fine, as long as they were careful.

Michiko was inconsolable, sobbing in the car all the way home from the doctor's appointment, the baby on her lap. Erika began to cry too, as if in sympathy, and when she wouldn't stop, Michiko shouted, 'Shut up! It's because of you!'

Erika screamed even louder, and George pulled over, imploring her: 'Please, Michiko, don't shout like that, it's not the baby's fault.'

Whenever he was home, it was George who would change nappies, mix up formula and feed the baby. He would bathe her, and at night, whenever Erika cried, Michiko would roll over and nudge George awake.

'The diabetes makes me so tired,' she would say. 'I have to look after her all day while you're at work. At night it's your turn.'

There was a crèche at the American Club. Once Erika was old enough, Michiko would leave her there with bottles of formula and instructions for the child minders, and sit poolside, sipping cocktails. She made new friends. Of these, the tall, blonde, glamorous Marit, whose husband worked at the Norwegian Embassy, became her confidante. She seemed so attentive, asking Michiko lots of questions and listening intently to her responses. Michiko wondered at their unlikely friendship: Marit didn't seem as interested as Michiko was in clothes, jewellery, or the lives of film stars, but she made Michiko feel as though she mattered. The maternal instinct seemed to come naturally to her, though she hadn't had children; she'd go to the crèche just to give Erika a cuddle. When the child cried, Marit would comfort her in a way that Michiko found impossible to comprehend or emulate.

When Lars was called back to Oslo for a week, Marit invited Michiko to bring Erika to stay with her at their embassy apartment. Michiko gaped when she stepped through the front door. You could have driven a limousine through the entrance. In Michiko's quarters there was an enormous European-style bathroom with marble tiles, and a huge, soft four-poster bed. They had staff: a cook, a housekeeper and a chauffeur.

In the evenings Marit and Michiko sat up late, talking, and Michiko told Marit about her childhood during the war. Oslo had been occupied by the Nazis, and there'd been a terrible shortage of food, just as there had been in Tokyo. She described how her parents and neighbours had grown vegetables on an allotment near their street; they raised rabbits and chickens and hadn't starved. Even in the darkest days of the occupation, Marit said, she and her brothers and sisters had never doubted their parents' love.

Marit would fetch Erika from her cot to dandle her on her knee, and tell Michiko what a lovely little girl she had. Michiko would smile, feeling something close to pain stirring in her chest. Sometimes when Erika pulled a certain expression, it reminded her of Michael so much that she could hardly bear to look at her child. When Marit offered her a little brandy nightcap, she'd gladly take it, and ask for more once she'd emptied her glass. It filled up the hollowness inside her, letting her forget her suspicion that something was wrong with her, that Marit had some aspect of humanity that Michiko did not. She would drink, and be soothed, and fall asleep on the sofa, and Marit would draw a blanket gently over her, put Erika into her cot, and switch off the lights.

In the embassy apartment, Michiko felt as if she were living that other life: the one she was supposed to be living.

When Erika was two, Michiko signed her up for pre-school each weekday morning. She organised additional childcare for the afternoon, or took her to the American Club crèche. It was a good way to get her used to other children, she told George, when he complained about the cost. She would drop Erika off early in the morning before heading out to the department stores. She'd then head to the American Club and have a few drinks with Marit before she picked Erika up again and returned home to the apartment and to George.

If it hadn't been for the child, Michiko suspected George would have left by now. The child was difficult; Michiko was tired all the time and found it increasingly difficult to control her rages. George was an empathetic man. She'd liked that about him at first, but now it just made her feel worse about treating him badly.

On a particularly hot Saturday afternoon in July, Marit introduced Michiko to an English friend of her husband who was in Tokyo for a few months. Julian Stanhope had an export business in Hong Kong and had come to Tokyo to open a new branch office. Michiko could tell he was rich as soon as she met him: he wore well-cut clothes and expensive-looking shoes, and had the relaxed look of someone who'd never had to worry about money. He had a deep tan – from a recent yachting holiday in St Tropez, he said – his hair was well-styled and his nails perfectly manicured. Julian was attentive and considerate, bringing Michiko cocktails and sitting at the end of her sun lounger while they drank to tell her how beautiful she was.

He was just as responsive as other men when she did certain things: licking an ice cream from the poolside bar in a particular way, or sinking down in her lounger with a sigh and lifting her arm over her head so her breasts rose up in her low-cut swimsuit, or looking directly into his eyes and smiling a little while she listened to him. He lapped it up. It was almost too easy. Even so, she took care not to mention Erika, slipping away to the crèche and heading home without saying goodbye.

Julian started to bring her gifts: small ones at first – some chocolates, a bouquet of roses. Soon he was bringing her jewellery: a pair of pearl drop earrings, a silver bracelet. He gave her a necklace with a heart-shaped padlock made of gold – 'because you've captured my heart', he said. She hid this from George along with his other gifts in a locked jewellery box she kept in her suitcase under their bed. It was where she kept Michael's ring. She hadn't been able to throw it away, hadn't known what to do with it. Ever since Obā had delivered the terrible news, Michiko had struggled to understand why Michael had given it to her. It threw her into unbearable confusion and pain whenever she looked at it. She laid the gold padlock necklace next to it and slammed the lid shut.

Marit was concerned – 'Do watch out for Julian, Michiko, he has a bit of a reputation,' – but Michiko laughed off her warnings.

When Julian bought Michiko a diamond pendant, she knew he was hers. One evening, he insisted on taking her out for a meal in town and wouldn't let her leave the club without him. She waved her wedding ring at him, told him she couldn't, that she was married and had a daughter who had to be to collected from the crèche. As she'd suspected, it didn't deter him.

'Get a divorce so I can marry you, darling,' he said. 'and I'll even take in your daughter.'

Early one Sunday autumn morning, Michiko prepared a full English breakfast for George, his favourite combination of fried eggs, toast, sausages, mushrooms and a large pot of tea. She waited until he had eaten it all before she told him, sitting at their tiny table in their two-roomed apartment, the toddler napping in the cot next door.

She was leaving him for Julian, she said. She was taking Erika to live with them in Hong Kong.

George's shock turned to pleading, then to tears. Michiko was taken aback to see him so upset; she'd thought he'd be happy to be free of her. She knew she should have been feeling compassion, or remorse, but instead she felt nothing.

George's tears gave way to anger, and he got up from the table, knocking back his chair. 'What about Erika?' he shouted. 'I'll fight for custody. You can't take my daughter away from me!'

Michiko lined up her knife and fork neatly on her empty plate, then dabbed her lips with her napkin. She looked up at him with a pitying smile. It was time to tell him the truth.

A Doll

It was a handmade doll finely sewn from cream-coloured poplin stuffed with kapok. Its blonde plaits, tied with white ribbon, were made from yellow wool. It wore a little red-and-white gingham bonnet over its golden hair, and a pinafore apron made of the same fabric. Its cheerful face was sewn on, and though it had become a little threadbare, it remained unchanged, despite the tragedies it witnessed over fifty years. Its eyes were of blue felt, and it had small strips of red felt for lips. The eyebrows, the nose, the eyelashes and ears were stitched lines of black thread. On its feet were tiny blue boots tied with white ribbon. Underneath the pinafore it wore the smallest of socks, a pair of underpants and a vest, and a white petticoat trimmed with lace. Made with care for a beloved child, it had once travelled many thousands of miles.

Erika

As soon as Erika lands in Okinawa she feels as if she's been here before; it's as if she's returning home. Even in the city, she feels a strange buzzing through her veins, as if her blood's recharging itself through the rocks, the trees and the ocean, as if she's drawing strength from this island and it's transforming her from a shadow into a solid body. She can't explain to Marcus why, for the first time since she can remember, she feels real, solid.

They decided at the last minute to come to Okinawa together. Felix is at a school camp in France; the timing is perfect. They've never been on holiday together before and it's the longest they've constantly been in each other's company. The continuous proximity doesn't seem to bother Marcus. If it does, he isn't showing it, but then, neither is she.

Coming here to the land of her ancestors, walking where her mother and father had walked, Erika feels herself brimming with a purpose she's never felt before. There are still so many unanswered questions. What circumstances brought her parents together? What became of her father? What was her mother like then? If she came to understand these things, Erika might be able to reconnect the fractured parts of herself. She wishes she could find the woman her mother called Obā, a distant cousin of her grandmother's. None of the Takigawas have been in touch with her. Erika doesn't remember Michiko ever mentioning her. Maybe she should go to Kudakajima, the small island where her grandmother had been born, to ask around. Surely somebody there would remember the Kudaka family.

She doesn't know how to begin her investigations and keeps putting it off. It doesn't help that she feels Marcus's presence restricting her somehow. It's as if he's become the veil between her and whatever it is she needs to experience. He's fallen in love with Okinawa and starts up cheery conversations about the islands with any strangers willing to speak English. He insists they go to the tourist sights he's marked out in his guidebook, and she's content to follow along at first, but after days of visiting museums, the royal mausoleum at Tamaudun, Shuri Castle and other busy tourist spots, Erika's starting to feel frustrated. His enthusiasm is an airy counterpoint to the weight of Erika's expectations about what she might, or mightn't discover here. They may as well be on separate planets. She knows it's unfair of her to expect him to understand. She has a strange, visceral urge to merge with the place, to pour herself into it, and Marcus's eagerness to stay in the lively city among the bustle of tourists is distracting her from it.

She's not sure exactly when or how she first heard about noro in Okinawa, but it's one of those things she feels she's always known about. Aunt Fusae once told her, years ago, that Erika's grandmother was supposed to have been one, but ended up leaving to be married in Tokyo. When Erika asked her mother what that meant, Michiko had been dismissive. 'Superstitious rubbish,' she'd said. 'Magical priestesses! Ridiculous. Some of them crazy.'

Ever since Okinawa's re-emergence in her consciousness, Erika hasn't been able to stop thinking about the way female power is woven through stories she's heard about the noro. She's been trying to share her excitement about them with Marcus. She buys herself an English-language book on Okinawan culture. Lying in bed one night in their hotel room, she flips it open at random and starts to read:

> *The indigenous people of the Ryūkyū Archipelago (also known as Okinawa) believe the first noro was the eldest daughter of a descendant of the goddess Amamikyū, who created the islands.*

Noro are considered to be priestess-queens, once consulted by the ancient Ryūkyū kings. Their practice has endured despite attempts at suppression after Japan annexed the islands and abolished the Ryūkyū monarchy in 1789. Along with yuta (shamanic mediums), they are classified as kaminchū, or 'people of the gods'. As befits a culture that accords spiritual supremacy to women, almost all are female. To some, the kaminchū are symbolic of Okinawan and feminist resistance. They are still consulted by those looking for solace, advice, blessings or cures, and in this sense noro are regarded as spiritual counsellors. Noro officiate at rituals to keep harmony between the living, the dead, and the spirits of nature. The role of the noro is usually passed on matrilineally.

Erika sits up in bed, spilling her chamomile tea. Her heart beats faster. 'Can you believe it? I opened the book and landed straight on a page about noro!'

'Amazing,' says Marcus, absorbed in a magazine.

'There's something here about another type of sacred woman.' She taps him on the arm. 'Listen: "Yuta receive their calling during their lifetimes, often after experiencing trauma. They are considered the intermediaries between the living and the dead, with psychic abilities. Some consider these abilities to be a sign of mental illness. They have been persecuted in much the same way witches were persecuted in Europe and America. For a period, "yuta" was used as a pejorative term, and for some time their practice was outlawed. However, some see the transformation of trauma survivors into kaminchū as a spiritual forging that transmutes their own and others' mental suffering." Oh,' Erika breathes, 'how cool is that?'

'Interesting,' Marcus says distantly, flicking through the magazine.

Erika wonders whether, like yuta, noro could end up punished with bad luck if they don't obey the call. She thinks of her grandmother's accident and her mother's chaotic life. Would things get bad for her too?

'I want to see a noro,' she says.

'You really believe in all that?' he asks, closing his magazine. 'Stinks of New Age bullshit to me.'

'It's part of Okinawan culture, Marcus.' She slaps the book closed. Talking to him about this is a waste of time.

In the diaries, Kei read that Obā had taken their grandmother to the island to see a noro the same day Michiko first spent time with Michael. 'She might still live on Kudakajima,' Kei wrote in her email. 'It's a couple of hours from Naha by bus and ferry; you could do it as a day trip.'

But that was almost forty years ago. Would the noro still be alive? If she was, she might be able to tell Erika where her Okinawan relatives are, what became of them. She'd be at least a hundred years old by now, but Erika knows that's nothing for the long-lived Okinawans. It's a long shot, but worth a try.

Kei had included the noro's number, which she'd found scribbled in Michiko's diary, at the end of her email. Shutting herself in the bathroom, Erika makes the call, taking deep breaths to calm her nerves. Her heart sinks when the sound of an automated voice tells her that the number's out of use.

The next day Erika and Marcus order cakes and frothy Okinawan buku-buku tea from a Makishi Market cafe. A striking woman who looks to be in her late fifties is sitting at a table across from them. Erika can't help but stare: she's masculine-looking, with thick dark eyebrows and sun-darkened skin unadorned by make-up. Her shining black hair is streaked with white and scooped into a topknot with an antique silver pin. She reminds Erika of an old photo she once saw of her grandmother Chiyo when she was young and healthy. The woman wears a dress so fine Erika can see through it to the tunic underneath; the dress is a light charcoal patterned with tiny squares of black and white.

The woman notices Erika staring, and stares back. Flushing with embarrassment, Erika stutters an apology, and explains that she's been admiring the dress.

'It's handwoven bashōfu,' the woman says in Okinawan dialect.

Erika struggles to follow. 'Bashōfu?'

The woman sighs, continues in Yamato Japanese. 'Bashōfu fabric. Made from banana plant fibres and coloured with natural dyes. It's a traditional Okinawan weaving technique.' She doesn't smile and looks at Erika in a way that unnerves her. She notices the silver knot ring on Erika's finger.

'That ring. Did you buy that here?'

'No, it was my mother's.'

The woman frowns. 'You don't live here. You sound as though you're from Yamato. How long are you staying in Okinawa?' she asks. 'Where do you intend to go in the islands?' Her eyes bore into Erika's, as if she sees everything.

'I'm hoping to go to Kudakajima,' Erika replies.

'It's not a place for a holiday.'

Erika is surprised by her forcefulness. 'Oh, I ...'

'You have to be called there,' the woman continues. 'It's a sacred island. There's nothing there except some houses, a shop and a school. There are secret groves forbidden to outsiders. Even Okinawans don't choose to go there. They only go if they're invited.'

She falls silent and drinks her tea: a dismissal. Feeling reprimanded and strangely shaken, Erika finds herself unable to speak. She turns back to Marcus, who's been watching them with interest. When she looks back a few minutes later, the woman is gone. Erika wishes she'd had the courage to tell her she wasn't going there on holiday. That she wants to find her family. That she's descended from Kudakajima women. That she is serious.

Erika spends the rest of the day searching for someone who can help her find a noro. Younger Okinawans she asks have never been to see one before, and seem puzzled that she'd want to. Older Okinawans appear reluctant to talk about them at all. Marcus rolls his eyes each time she brings up the subject.

She finally manages to get hold of a number from the owner of a Tsuboya coffee shop. He flicks through his phone, writes the number on a piece of paper.

'She lives in the north, in Nago, on the Motobu peninsula. She comes here to Naha twice a week to consult with her city clients,' he says. 'They say she's powerful. You'd better ring for an appointment straight away if you want to see her before you leave these islands. She gets pretty booked up.'

That evening, Erika shuts herself in the hotel bathroom again and rings the number. A young woman, the noro's daughter, answers the phone. 'We've been waiting for you,' she says.

'They probably say that to everyone who rings up for the first time.' Marcus says, when Erika tells him. But he decides to come with her all the same.

'I thought you said it was all bullshit,' Erika says, with a sly grin.

'Just curious.'

Their taxi takes them through narrow, twisting streets to a house hidden among trees. They pay the driver and walk through a sturdy, round-edged, white stone gate into a courtyard with three smooth boulders, each a different size and colour, pleasingly arranged in a cluster at its centre, like three people embracing. The rest of the courtyard is overflowing with plants, shells and rocks. Water lillies grow in a stone basin in the corner, and the water's surface ripples with the flicker of golden koi carp. The air feels thick with torpor; Erika wades through it like a sleepwalker, hardly noticing Marcus beside her.

They enter the traditional Okinawan house, its terracotta tile roof protected by a fierce-looking stone shīsā lion. The noro's daughter invites them inside. They remove their shoes and step up into a sunny room. There's a sofa next to a large tank full of bright fish. The daughter gestures to it. 'You can wait here,' she says to Marcus.

He elbows Erika and points to the fish. 'See those?' he whispers. 'They're the noro's previous clients.' He ignores her glare and watches them swimming about.

Erika follows the daughter through a sliding door into a large room. Sunlight gleams off pale wooden-panelled walls and a tatami floor. There's a smell of jasmine and sandalwood incense. A wooden statue of the goddess Benzaiten, with her flowing robes and lute, stands in the corner next to a cabinet full of conch and spider shells. An altar with ancestral tablets and incense along the wall reminds Erika of her own back in London, though this one is much bigger. It's arranged with offerings of tangerines, rice cakes and several bottles of awamori liquor. Looks like the noro's ancestral spirits like their alcohol too.

The noro's daughter motions for her to sit. Erika folds her legs neatly underneath her on a zabuton cushion and the woman brings her a cup of coffee and a slice of cake. It could be any ordinary home if not for the statue, shells and incense, and the strange, hypnotic feeling in the room.

As Erika raises the coffee cup to her lips, the noro walks in. She has a stern expression. Her hair is pinned in a topknot, and she wears a turquoise blouse with a long skirt patterned with blue flowers. Erika guesses she might be in her late sixties or early seventies – the age her mother would have been, had she lived. There is nothing to indicate her status – none of the loose hair, white robes and crown of leaves Erika's seen in pictures.

Erika sees the noro notice her hesitation. 'I … I expected white robes,' she explains.

The noro meets Erika's eyes and smiles, and her face opens and glows, as if the sun is shining from it. 'They're for rituals only. Quiet now, please.'

The noro closes her eyes and bows her head. She makes clasping gestures with her hands. She mutters under her breath, rocks back and forth a little. She suddenly opens her eyes to look at Erika. 'They're glad you came back,' she says.

'I've never been to Okinawa before. Who do you mean, "they"?' asks Erika.

The noro continues as if she hasn't heard, and Erika wonders if Marcus is right. Maybe this is bullshit.

The noro suddenly opens her eyes, as if Erika had spoken the words aloud. She notices Erika's ring, stares at it.

'An en-musubi ring. Your mother's?'

Erika flushes with shock. But then, it was a question. She nods.

'It has drawn you back here. There are things that must be finished.'

'Excuse me?' Erika shivers, despite the warmth of the room.

'Tell me your birth date.' Erika tells her, and the noro makes calculations with a pencil on a pad. 'What do you wish to know?'

'About my grandmother's family. They're from Okinawa. And about my father. My mother met him here. I never knew him. He's American.'

'How long has your mother been dead?'

Good guess. Erika is wearing her ring, after all. 'Twelve years,' says Erika.

'Where did she die?'

'London.'

'It was not a good death. Where are her remains?' The noro is brisk, business-like.

'I don't know what to do with them. Most are in her family grave in Tokyo. The rest are in an urn, at home, with me.'

'You must put your mother's bones into your father's family's ancestral tomb.'

'That's impossible,' Erika says. 'I don't know where my father is. Like I said, I've never met him.'

'Hmm,' says the noro, and closes her eyes again. She nods and twitches her mouth as if she's listening to someone. Then she says: 'This does not matter.'

Erika can't speak; she's shocked at the anger that overwhelms her. She wants to shout, *Of course it fucking matters.*

At the exact moment she thinks this, the noro opens her eyes and looks directly into Erika. It feels as if she's reached into Erika's chest with her fingers and is tugging at something inside. Erika's rage evaporates so suddenly she wonders if she's losing her mind.

'There is a doll.'

'Doll? What kind of doll?' Erika flounders about for meaning. She wonders again if she's made a mistake, coming here. How could she have been so gullible? Marcus will dine out on this for days.

'There *was* a doll. It no longer exists. It was of great significance to your mother. When it was destroyed, it destroyed her.'

Erika gasps. The realisation hits her like a lightning bolt. She remembers it, the soft fabric doll with the red gingham dress she'd found wrapped in tissue in a box in the top of Michiko's wardrobe. Erika scrabbles for a foothold on reality, as though she's clinging to a crumbling cliff. The tangible world is shifting, slipping sideways, revealing something unsettling beneath. She feels a chill creep into her. She's wondered too many times recently about her state of mind: doubting its stability, unable to trust her own judgement. She doesn't know what to think any more.

'Yes,' she whispers, finally. 'There was a doll.' Erika hopes the noro will say more, but she's closed her eyes again, muttering and rocking.

She had always thought drunkenness was the reason for Michiko's extreme reaction when she found Erika with it. But Erika remembers now her mother's inhuman howling, her face contorted with fury and distress as she hauled Erika into the wardrobe and locked her inside. She remembers the scratch of plastic garment bags crowding her in the suffocating darkness, remembers wetting herself in terror as she listened to her mother sobbing and wailing for what felt like hours afterwards; remembers her own wretchedness, knowing she could torture her mother without even meaning to, without understanding why, when all she felt was softness in her heart. She remembers the look on the amah's face, later, as she released Erika from the wardrobe; how she put her arms around Erika and took her to her quarters, and Erika feeling ashamed for her, that she should waste her kindness on such a criminal child.

Erika realises, now, that something terribly wrong must have happened in her mother's life.

Later that same night, after the amah had put Erika to bed, there had been a smell of burning, and the sound of Michiko and Julian fighting. The memory looms out at Erika from the fog of her unconscious. She did not recognise her mother's pain, let alone help her to fix it, and now it is too late. She swallows, feeling a dull ache press into her throat. Her eyes fill; the room is swimming.

'Now,' the noro is saying, 'you must find your place in the world.' She speaks quickly, and Erika wipes her face, forcing herself to shift her focus; she's unused to the Okinawan accent and struggles to concentrate. Something about elements expressing themselves through nature: trees as an expression of air, sun as an expression of fire, rock as an expression of earth. 'Offer your gratitude to the elements of air, earth, fire, water,' the noro is saying. 'Pay respects to them before you pass through.'

'Sorry, what?' says Erika, still reeling. 'Pass through where?' She can't get a grip on what the noro is telling her.

'Come to Nago, to the north,' says the noro. 'I will carry out a ritual of mabui-wakashi for you.'

'I know *mabui* means "spirit",' says Erika. Her hands feel cold and clammy. 'What's *wakashi*?' She's almost afraid to hear the answer.

'It is a rite to remove a mabui from a person, a place or object. Your mother's mabui still clings to you,' she says. 'It is bound to you through the objects you share, and it struggles to be free. It is not at peace.

You must let it go, or it will make you ill.' The noro reaches across the table and grasps Erika's hands in hers. She stares at the scar on Erika's hand for a long time. The noro closes her eyes again, nodding and murmuring, and Erika feels the adrenaline leave her body, as if she's had a couple of Tramadol. Her body is buzzing, probably from sitting on the floor too long, but the heat of the noro's hands sends trails of sensation up her arms. Erika's chest feels full, as if something were about to burst out of it. She fights the urge to lie down on the tatami and go to sleep.

'Come back to Nago,' says the noro, her eyes still closed. 'First, travel to Kunigami-son, and from there, walk into the Yanbaru forests, to the largest waterfall in the Motobu mountains. Do not forget. You must pay your respects to the elements as you pass through. Walk without fear. You will find the utaki, the sacred places. At every single one of them you must pay your respects. And then you must come to me.'

With that, the consultation is over.

Michiko

The Vietnam War had ended, and Junko Tabei had just become the first woman to reach the summit of Everest when Michiko moved into Julian's huge Hong Kong apartment high up on Victoria Peak. She loved living in such luxury: designer leather furniture, fine art, mirrored walls and shag pile rugs; there were even gold taps in the marble bathroom, just like the ones Michiko had dreamed about. The apartment had floor-to-ceiling windows and enormous balconies looking out over the harbour; a well-kept garden full of flowers, a heated pool and a jacuzzi. A gardener came several times a week, and there was a chauffeur as well as a live-in amah to do the housework and take care of Erika. This, at last, was the life Michiko had always imagined, the life she deserved after all her suffering.

The money available to her seemed limitless, and Julian encouraged her to buy herself nice things. She went to Lane Crawford so often the shop assistants knew her by name, calling her Mrs Stanhope – they didn't have to know she wasn't married yet – and, familiar with her tastes, they'd direct her to the latest dress or necklace or shoes they thought she'd like. Resplendent in couture and glittering with jewellery, she went out with Julian almost every night to dinner parties and restaurants where she charmed everyone; at weekends, his expat friends invited them to stay on their yachts or in their holiday villas on Lantau or Macau.

It would all have been so perfect if it hadn't been for Erika. The girl was a bottomless pit of need. Whenever Michiko was home, the child followed her everywhere, getting in the way, driving her wild with irritation. Goodness knew she tried to bond with her; she took the child clothes shopping, or for afternoon tea and ice cream at the Ritz-Carlton. But Erika would sit, refusing to talk, looking at Michiko with accusing eyes. The child wandered off in Lane Crawford once; Michiko had to look for her everywhere. When she finally spied her in the toy department on another floor, her relief turned to rage; she knew Erika had done it on purpose to worry her. She left her behind to teach her a lesson, although halfway down Queens Road she changed her mind, instructing the chauffeur to turn around. Sometimes she regretted telling George the truth; he would have taken Erika with him when he left, and he'd have been none the wiser. Erika's brooding silences grew more frequent, as if her daughter could read Michiko's mind.

Although there wasn't a day when Michiko wished she hadn't become pregnant, she felt guilty she couldn't be the mother this child wanted her to be. She had to remind herself that it wasn't Erika's fault she had been born. Sometimes a thought would rise unbidden into her consciousness: of another child that had been born, but not lived. She would trample it back down. The frivolous distractions life with Julian offered made it easy to forget.

It was a good thing Erika had grown close to the amah. It was convenient having someone in the house with a knack for settling this strange and difficult child. Marit had the knack too, but Michiko didn't see her again after that day on their friends' yacht when the silly girl nearly drowned. Marit stopped returning Michiko's calls. When Michiko tried to visit her while on a trip to Tokyo, the embassy housekeeper said that Marit was too busy to speak to her. Erika must have done something to upset her.

The child was her punishment, but Michiko didn't know what for. She couldn't look at that small face, couldn't see that resemblance without feeling anguish; couldn't forget that it was the pregnancy that had made her ill. Years passed and Julian never proposed to Michiko; soon their relationship was fraying. She was certain she would have been married long ago if it weren't for Erika. The glamour of the parties, the cocaine, the yachts, the cocktails, all helped to bury Michiko's agitation, at least to begin with, but whenever she came home, there Erika was, her wreckage from another life.

Michiko came home from lunch at the Cricket Club one day to find the bedroom ransacked. The drawers were open, their contents jumbled. A box of photographs lay upturned on the sofa, pictures scattered across the cushions; jewellery sat in tangles on the dressing table, expensive dresses, coats, lingerie, shoes, scarves, in crumpled piles on the floor. There was a chair next to the open wardrobe, and all the boxes inside had been pulled out and upended, even the ones hidden at the back of the top shelf, which contained her private things that nobody, not even Julian, ever saw. Her immediate thought was that they'd been burgled; she was about to shout for the amah and ask her to call the police. But what she'd thought was a mess of clothes on the bed turned out to be Erika, curled in a ball under Michiko's mink coat. She'd eaten most of a packet of chocolate biscuits. Crumbs littered the sheets, and chocolate was smeared everywhere – *on the fur coat too, my god!* Michiko felt molten rage surge into her body. She stalked over to the bed and whipped the fur coat off the child's sleeping body. And then Michiko saw what Erika was holding.

Erika became even more challenging as a teenager. She behaved badly, Michiko suspected, just to get a reaction from her. They were constantly at war. These conflicts made Michiko feel ill, yet Erika seemed unable to comprehend this, persisting in her attacks no matter what her mother did. She had a special knack for choosing moments when Michiko was in a hypoglycaemic slump, or when things were going particularly badly with Julian, to test her patience. Michiko would try, and fail, to control her own rages. She'd feel them building deep inside her, and they'd erupt so violently, often without warning, that she barely knew what she was doing. After the firestorm had passed, she'd remember her own father striking her as a child, and, remorseful, she would give the amah the night off and retreat to the kitchen to prepare her daughter's favourite Japanese dishes. Michiko had bought a fine hybrid Kamagata when she first married George, choosing it with care from a knife vendor in Kappabashi; she would take this knife and purge her sins and her violence with it, chopping, dicing, slicing. Julian would be elsewhere by then, having escaped the house at the first sign of turmoil. As she prepared food for her daughter, she'd feel her hard edges soften into something that felt close to maternal. Sometimes, if the argument had been trivial and blown over quickly, Erika would slip into the kitchen to watch her mother. One day, while Michiko was distracted, roasting sesame seeds to grind into a goma-dare sauce, Erika quietly picked up the Kamagata knife and began chopping a bunch of spring onions. Michiko had barked at her to leave it, that the knife could only be handled by an experienced cook, but then she saw how naturally Erika held it, how swiftly and efficiently she cut the spring onions into fine rounds. How she had learned to do this, Michiko didn't know, but she let Erika carry on as she stood quietly watching, impressed.

There was a routine. The orderliness of setting the yellow Formica table in the kitchen calmed Michiko's nerves. A large teapot for hōji tea. Two yunomi teacups: Michiko's, of blue-and-white Hasami porcelain, Erika's with hand-painted goldfish. Two pairs of chopsticks: Wakasa lacquer for Michiko, Erika's decorated with Lady Oscar from the shōjo manga Berusaiyu no Bara. When Erika complained she was too old for such chopsticks, Michiko replaced them with a pair of hinoki chopsticks from Daikokuya in Tokyo. Michiko would then place crockery for the food she was making: black Setoguro plates for tonkatsu, rectangular blue-and-white Seto dishes for grilled himono fish, earth-coloured Raku bowls for rāmen or kitsune udon. If there was rice with the meal, which was almost all of the time, she would set their ochawan beside the rice cooker, the red lacquer shamoji rice paddle laid ready on top of them.

She had bought the chawan rice bowls, just for the two of them, in Tokyo. They were made by the same ceramic artist: Erika's striped red and blue; Michiko's spiralling with dots of pale-blue wash. The patterns were completely different, yet the bowls looked as if they belonged to each other. They were rounded, not conical, so that they nestled comfortingly in the palm as you ate. In the kitchen, far from the gold taps, the Lalique crystal and the silk sheets, the rice bowls connected Michiko with something she'd lost long ago, grounding her in a no-man's-land where she and Erika could lay down their weapons and come together for an hour's truce while they ate.

She would call out that the food was ready, and Erika would creep into the kitchen, her face often red and swollen from crying, and quietly take a seat. Michiko would scoop a mound of freshly steamed rice into the red-and-blue bowl, another into her own, and set the tonkatsu, or the tempura, or the fish on the table. They would sit together, eating in a silence that was not altogether uncomfortable. When they were done, Erika would wash and dry the dishes, then retreat back to her room. It never took long, though, before arms were taken up again.

Their fights grew so frequent and terrible that Julian would disappear for days. Michiko never knew where he had gone; if she asked him, he'd give vague answers, saying he'd been called away from the office at the last minute to go overseas on business. She intercepted one of his credit card bills and saw a charge for the Ritz-Carlton. He had not been away at all. The price could only have been for a suite. There were other charges, at jewellers, at restaurants. He had not bought her a gift for months. Whenever he came home from these absences, she would confront him. Their fights became physical.

As if it weren't enough that her daughter's presence was driving Julian away, Erika had to keep bringing up incidents from the past, yelling about emotional and physical abuse. She brought up the incident with the doll several times. Michiko couldn't bear thinking about that day – Erika knew this, but insisted on talking about it as if she were the innocent victim, the one who suffered. Michiko blocked her ears, but could still hear Erika shouting.

'You traumatised me. You were always drunk. You're *still* always drunk!'

'Always blaming others for your behaviour. ' Michiko could not believe what she was hearing. 'You don't know what trauma is!' Why did this girl have to keep picking at these scabs, stopping the wounds from healing?

The day Julian told Michiko he was leaving her, that he was selling the apartment and moving to London to live with his new fiancée, Erika took over the sorting and packing with the amah. She had been unperturbed, happy even, at the news.

Michiko spent those weeks in a drunken stupor; the morning Julian broke the news, she drank an entire bottle of vodka. She was glad, then, that Erika was there to organise everything, so unexpectedly business-like. There was no recognition of common-law marriage in Hong Kong, and legally, Julian owed Michiko nothing. Erika negotiated a sum with him that would ease the separation; she agreed that some of Michiko's jewellery, fur coats and couture should be auctioned to contribute to their funds. When Michiko had moved in with Julian, Marit had suggested she ask Julian to pay money into a trust fund for Erika's education; he had been eager to please Michiko, then, and had complied. Erika wanted to train professionally as a chef; the money would go towards her fees at Le Cordon Bleu school in London. Going to England made sense. Michiko agreed, thinking that if she followed Julian to London, she might be able to persuade him to return to her.

For months Michiko was in a daze, cut through with sharp moments of awareness – of Erika sobbing as she hugged the amah goodbye; the truck driving away the shipping container loaded with their things; the flight to London, economy class. She and Erika moved into a small flat in Chelsea, not far from where Julian was living with his whore. Michiko turned up drunk on his front door step so often that Julian's pregnant wife – another stab of betrayal, this happening so quickly – eventually called the police. Michiko would go for long walks along the Thames and consider jumping off one of its bridges. Erika had turned seventeen and had started her course at Le Cordon Bleu. When she came home, she mostly kept to herself in her room, though she did the housework and cooking that Michiko was finding increasingly difficult.

There were times when Michiko almost felt grateful that Erika was around but most of the time she wished her daughter would just move out and leave her alone. Erika would shout at her to stop drinking and pull herself together, or would force her to go to the doctor. Michiko would remind her that if it hadn't been for Erika, she wouldn't have diabetes, and Erika would scoff and tell her to stop being ridiculous. Michiko knew too, deep down, that she was a mess, that she wasn't well, but she didn't know how to fix herself. Her health continued to deteriorate. There were no longer the distractions that kept memories from slashing into her consciousness; only the drink kept them at bay. Erika didn't understand.

'If you don't stop drinking you're going to lose your toes! You're going to go blind!' Erika was always yelling such things at her.

Michiko would simply splash more whisky into her glass.

There was a terrible day when Erika confronted her with a letter from George. The girl had managed to track George down, goodness knew how, and had written to him. It was an unspeakable betrayal, a scraping open of a long-knitted scar. Her daughter clearly wanted her to bleed.

Erika shouted again and again, 'Tell me what happened, I have the right to know!' and Michiko ripped the letter to pieces. Erika became hysterical then, red in the face, screaming, until Michiko slapped her, to make her stop. Erika curled in on herself; there were a few beats of silence. But when she stood up and faced her mother, she had stopped crying, and her expression had been terrible, frightening. She had walked calmly into her room and packed a suitcase. Michiko did not stop her as she ran down the stairs, slamming the door.

How pitiful Michiko's life had become. It was typical that Erika should abandon her when Michiko needed her most. As if it weren't enough for her to have driven Julian away, as if it weren't enough that she'd likely had something to do with the restraining order he'd taken out against Michiko, Erika had left her own mother to suffer alone. Crumpled on the floor, surrounded by the mess of broken lamps and chairs, Michiko tried to catch her breath. She felt dizzy, disconnected. How had everything come to this? It wasn't meant to be this way. She was so tired of fighting. She crawled to the bedroom and pulled out a vodka bottle hidden in a shoebox that Erika hadn't managed to find; she unscrewed the cap and took a long swig. Then she lay on the floor, looking up at the ceiling, and felt everything spinning out of control.

A Fate-binding Ring

Weighty in the hand, it is a traditional Okinawan silver ring designed for a woman's finger. Two strands of beaten silver run side by side to girdle the finger before looping together, rising and twisting upwards into a large, simple four-loop knot that forms the ring's crown. Seemingly without end or beginning, the two strands are eternally bound together in a symbol that resonates across cultures; one that contains the universal idea of one person bound by fate to another, or to a place. Held within the knot of this en-musubi ring is a promise, inherited by one hand from another, to return to the place that binds them both.

Erika & Michiko

Erika says little about her appointment with the noro. She ignores Marcus's joshing on their way back to the hotel; when he suggests they take a walk down Kokusai Dōri to explore new bars and restaurants to try out that evening, she says she's tired and needs to rest, and tells him to go ahead without her. She feels drained, as if she's recovering from a fever, and sleeps soundly with the curtains drawn until he returns. She feels a little like her old self by then, and they go out to eat a quick bowl of Okinawa soba, then spend the rest of the evening trying out different types of awamori at an izakaya bar. Marcus doesn't suspect anything is amiss.

Erika wishes she could unburden herself to him, but hasn't been able to find the words to describe what took place during that hour with the noro. She's afraid Marcus will make fun of something she still can't understand; all she knows is that it has shaken her to her core. Marcus interprets her reticence as a silent admission that the visit has been a waste of time and continues ribbing her until she tells him she plans to head north to see the noro again. When his amusement turns to incredulity, she distracts him by pretending to be drunker than she is, and orders another bottle of awamori. She raises her glass. 'To us, and our romantic holiday,' she says, slurring. 'I'm up for more sightseeing tomorrow. How about you?'

They eat breakfast late the next morning in a hipster cafe just off Kokusai Dōri after stopping off at a chemist for some paracetamol. Erika looks through the guidebook. She's had enough of museums and tourist spots. She wants to get away from the city, find somewhere wild, away from all the noise and the distraction. She's about to suggest they take the bus north together when she sees in the guidebook that there's a shrine in Naha, a twenty-minute walk away, perched on a low cliff overlooking the sea. 'Check it out,' says Erika, sipping a second cup of coffee. 'The photos look amazing.' She turns the guidebook to show Marcus. 'It's called Naminouegū. It means "above the waves". Let's go after breakfast.'

They turn off Kokusai Dōri and head for the sea. Shops and restaurants give way to tree-lined streets with low-rise residential apartments and traditional tiled-roof houses half-obscured by lush vegetation. They forge on, following the signs for the beach. Ahead of them, a huge concrete bridge fills the view.

'Are we going the right way?' asks Marcus, shading his eyes from the late autumn sun. 'That monstrous thing looks like it doesn't belong beside a pretty beach.'

Erika consults the map, and nods. 'Yep. Right up ahead.' The damp salt scent on the breeze confirms they're near. Expecting to walk several minutes more, she's surprised to find they've arrived. There's a small paved area with trees and benches; a few people are gathered there for a picnic. Behind it, a broad sweep of steps brackets the white sand and sea with the big bridge just across the water. It is all so unexpected, somehow: the dazzling white of the sand, the enormous grey bulk of the bridge, the clear azure water. A few people bob about in the waves.

'That view's pretty disappointing,' says Marcus. 'They don't show that bridge in the guidebook photo. Why the hell would they build it there?'

Two men with blond crew cuts are standing close by, and one of them, overhearing, calls out, 'Ugly, isn't it? They thought it would be a good idea to build that back in the eighties.'

'You guys American?' asks Marcus.

'We're stationed here, up at Ginowan,' one of them says. 'We're down here for the weekend for some R&R,' he adds, gesturing at his swimming shorts.

Erika is suddenly overwhelmed by an inexplicable fluttering inside her. It reminds her of the terror and excitement she used to feel as a

239

child, waiting for her turn on a rollercoaster. Ignoring the conversation Marcus is having with the Americans, she drops her backpack at the bottom of the steps and takes off her shoes, sinking into the soft sand. Her feet are hot and tired from walking, and beneath the sun-warmed top layer, the sand is cold and soothing. She'd wanted to visit the shrine first – she can see its roof peeking out above a cluster of trees up on the bluff to their left – but her gaze keeps being drawn back to the waves that lap gently at the dazzling white sand. She doesn't care if she's being rude. She stands with her back to the men, unable to look away from the sea.

The water is clear like crystal, a witness without judgement. It's been lapping the shifting white sands of this beach for eons, Erika thinks, from a time before the shrine on the cliff was built, continuing ceaselessly while these sands were fought over by kingdoms and nations. She imagines it reflecting the flames of Naha as it burned sixty years before, the city's people running across the sand to escape the American bombardments. She imagines fishermen, troubled souls, priestesses and warriors standing where she stands, turning to the sea, towards Nirai Kanai, the underwater realm of the gods. She imagines soldiers, pleasure-seekers, families, and those who stood at crossroads in their lives, not knowing which way to turn. The sand is made bright by the bones of sea creatures, she thinks, continually replenished as they die and drift and fragment into tiny grains of sand, becoming a part of this place.

She steps forward until the water laps at her toes. She doesn't draw back. She stands, swaying. She feels sleepy, spellbound, but her knees are trembling and her heart racing at her proximity to the salt water, her body feeling as if it's being overridden by a force outside her. It's pulling at her, drawing her towards deeper water, as if the bridge were a magnet and she a helpless scrap of iron.

'Hey!'

She starts as Marcus puts his hand on her shoulder. She sees her feet in the water, stumbles backwards.

'You okay?' Marcus asks. 'What are you doing?'

She nods, but she's shaken. 'I'm not sure … I feel kind of weird,' she says, twisting the silver knot ring around and around on her finger. 'For a moment I felt like I wanted to get in the water.'

'That's great! It would be good to mend that phobia of yours. Sun's out, it shouldn't be too chilly.' He starts pulling off his shirt.

'I'm not going in.' She backs away from the water.

'You want to go to the shrine first?' he asks.

She shakes her head and sits in the sand.

'What's going on?' Seeing her expression, Marcus puts his shirt back on and sits next to her.

'I did something awful,' says Erika, running her fingers through the white sand, 'I've never told anyone before.'

Marcus looks at her and waits.

'Michiko was a horrible mother, but she liked to cook for me. She'd treat me in the worst possible ways, and then she'd go off to the kitchen and make all my favourite things to eat. If we bonded at all, it was over food; cooking it, eating it. We'd sit together and have a few moments of peace. We didn't talk much, but it was enough. The night she died, she called me and asked me to come over to her flat and eat with her. She sounded sober, said she'd cook something special for me. But I forgot.'

'Forgot?'

'Well, sort of forgot. I'd only spoken to her that morning, so it was in the back of my mind, but she'd been so awful to me the day before, I was still angry. I went out with some people from catering college for a drink. The next morning, I realised what I'd done and I rang her. I felt pretty bad. But she didn't pick up.' Erika closes her eyes and takes a deep breath. She feels dizzy.

'Honey, you don't have to tell this story now,' says Marcus, stricken.

'No. I have to. Like I said, I've never told anyone before. It's time I did.'

*

Michiko hadn't told Erika yet that she'd made her decision; she wanted to save it for the dinner. She'd found herself tripping over more often lately — the pins and needles in her feet were turning into numbness — and she was seeing dark patches in her vision that hadn't been there before. She'd gone to the doctor and asked for help. She wasn't sure if she could go through with it after all this time, but she had no choice. Michiko rang the number the doctor had given her and was told where to go for the next meeting. She wanted to invite Erika to dinner so she could ask her for her support; she was sure she'd give it — Erika had shouted at her enough times to stop drinking. Michiko just had to persuade her that she was serious.

Tonkatsu was one of Erika's favourite dishes. Michiko prepared the flour and panko breadcrumbs in bowls ready for the escalopes. She washed the rice, slowly, carefully, without losing a grain, and set it aside in the cooker to soak. She arranged some white tulips in a vase and put them in the middle of the kitchen table. She set the two rice bowls beside the rice cooker, and laid out the pot and yunomi for hōji tea. She got her black Setoguro plates out of the cupboard. They rattled a little as her hand shook — she hadn't had a drink since she'd made that call. She'd tipped all the bottles she had in the house into the kitchen sink, terrified and elated as she watched the shōchū, the vodka, the whisky and the wine swirling down the plughole. She'd lined up the empty bottles beside the bin.

Michiko looked up at the clock. Erika would be there in a couple of hours. She made herself a pot of tea so she wouldn't think about drinking. She wondered how her daughter would react, whether she'd believe her. Whatever Erika said, Michiko told herself, she had to remain calm. She needed her daughter's support. It would be a new start for both of them, and though she knew she'd never be the mother she ought to have been, she wanted to make things right.

*

'I didn't even tell the police, you know, when they did their routine checks, asking lots of questions. I just told them that I'd only been trying to get in touch with her since that morning because I hadn't heard from her the night before. That she was a depressive, diabetic alcoholic. I phoned again and again that morning, and she still didn't pick up. I thought she was probably passed-out drunk as usual. I decided to leave it until later in the evening. When she still didn't answer, I went over to her flat after college and let myself in. I always kept the key with me, even after I moved out. I worried about her, you know. Despite everything. First thing I saw when I let myself in was a row of empty bottles by the bin, so I thought, here we go again.'

*

Something must have happened to delay Erika. Michiko knew she usually finished catering college around five. Maybe she'd had to go on somewhere unexpectedly; she'd probably ring soon to let her know what was happening. Michiko would usually be well into her second bottle of wine by now; she was sweating and starting to feel agitated. She wandered into the sitting room, and paced back and forth a few times, unsure of what to do.

The Chinese bronze lamp cast a light onto the Korean cabinet. It was dusty; she walked over and ran her finger across its top, leaving a streak in the London grime. There were things inside that cabinet she hadn't looked at for a long time; things she'd put inside for safekeeping when she and Erika had left Hong Kong. Her diaries were in there too; she hadn't written one for years now. She opened the metal clasps and reached inside, searching through the piles for the one she'd written in last, when things were starting to go wrong with Julian. She'd filled less than half of it. She could see from the handwriting that she'd been on a downwards spiral; the last entry was on the day she'd found Erika with the doll. Her heart contracted. She took the diary to the kitchen table and found a pen. She wrote frantically without keeping to the lines, filling blank pages, filling the time.

When she was done, she slid the diary back into the cabinet. She ran her fingers over the others. One day, when she was feeling better, she might read them again, but not now. She wasn't ready to be reminded of the girl she'd once been, full of energy and optimism for a life that should have been different to this one.

She wondered if she should switch off the rice cooker so it wouldn't burn the rice, but decided to leave it on. She tried ringing Erika's mobile phone again, but it went straight to voicemail. Michiko didn't leave a message. She was looking forward to telling Erika her news face to face. She made herself another pot of tea. She was sure the door buzzer would go at any moment.

*

'I went into her bedroom and saw her lying in the bed with the covers over her face. I thought she was passed out from the booze. I remember feeling relieved she'd managed to put herself to bed for once, instead of passing out on the floor like usual. I hated having to lift her up to get her into bed. I went to the sitting room, and I remember being surprised at how tidy everything was. She hadn't turned out the lights. I went through to the kitchen and there was food laid out ready on the table. I felt terrible. The rice cooker was still on.'

*

She decided she should fry the tonkatsu. If Erika was going to arrive late, better that the food be ready. Michiko felt herself waver between indignation and fear. She needed Erika to come soon. Maybe if she fried the tonkatsu, it would summon her, the way it used to summon her from her room after their fights. She picked up her Kamagata and started shredding the cabbage, fast and efficient despite the slight tremor in her hands, dissipating her alarm. She scooped the cabbage onto the Setoguro plates; after she crumbed and fried the escalopes, she'd slice them up and lay them on top. When Erika arrived, Michiko would pour the Bulldog Sauce over each dish, boil the kettle for more tea, and they'd sit down to eat and find their peace. Mothers and daughters, they were connected whatever happened, weren't they? There was a time when Erika wouldn't leave her alone, following her all around the house. Michiko hadn't liked it, then. Now she longed for Erika to appear on her doorstep. Michiko would open her door, smiling, and she would let her daughter in.

*

'I went into the bathroom. There were at least a dozen empty insulin bottles in the sink, and a bloody syringe. I wasn't sure if she'd used all of those at once, but I think I already knew, then. I felt sick. I went back into the bedroom …' Erika's face folds in on itself. She tries to hold it in – Marcus is watching her, wide-eyed – but she can't.

Erika's surprised how badly Marcus takes it when she confesses her plan to ride the bus an hour north into Motobu and hike to the waterfall in the Yanbaru forest without him. He seems apprehensive, and keeps asking if she's all right after what she told him the day before. She says it was good for her, to finally let it out, that she feels better now she's shared her burden with someone. He doesn't seem convinced.

'I need to go up there by myself because … because I need to be alone to connect with that landscape,' she says.

'Can't you "connect to the landscape" with me there?' He makes inverted comma motions with his fingers.

Erika squashes down her irritation. 'Please try to understand. It's not personal.'

She feels bad, telling him about her decision at such short notice, but the compulsion she's started to feel since seeing the noro is too strong to make her change her mind.

'Surely you understand the need for space. You're like me that way.'

'This is different,' he says. 'I'm worried about you.'

She promises Marcus she'll be back in time for dinner, pushing her guilt aside. She writes down the time the last bus arrives back in Naha, hoping he'll be there to meet her. She puts on her hiking boots, shoulders her backpack and heads for the bus terminal to begin her journey north to the mountains.

She feels her old self unravel as the bus takes her further north, past the military bases, away from towns and suburbs. The other passengers have gone by the time the bus reaches Motobu; when Erika steps off at Kunigami village, she puts her head down and walks swiftly away from the few people hanging around near the shops. She forges on into the wilderness.

On her way up to the waterfall, Erika stops at each utaki and pays respect as she passes, just as the noro asked her to do. Some are obvious shelters built of pale stone, scattered with incense ash; others are simple hollows under trees and rocks. She burns incense and puts her hands together, head bowed, eyes closed. She feels how momentary and insubstantial her place is in the universe; she could just blow away like a dandelion seed in the breeze.

The flat path along the river grows steeper, and Erika's skin slickens with sweat. She takes off her jacket and ties it around her waist. The river babbles softly at first, lilting, crooning; Erika feels the sound reverberate around her skull, as if the river were murmuring in her ear. The walkways skirt sheer rock faces that drip with water, ferns sprouting from cracks; a lizard signals the way with its bright-blue tail. All around her, the trees are so tall she can't see their crowns, even when she leans so far back it makes her head spin. She keeps walking the dirt path, stepping between tree roots, up, and up. She spreads her shoulders back, opens up her chest the way you'd split a crusty loaf of bread with your hands, and draws in the air, the sun, the trees, the wind, the river, the rocks. She feels herself filling up with the green she's breathing in, turning transparent, merging with the landscape around her.

She crosses a suspension bridge over a ravine. At the sight of the river flowing far below at the bottom of the gorge, she feels her body hollow, a small bird fluttering inside. Everywhere she looks, the earth is spilling over with boulders and trees and vines and ferns. The river is calling louder now, sliding and skipping over rocks below, tumbling in a hurry through the gorge. Erika imagines what it would feel like to fall through air down onto those rocks, wonders how long it would take to land.

When she reaches the other side of the bridge there's an abrupt drop in the temperature; Erika shudders and puts her jacket back on. Apart from the sound of the river and the moaning of the wind in the trees and rocks, there's nothing, not even the sound of birds, as if the earth holds its breath, waiting, and the air is thick. A lightning flash of fear strikes her and she stumbles. She starts walking faster.

'You have a right to be here,' she whispers to herself, again and again, in time with her footsteps, 'You have a right to be here, you have a right to be here.'

She comes to a large crevice in the rock face, a monumental, inverted V-shaped crack so deep and dark she can't see inside it. She takes her camera from her backpack to take a picture, and freezes. Cold terror swamps her and she lurches away, almost dropping the camera. She trips and falls and pants up the mountainside until she comes to a tall tree with a great nest of moss-covered roots. She curls inside, waiting for her heart to stop hammering. She looks back at the crevice in the rock now far below, then breathes out and laughs. She's losing her grip on reality. It's just a crevice in a rock, Erika, for god's sake.

The swollen river is reckless now, pitching from one craggy boulder to another in a succession of small waterfalls that swirl into limpid pools. She feels the river drawing her in, just as the sea did at Naminoue. She imagines herself surrendered to the river, her body churning and tumbling and tossed over the boulders into the gorge below. The thought doesn't frighten her as it might have done, and she feels herself unravelling.

Beneath the rumbling of the river beside her is a low reverberation, an uninterrupted thunder. It grows louder the higher she climbs. She follows the curve of the path, and gasps as she comes upon it suddenly: plummeting through a violent gash in the mountainside, roaring, the waterfall is astounding, monumental, like a living, breathing giant.

She perches on a boulder, breathing heavily from the climb. Already the massive presence of the waterfall is tugging at her, as if it wants to possess her. The deafening white noise of this colossus of water reverberates in every cell of her body. It's singing to her, bewitching her, a choir of sirens luring her to the rocks.

She sits for a long time, dizzy, entranced by the vertiginous wall of white water crashing down in front of her. Anything seems possible now. Her father on this island, right now, loving her mother still, ready to welcome his daughter, who loves them both. The three of them connected, in a triangle of forgiveness and reciprocated love.

She gets up to stretch her legs and stands, eyes closed, in the spray at the edge of the churning pool below the falls. She removes her shoes and socks and walks straight in, through the shock of the icy water, across the slippery stones. Her feet ache with it, but she stands there staring until her feet go numb. It is easier to surrender to the pain.

A vast boulder beckons from the other side of a torrent that forces its way through a narrow gap in the rocks. She must go to the boulder, cross the churning river. A thick crack cuts upwards through the rock face behind it, levelling into a ledge high at the top of the falls. She will perch there, close to the force of the water that would sweep her away. She wants to feel the spray on her body, imagines the water surging onto her head, dissolving her so she merges with the thunder, the spray, the rocks, the way Buddhist monks stand beneath waterfalls, praying, shivering, enduring. The force of the icy water cleansing the body of its sins. She could not ever have imagined doing this, before now.

She removes her clothes. She doesn't need them now. She folds them, tucks them into her backpack. She glances at the silver knot ring on her finger that binds her to her mother. She does not want to break the bond. Erika makes her way to the rock face, feeling the pull of the waterfall. There's no time to waste.

Ojyuzu

It is a ritual object looped over the left hand and held between the palms when paying respects to the dead. A small circle of prayer beads, a talisman passed down three generations. Its size and ascetic simplicity are markers of Sōtō Zen: fifty beads of polished ebony half a centimetre across and two smaller beads of orange–pink coral are strung onto a circle of fine silken braid the colour of dark wine; two quartz crystal beads – one spherical, the other cylindrical – unite its two ends, forming a closure in a form faintly reminiscent of a skull. The circle is closed by a knot, and its two threads emerge from the crystal beads and end in tassels trimmed into two velvet-soft orbs about two centimetres in diameter. A sacred sum, the fifty-four beads are half the one hundred and eight of humanity's darkest desires, the cravings and sins that keep us earthbound.

Erika

She sees herself. She is in a white bed in a bright room, white bandages with dark stains under the glinting metal frame caging her skull. She sighs and descends, understanding the wires and tubes connecting her body to the machines around her bed are binding together the frayed threads of her life. In her body now, she feels the chill in the backs of her hands where needles feed blood and quickening fluids from bags hanging dark in the air above her.

So soothing, the sound of slow heartbeats counted out in soft electric signals, measuring the life force in each pulse, calculating percentages, from second to second, of oxygenated blood. Cold air whispers through a tube in her throat; she feels it, dry and rough, and her body's impulse to cough explodes white fireworks in her skull. It is painful to be in this body. She knows it is not the machines that decide whether to mend or snap those frayed threads.

Beside her, a man with dark hair sits with his head in his hands.

*

Erika swims through morphine depths, surfaces. Her head feels tight, hot. Pain spikes through the fog. She stares at the curtains around her bed, uncomprehending. Her room in Hong Kong? The hotel room in Naha? The cabin of a boat? A woman in blue stands next to a machine beside her, ripping her from one reality into another. A band tightens around her arm, forcing blood into her fingers.

A machine ticks and beeps. She wonders where Marcus is. She's so tired. She closes her eyes.

*

She stands facing the waterfall, immense now she's closer. Its spray dampens her face, its force pushing air outwards, caressing her hair, chilling her face. Something is shimmering up at her from the pool by her feet, a smooth stone so different from the others that she scoops it from the water. It fits in her hand like it belongs there, and in the light it is iridescent, changing colours. She leans over to her backpack, slides it into a pocket. She's ready now. Her bare toes, numb with cold, curl tightly onto each stepping-stone as torrents of water blast between them, juddering down the cavernous drop to her left. She is not afraid.

*

Voices pull her back to the surface. Her skull pulses: expanding, shrinking, expanding, shrinking. Marcus. He's here in Hong Kong? Or is this London? He's talking to someone, a woman. She forces her eyelids open, just a sliver. Voices: *I don't know … slippery rocks.* She is hallucinating, seeing him stooped with a crumpled wet face. Voices again, fading in and out: *Yanbaru … powerful place … a lot of people get into trouble there.* She feels a soft thump near her feet. Marcus putting her backpack on the bed, rummaging inside it. She can feel by the way he moves that he's flustered.

*

He rummages in the backpack, and a small tasselled circle of beads tumbles out.

The noro has come in white robes, and bows her head, whispering secret words. Her hands held over those needle-prickled hands, vibrating heat in an exchange of something unknowable. The noro sits for an eternity, speaking with the unseen. When she stands and raises her palms to the ceiling, the power of her appeal unfurls through the solid structures of the building.

*

Staples prickle and scratch under bandages. The metal cage around her head is clamped too tight. More morphine. She will ask, if she can. Her voice is sandpaper in her throat, and no sound emerges.

*

She holds tight to the boulder behind her with one hand and steps back onto the stepping stones, shifting her weight and swinging her body across, clutching one rock after another until she reaches the other side of the churning pool. She catches her breath, looking up at the rock face she will climb. She flattens her cheek against it and listens. The waterfall is singing to her.

Barefoot and naked, she's a forest creature, agile, climbing. She grasps the crack in the rock with her fingers, finding footholds for her toes, levering herself up. Another fingerhold, another foothold, up and up.

*

She drags her attention back to her body. There's something looped around her left hand. She lifts it close to her face, struggling to focus. Why is this here? It's the ojyuzu she last saw Michiko clutching years ago, wretched with grief when her mother Chiyo died. Reality is sliding away again. She will ask if she had visitors in the night. She opens her mouth to speak, but still, no voice comes.

*

Up and up she climbs. It's easier than she expected. She's high up now, vertiginous, the waterfall deafening, the pool shrunken below. She inches her way through billows of spray that shroud her in clouds. The ledge is close. Just a few more metres and she will reach it. She shifts her hands to the next crack in the rock, shuffles her right foot forward. One more manoeuvre and she will reach it. Lifts her left foot clear of the rock, searches with her toes for a foothold, but there isn't one. She feels the toes of her right foot start to slide, but she remains calm. She tries to adjust her position, using the strength of her arms to find another purchase on the rock, but there is only soft moss, wet and slippery. Her toes scrabble at its surface and slide off, leaving her hanging, just for three seconds, by the tips of her fingers.

The lightness of the air she falls into is delicious. The rush in her ears, the roar of the water, her stomach and heart flying up into her throat, soaring, weightless.

*

Voices, different languages, different accents: *depressed skull fracture, we had to operate ... hikers found her ... unconscious for two days now ...* Marcus: his voice pretending lightness, masking panic. The heavy lull of morphine. So sleepy. She drifts.

*

She drifts deep and dark. No fear, only mild unease. She floats through grey, fringed with black void. Water presses in on her, heavy, like swaddling. She feels no pain. She's tired. It's tempting to stay where she is, but she's not ready. Her chest tightens for air. Where is the air? Panic floods in a cold rush, heart hammers. She kicks towards the rippling mercury mirror overhead with inhuman strength, forging through the mass of water pulling her down. Terror forces her body to kick upwards, upwards; she rises towards the surface, ears cracking, lungs twin meteors burning up on re-entry. She bursts through to the other side of the mirror and heaves at the shock of fresh air, spluttering, spewing, gulping oxygen and salt water in turn as waves slop into her choking mouth, batting her face as she fights and thrashes. Her lungs burn. As she flounders and vomits, tears merging back into the sea, a figure plummets from the dark shadow of the boat, the sound of the loud blooshh *resonating across the surface of the waves, hurting her ears, which are tight as drumskins with water. Her body cannot sustain the fight. Tiredness takes over once more, and all goes dark.*

She drifts through light and dark, sensations flitting across her skin, like clouds. She senses movement, touch, pain. Her arms pulled by cold, tight fingers. The bruising blow of a hard edge. A scraping on her legs of dry wood. Burning lungs. Urgent voices.

'Where are her water wings?' Drifting back into the dark.

'There! One in the water!'

The feel of a mouth on hers, her nose in a cold-fingered pinch, an odd sensation in her chest, of lifting, falling. Vomiting water, coughing and choking. Cold shaking hands, pulling her this way and that, her body a doll. Bile burning her throat. Then again, darkness.

She re-emerges into pale light. Softness beneath her head, the bliss of

253

dry sheets. Heavy chest, aching body. A patch of cold wetness against her cheek, from lungs, or eyes. She lets herself be rocked, distant sounds of water slapping on wood as she listens to voices pierce thin walls. Words rise and fall; some murmur, others shoot like bullets. Sharp words like these a signal to hide, stay small and quiet: she knows the drill. She takes tiny breaths so air won't catch at the rawness of her throat and make her cough. She shivers. Her head burns hot.

A man's voice, Julian's: 'Mistake ... fuck's sake!' It strains against a quiet, steely voice: Marit's.

'... drinking ... could have killed her!'

A third voice, familiar: her mother. She hears her drawl, loud, sudden: 'Oh, Marit, never mind. Erika is okay.'

She hears voices next door again, fragments of sentences. Marit's voice: '... needs a doctor, Michiko ... don't ... hospital ...'

Her mother's voice too low to make out the words.

Marit again, clearer: 'Please, Michiko, you must ... she needs ...' A clink of glass. 'No ... too drunk ...' Another clink. '... stop ...'

Her mother. The familiar irritation in the slurred voice: '... need it ... sick of her!' The last words shouted.

A moan, and a thump against the wall next to the bunk. She reaches out and strokes the wooden panels, imagining her mother's body on the other side. Shuffling close, she lays her cheek there.

Silence. She drifts downwards, sleeps again.

A Water-Tumbled Stone

It is perfectly round and perfectly smooth. It is pale, though not of any single colour. In the light, its opalescence changes from pink to blue to purple to green to yellow as it is turned and examined. It radiates an airy iridescence that belies it density, its weight. It is small, or perhaps large enough, to fit an adult woman's palm. When the hand closes around it, it is perfectly hidden. It is a stone so unlike the others that were around it that its difference is a question. It belongs where it was found, but it also belongs here, belongs there. It is a solid object formed millennia ago, spat from the core of the planet. It is changed, by heat and violence, but is still the same. A liminal object, a threshold to the new, an instrument of change.

Erika

'You really scared me, Erika.' Marcus plucks grapes from the bowl on her bed tray. 'That was one hell of a thing to do.'

'I'm sorry. I don't know what came over me.' Her voice is hoarse.

They sit, silent. An elderly man is visiting his wife in the bed next to hers, talking loudly in Okinawan dialect. Erika doesn't understand a word. A thought flits across her mind: I ought to learn Uchināguchi.

'When the noro called to tell me you were here I thought the worst.' Marcus draws a breath. 'You know, after that thing you did to your hand, and especially after what you told me the day before you came up here. I panicked when you went missing.'

'The noro?' she asks.

He nods. 'When you weren't on that last bus from Nago I didn't know what to do. I ran all the way back to the hotel. I was searching through your stuff for her number and freaking out that I couldn't find it, and that's when the phone in the hotel room started ringing. It was her. I don't know how she knew to call me.' His voice cracks. 'I called the hospital, and they told me you'd been found with a fractured skull at the bottom of a waterfall. I got a taxi here as quickly as I could. I sat through the night here not knowing whether you'd pull through ... I didn't know what to think.' He wipes his eyes.

She takes his hand, the drip tugging at the needle. 'It was an accident, Marcus, I promise.'

He blows his nose and clears his throat. 'Erika, I've been thinking ...'

'Marcus ...'

'Please, let me finish.' He squeezes her hand. 'I didn't understand what was going on with you, before. You're not exactly an open book.'

Erika gives a wry smile. 'I don't understand myself, either.'

'You seeing the noro. I didn't realise what it meant to you.'

'I'm still not sure what any of it means, to be honest.'

'You know she came to see you?'

So it wasn't a dream after all. Erika sifts through her memory, wondering what else had been real. Or is she still dreaming?

'She did some kind of ritual while I was here. The nurses knew her. One of them told me she comes in here to see people all the time. Here,' he says, handing her a small box. 'She left this for you.'

Erika opens the lid. Inside there's a small drawstring bag sewn from yellow bingata fabric, closed with red string. She can feel something gritty inside. There's a spider shell, striped cream and honey, its body the size of a fist, its pointed fingers splayed as if searching for Erika's hand. A small hand-written note in hiragana, reads: 'Sacred salt from the sea at Kōri island; the shell is from the sands below Nakijin Castle. For protection.'

The old man visiting his wife in the next bed has turned on the TV, and is talking loudly over the sound.

'Erika,' says Marcus. 'You should go do your own thing. Without me.'

She looks at him, alarmed.

'Felix had to stay with his mum while I've been with here with you, and each time I talk to him on the phone he sounds upset, asking when I'm coming home. I love you, Erika, but it's not going to work the way things are. I didn't know when else to tell you.' His voice breaks.

Erika feels a pressure rising in her throat, swallows.

'You have to do what's right for you,' Marcus says. 'I have a feeling you won't need me around for that.'

A fat tear plops onto the sheets. It's too much to take in. Her head still hurts.

'Don't cry. It's a chance for a fresh start.'

Her metal halo is removed, and she's discharged. She'd worried about the impact on Marcus's job, on his son, and about the extra costs, but Marcus has been given compassionate leave and the travel insurance has covered all the expenses, including a business flight back to London. Marcus's ex has already suggested Felix stay with his father a few extra weeks when he gets back so he can make it up to him. The thought that this will be easy to do now Marcus won't be staying with Erika any more pains her more than she expected. When the nurses wave Erika goodbye as she's wheeled to a taxi she struggles to hold back her tears.

Erika calls Kei from the airport business lounge. Her cousin had been surprised at Marcus's phone call, almost a month ago now, telling her they'd decided to stay in Okinawa for longer. Erika had made him promise not to tell her why. They haven't spoken to Kei since, so she now probes for details; whether they've discovered anything about their grandmother's family or about Erika's father, whether they went to Kudakajima and saw a noro.

'No exciting discoveries. We did some sightseeing. I went hiking in the Yanbaru mountains. I had a little fall while I was up there.'

'A fall?'

'I had a few weeks in hospital, actually.'

Kei insists she'll meet them at Narita before they board their connecting flight to London. Nothing Erika says dissuades her. 'I'm meeting you off the plane,' says Kei. 'We'll have a few hours before your next flight. I can be there by the time you land.'

She's there, brow furrowed with worry. Marcus wheels Erika into the domestic terminal, her head and neck bandaged above the neck brace, the bruises around her eyes faded green and yellow. Kei lets out a yelp and her hand flies to her mouth.

'It's not as bad as it looks,' says Erika. 'I'm much better than I was.'

'You look terrible!' Kei is hovering over her, horrified.

'Thanks.'

'Your eyes are all bruised and swollen!'

Erika wants to get away from the arrivals hall. People are stopping to gawk. 'It's a very small skull fracture and it's mending.'

'A skull fracture?'

'I was lucky. Or I have a head made of concrete. I get headaches, but they say there's no lasting damage. Maybe the knock on the head will make me less stubborn.'

They go to a Japanese restaurant near the viewing deck. Erika and Marcus have decided not to tell Kei about their decision to break up just yet. Erika knows she won't be able to handle her cousin's response; Erika will just end up crying, and crying makes her head hurt. Marcus wheels her there, both of them pretending; she smiling up at him, Marcus reaching down to touch her shoulder. It's a good act; Kei notices nothing.

While the waitress brings their tea and azuki red bean pudding, Kei pulls a package out of her bag, as if she's too impatient to wait.

'I've got something for you,' she says to Erika. 'I'm sorry,' she says to Marcus. 'I can only tell this my cousin in Japanese.'

'No problem.'

'What is it?' Erika asks Kei.

'I kept working on the diaries when I got home. I still have a few more to go, but here are the ones I've done,' says Kei, handing Erika the package. 'The last one she ever wrote in is in there, but it's different from the others. She'd written her last proper entry when she was in Hong Kong, in the usual way, keeping to the lines for each day. Then there was a gap, and then pages and pages of continuous writing. It looks like she wrote it years later. I think you should read it, it's important.'

Kei has marked the page with a Post-It. Erika opens the diary and starts reading, blinking so she can focus. Her head is hurting, and she frowns at her mother's words on the page. The writing is shaky, but Kei's furigana against her mother's kanji helps steady her reading. It's one long stream of consciousness, Michiko reflecting on her life. It seems so out of character. Each revelation stabs through Erika, knife-bright. Michiko's father's cruelty. Her dead school friend, Maki-chan. The bombed house. The starvation during the war. The terrifying things she witnessed. The GI. The doll. Her dream for a better life, and then, meeting Michael in Okinawa, the happiest she'd ever been in her life. The call from Obā.

'My god, he was married. She didn't know.' She gasps as she reads, and Kei reaches for her hand.

Erika's birth. The depression. The diabetes. George. Julian. The fighting. The day she fought Erika for the doll …

'She burned it in the garden,' Erika whispers.

Moving to London. Her despair. Erika moving out. Her loneliness. Her illness. How she's had enough of drinking. Erika's chest begins to tighten. 'No … no, please, no …'

Michiko deciding to commit to a twelve-step program. Michiko's hope that Erika will support her through it.

'No … no… I can't believe this …'

Michiko wondering where Erika is, why she's late. Her regrets at not having been a better mother. How she hopes she and Erika can start again.

'No!'

Marcus half-stands, but Kei is quick to leap up and hold her cousin, who has crumpled in her chair. People are turning around to look as Erika sobs.

She doesn't care that she's in a public place. She howls.

When she gets home, Erika sleeps for so long that it worries Marcus. When she finally wakes up she feels well enough for a bath. The nights are colder, and Marcus goes to switch on the bathroom heater and turn on the taps.

'There was something else in Kei's package,' says Erika, as she sits on the sofa waiting for the bath to fill. 'A letter. Kei stuck a note on it that said it had been tucked into the back of Michiko's Okinawa diary. I guess Kei was going to tell me about that at the airport too, but then I fell apart.'

Marcus goes to sit next to her on the sofa and starts to put his arm around her, then draws it back as if he's suddenly remembered, but Erika takes his hand and gently pulls it back around her again. There'll be time to put an end to these habits.

'It was meant for my uncle Kensuke, but Michiko never sent it. The way things turned out, it was just as well she didn't.' Erika sighs. 'She wrote it when she was in Okinawa with my father. Didn't seem like he was a typical American GI. He was born and raised in Okinawa. He even spoke Uchināguchi.'

Erika smiles at the thought. The way her mother wrote about Michael painted a different picture to the one she'd created in her mind. Things were never as straightforward as they appeared.

'She was asking my uncle to persuade my grandfather to let her stay in Okinawa. She wanted to take her mother to live there with her too. She said it was as if Okinawa had brought my grandmother back to life. It's a happy letter.'

Erika remembers how she felt when she set foot on the island, as if new blood were flowing in her veins. Her mother had written that she had gone to Sēfa Utaki, the sacred place where noro had worshipped the spirits of nature for millennia. Erika wishes she'd gone there.

Her bags have been sitting, still unpacked, in the corner of the bedroom. There'll be clothes in there that need washing. She empties her backpack onto the bed, pulling out her jacket, her wallet, her camera, her water bottle, the shell and the bag of salt from the noro.She remembers the en-musubi ring. She'd completely forgotten about it. Where is it? Everything her rescuers found at the waterfall had been put back in her rucksack. She scrabbles around in the bottom of the pack but it's not there. They'd have removed it before her surgery, but surely they'd have put it into safekeeping along with the dress ring and bracelet she'd been wearing on her other hand. She tips the rucksack upside down and gives it a shake. Something falls out and bounces on the bed. It's the smooth pebble she found at the waterfall; seeing it again makes her heart race. She weighs it in her palm. It's heavier than its size suggests, a dense, rounded mass of grey stone cut through with sparkling streaks of white. She closes her fist around it, and it quickly grows warm. She holds it in the light and the white streaks glow like shooting stars. She holds it to her mouth. Tiny reverberations against her lips, as if its surface were a thin membrane. She thinks she feels something tremble and turn inside it, like an embryonic creature inside an egg, but when she looks again, there's nothing there. It's just a stone. She picks it up again, feeling its smoothness with her lips, and then she kisses it, like a gambler kissing dice for luck.

There's an unspoken agreement not to mention the impending separation, although there's a blanket of despondency over everything. It makes Erika so sad she wants to blurt out that she wants a committed relationship with Marcus after all, that she can change, that she'll meet Felix and be a constant presence for him. She's not sure if this is true, or whether what she feels is love, but if the pain she feels at the thought of never seeing Marcus again is a measure of it, then yes, she loves him. But she says nothing.

Sarah pops in to help out when she can. She comes over with funny stories about strange customers and the latest dramas in the kitchen, but to Erika they feel like a relic of another era. Luca has made her a huge get-well card with a drawing of Erika on it; Sarah sticks on the fridge. Whenever Erika shuffles over to get herself something to drink or eat, the massive moon face beams out at her. The stick figure wears a pink neck brace and an enormous red grin. The eyes are crinkled into a smile – he's recently learned to draw sideways Cs to represent happy eyes, with long eyelashes. Black curls tumble out over the top of the bandage wrapped around its head, and on top of it he's drawn a golden crown.

Sarah took over cooking and cleaning for Mrs Mackenzie while Erika was away, and she'll carry on until Erika's well enough to manage it again. Erika goes upstairs one evening to see her neighbour, taking Marcus with her. Mrs Mackenzie smiles at them both, saying, 'My dears, you're such a lovely couple. When are you going to get married and start a family? Any fool can see how much you love each other.'

They laugh in high-pitched voices, as if Mrs Mackenzie has just told a hilarious joke, and shift uncomfortably next to each other on the sofa.

Sarah has come over. The three of them devour a mountain of spaghetti bolognese that Marcus cooks for them and empty two bottles of red. They flop on the sofa. Luca is asleep in the spare room. Quiet music plays.

'I've made a decision,' says Erika.

The other two look at her, and wait.

'I'm going to sort out that business with my mother's bones.'

'Did that priestess woman tell you to?' asks Sarah. 'What did she say you should do with them?'

'Nothing that was going to work for me. I'm going to get them ground up like they do here.'

Sarah and Marcus look at each other.

'I found a crematorium in North London that's done a few Japanese funerals; they know the traditions. They say they can put my mother's bones through what's called a cremulator, turn them to powder. I can't keep that urn in the house anymore.'

'What will you do with the ashes?' asks Sarah.

'I'm going to scatter them,' says Erika. 'In the sea, in Okinawa.'

'I hope you won't mind me saying I'm proud of you,' says Marcus later that night. 'You couldn't even bring yourself to talk about it a few months ago, let alone make a decision.' He lights a joint and passes it to her and she takes it, squinting at him through the swirling lamplit smoke as she draws. With the black stubble of her hair that's starting to grow back and the surgical scar still visible she looks punkish and fierce, like a different person.

They're still sharing a bed each night, more for comfort than anything. It lets them pretend for the moment that nothing's going to change. That night, Erika turns to him, her face so close she can see the soft blue–grey ridges in his irises, and she cups his cheek in her palm, as if she's trying to feel what he isn't telling her. He traces his fingers down from the dip in her throat below the neck brace, across to her shoulder where the koi carp is permanently suspended in its attempt to swim free. When he continues down the centre of her chest and belly, she shifts towards him a little, and doesn't tell him to stop. He's afraid of hurting her; he's slow and gentle, so as not to jar her, and she is filled with him, with the love she doesn't know how to take in.

Erika takes the Tube to the crematorium on a freezing grey January day. She hands over the tiny urn and the undertaker checks the death certificate. She waits in reception and staff fluent in professional sympathy offer her tea and biscuits. Not long afterwards, a man with a solemn face returns with the urn in both hands. The lid has been taped back on.

Back at the flat, Erika places it on the Korean cabinet. She empties the offering cup, washes it. She makes a pot of gyokurō tea, pours some into the cup and places it on the altar. She's cooked some rice. She puts some in her mother's rice bowl and puts it next to the tea.

'Here you go,' she says, feeling self-conscious. She takes the waterfall stone from the pocket of her jeans and places it on the altar, a fragment of the land where her mother belonged. She lights a candle and holds two sticks of incense to it. She wafts out the flames with her hand and smoke drifts around her head in a fragrant cloud. She pushes the incense into the soft ash of the kōrō bowl. She loops her mother's ojyuzu around her left hand, and taps the wooden stick against the orin bronze bowl on its brocade cushion with the other, twice. The sonorous reverberation shimmers in waves, filling the room, filling her head, lingering. She puts the stick down, clasps the ojyuzu between her palms. She closes her eyes and bows her head.

Erika picks up the crystal Bodhisattva that Kei gave her, polishes it with the sleeve of her jumper and puts it back beside a photograph of Michiko taken just after the move to Hong Kong. Her mother looks happy. The look in her eyes reminds Erika of her own.

All That Remains

The tiny pile of ash looks like nothing, like dust, just enough to spread across the bowl of a small spoon. 10It is made up of tiny grains of different colours: beige, grey, cream, white. It is made of the dead, the way the sand on the island that this ash belongs to is made of the dead. Sand and ash, the bones of dead creatures of the sea. This tiny pile of ash is so insubstantial that it would blow away with a puff of wind, and disappear, merging with the sky, the earth, the sand, the sea, the stars.

Erika

There's something hypnotic and comforting about airports. Not in the hustle and bustle of the arrivals hall, or ranks of check-in desks and queues of people; it's once she's passed through customs and immigration and into the muffled innards of the airport that Erika feels a kind of peace. Still on British soil, but no longer in Britain. She's in no country, a threshold to everywhere. She looks up to check how long she has before boarding.

Sarah and Luca come to see her off. When Erika cries as she waves goodbye, her tears are not really for them. She's only going to Okinawa for three months. At least, that's the plan.

The urn is in her shoulder bag. It's small and takes up little space.

It's empty.

*

She's finished packing and sits on the bed with it, figuring out whether to put it in her suitcase or in her carry-on bag. She removes its brocade cover, opens the pine box and takes out the urn. She peels away the sticky tape around its lid and lifts it off. She's shocked at how little ash is inside. The small gritty pile of cream and white and grey, spread in a thin layer across the bottom of the urn, barely amounts to a tablespoonful. That's all there is. All that agonising over something so insubstantial. She stares at it and when she starts to cry, she feels she might never stop. She opens her mouth and howls like an animal, tears plopping onto her trousers.

Erika had not understood until it was too late. In an alternative universe, her mother is healthy, living a life on an island where she feels whole, a life that makes up for all the horrors of war.

Her crying is relentless, as if it has taken her over, and she surrenders gladly, purging herself of pain. Tears spill down Erika's face, splashing onto her hands, splashing into the urn. She reaches a finger inside to wipe them away, but they've already trickled down, darkening the edges of powdery grey. This will not do.

She breathes long and deep, trying to stop her sobs, but her tears continue to flow. She thinks she has stopped crying, but she has not. She steps outside of herself, observing. She sees she is made of two shimmering mists that long to merge and become whole, become solid. Reality shifting, slipping again. She wonders if she's in a coma dream, or on a boat in the South China Sea, or in a hospital bed, or at the mercy of a waterfall, as she falls through its anointing spray. She wonders if she is sitting on Naminoue Beach, where a grieving man with golden hair and a kind, gentle face pats the sand next to him, asking her to sit down and become a part of that place.

Her fingers are wet, covered in ash. Or perhaps it's sand, the bones of dead sea creatures. She raises her fingers to her lips. She tastes the saltiness of the sea; maybe it's the salt in her tears. The ash is grit between her teeth, tasteless, like sand. She is running her fingers through the sand, bringing her fingers to her lips, its dusty, gritty abrasiveness making her wince and shiver, but she must keep going, because all of this, this heart-home, must become a part of her. She keeps going, keeps going, until there is nothing left.

There had been a time when all she'd wanted was to take refuge in her mother, to return to her. She had once been a part of her, and her mother had cast her out in agony. But now, wherever she goes, she knows she is safe, knows her mother will forever be a part of her.

Love, revenge, redemption.

*

Erika jolts at the loud airport announcement: 'This is a final boarding call for passengers on British Airways flight number BA005 to Narita. Please proceed to the departure gate immediately.' Erika collects her bag from the floor by her feet and stands up. Deep and low within her belly – alchemy. She doesn't know it yet, but inside her, new life stirs.

Acknowledgments

The seed for *The Things She Owned* was sown years ago in London, when I had a career incompatible with a writing life. It was after migrating to Australia that I found a way to sprout that seed to maturity. A federally-funded APA scholarship enabled me to embark on a creative writing PhD, and an early version of this novel was submitted as part of my thesis at the University of Adelaide. More recently, a project development grant from Arts South Australia bought me the time I needed to prepare my manuscript for publication. I am truly thankful to my adoptive country for this assistance, coming as it did at this project's most crucial points: the start and the finish.

My thanks also go to the Eleanor Dark Foundation for the award of a writing fellowship at Varuna Writers' House in the Blue Mountains in 2014, when I completed the first draft of this novel, and again a few years later for a Varuna Affirm Press mentorship, when I embarked on the last. As its name suggests, Affirm Press offers this wonderful opportunity each year in partnership with Varuna. It led to the publication of this novel, for which I am deeply grateful.

Travel funding awarded by the English department at the University of Adelaide enabled me to carry out my research in Okinawa, Cambridge and London.

I feel lucky to have benefitted from the excellent HARDCOPY program twice over, run by the ACT Writers Centre. The teaching, industry advice and support from Nadine Davidoff, Mary Cunnane and Nigel Featherstone have proved invaluable.

An excerpt from this novel was published in slightly altered form in the short story anthology *Breaking Beauty*, edited by Dr Lynette Washington and published by Midnight Sun Publishing. My thanks to Lynette and to Anna Solding for this opportunity.

Many people have been vital to the process of getting this book out into the world. I owe my gratitude to Linda Dixon Howard, the first to recognise and encourage my childhood propensity for story-writing; to Albyn Hall, whose early advice set me on the right path; to John Stammers, Paul Laffan and Bill 'Swampy' Marsh.

My deep appreciation also goes to Dr Sue Hosking, for her thoughtful guidance and eternal patience while coaxing me through my PhD; to Dr Carol Lefevre, for her invaluable lessons on craft, for inspiring conversations and for her friendship, and to Dr Shoko Yoneyama, for introducing me to Okinawan rituals of the sacred feminine.

I am privileged to count talented writers as friends, who have read drafts, shared opportunities and offered encouragement. My love and thanks go to Dr Rebekah Clarkson, Alison Flett, Dr Rachael Mead (my long-time running companion), Molly Murn, Dr Anna Solding, Dr Heather Taylor-Johnson and Dr Lynette Washington.

Thanks also to Craig Harrison, Emma Anderson, Rachael Mead, Kara Jung and Lynette Washington for sharing their spaces, allowing for writing retreats in beautiful places.

My heartfelt thanks to the team at Affirm Press; to Ruby Ashby-Orr, my editor and the best manuscript midwife a first-time novelist could wish for; to Coco McGrath and to Martin Hughes, who saw potential in earlier drafts and kept the faith. Thanks also to Alissa Dinallo for her beautiful and thoughtful cover design.

To my father, Miles Dodd, my love and gratitude for his support which has led me to a place where I can pursue a writing career, and for his infectious enthusiasm for books which influenced my childhood reading. To Dr Jocelyn Probert, his partner, and my ideal reader, my love and thanks for helpful feedback on this manuscript, for friendship, and for bookish conversations.

My mother, Akiko Yonekubo Dodd, was a storyteller and avid reader. Bright, beautiful, funny, imaginative, she died too young in 1995, leaving an irreparable hole in my life. While I have drawn on her experiences of trauma as a child growing up in wartime Tokyo, the character of Michiko is purely fictional.

To Paul Arguile, my partner, who bore the weight of everything while I ploughed through countless drafts of this novel, thank you for your love and support, for your encouragement and your faith that this novel would make it out there, even in the moments when I doubted it. All my love to you.

Glossary

Terms are in Japanese unless otherwise stated.

Words are read phonetically, exactly as they are spelled.

Vowels remain constant in their pronunciation, as follows:

a, as in apple

i, as in seat

u, as in spoon

e, as in bed

o, as in ox

Vowels topped with a macron, are elongated: ā, ī, ū, ē, ō

*

amah (Cantonese) – a woman employed by a family as a servant to do domestic chores and care for their children

arigatō – thank you

awamori – strong Okinawan liquor

beni-imo – purple yam

bentō – lunchbox

Berusaiyu no Bara – The Rose of Versailles, a 1970s *shōjo manga* comic

bingata – brightly-coloured traditional Okinawan textiles

buku-buku cha – Okinawan tea frothed up with a whisk

chāhan – Japanese version of Chinese fried rice

chawan – rice bowl. Usually prefixed with 'o' (ochawan) to denote respect towards the object

chindonya – colourfully dressed wandering street musicians playing drums, bell-gongs and wind instruments to advertise local businesses

chōzubachi – water fountain for purification before paying respects at a Shintō shrine

dagashiya – old-fashioned candy and snack shop

dōzo – go ahead; here you go; please help yourself

en-musubi – fate binding

fuchiba jushi – Okinawan pork and vegetable dish

furigana – phonetic characters, either hiragana or katakana, written against kanji characters to make them easier to read

furoshiki – cloth used for wrapping

futon – bedding laid out on the floor; this term includes both the base mattress and the quilt cover

gaijin – foreigner, literally 'outside person'

geta – traditional Japanese footwear, usually made of wood held to the feet with a fabric thong

giri – obligation

goma-dare – ground sesame sauce

gōya – bitter gourd grown and eaten in Okinawa

gōya champuru – Okinawan dish made with bitter gourd, tofu, pork belly and egg

habu – poisonous snake native to Okinawa

hāfu – term used to describe mixed-race Japanese, literally 'half'

hajimemashite – pleased to meet you

hibachi – fire pot, usually used indoors, containing charcoal for heating and cooking

himono – dried or semi-dried fish

hinoki – Japanese cypress

hinomaru – the red rising sun motif on the Japanese flag, sometimes referring to the controversial Imperialist Japanese flag, which includes rays extending out from the sun

hōjicha – a variety of fermented Japanese tea

ikebana – Japanese flower arranging

itadakimasu – equivalent of 'bon appetit'

izakaya – drink and snack bar

izaiho – an ancient Okinawan ceremony to induct women to shamanic priestesshood

jīmami tofu – Okinawan peanut and potato starch tofu

jizō – like a bodhisattva, a small stone statues depicting Budda in the form of an ascetic monk who guides and aids others

kamishibai – traditional storytelling with storyboards

kampai – cheers

karī (Okinawan) – cheers

katsuobushi – shavings of dried bonito fish, used as a condiment

kitsune udon – a variation of udon noodle topped with seasoned fried tofu skin. *Kitsune* means 'fox'. This dish is named after the Shintō fox god, Oinari-san, who is said to love fried tofu skin

kōrō – incense burner

kucha (Okinawan) – fine clay from Okinawa

kunpen (Okinawan) – traditional Okinawan sweet with peanuts and sesame paste

kyokujitsuki – the Imperialist and militarist rising sun flag, where red rays extend outwards from the sun in the centre of the white flag. It is considered offensive, especially by other Asian nations, due to Japan's actions during the Second World War.

mabui (Okinawan) – spirit

mabui-wakashi (Okinawan) – traditional Okinawan ritual for returning the spirit to someone who has suffered its loss through an accident or mental shock

mimigā (Okinawan) – traditional Okinawan dish made of thinly sliced pig's ears

275

minshuku – traditional bed and breakfast lodgings

misoshiru – miso soup

mizuyōkan – gelatinous dessert made of azuki red mung bean paste

monpe – traditional loose-fitting trousers

mugicha – roasted barley tea served cold and drunk in summer

nakami jiru – Okinawan soup made of pig's stomach and intestines

nameko – a type of small mushroom with a gelatinous coating

Nirai kanai (Okinawan) – a mythical paradise in the Ryūkyu religion where the gods are thought to reside

nōkotsu – ceremony for the interment of cremated bones forty-nine days after death

noren – fabric dividers hung over doorways, between rooms or on windows

nori – thin sheets of dried seaweed

noro (Okinawan) – traditional Okinawan shamanic priestess

obā – familiar term for grandmother, or a woman of a grandmother's age. Equivalent to 'granny'

obachan – familiar term for an aunt, or a middle-aged woman. Equivalent to 'auntie'

obi – a belt sash used on a kimono or yukata

Obon – Buddhist festival celebrated on the 15th day of the 7th lunar month (usually August/September) to honour the spirits of dead ancestors, which are thought to return to the living world around this time. It is a joyous occasion for family reunions

ochawan – rice bowl, prefixed with the honorific 'o' to denote respect towards the object, since rice is considered sacred

okāsan – mother

omamori – protective talisman

omocha ga okottchatta no (Tokyo dialect) – 'I dropped my toy', literally, my toy fell down

onē-chan – familiar term for an older sister, or a young woman in their teens or twenties

onī-chan – familiar term for an older brother or a young man in their teens or twenties

omiyage – a gift or souvenir expected to be given to friends, family, co-workers and business associates whenever one travels within Japan or overseas

omocha – toy

ongi – debt of gratitude

oni – horned ogre or monster

onigiri – sticky rice balls, usually with a savoury centre, or with savoury condiments mixed into the rice. Usually encased in nori seaweed sheets

oyunomi – teacup

pan-pan girl – derogatory post-war term for sex workers known for servicing American occupation forces

panko – Japanese-style breadcrumbs, with larger, crisper pieces than the Western version

rafute (Okinawan) – Okinawan pork belly dish

raku – lead-glazed Japanese earthenware, more luxurious than a minshuku and

usually located beside a hot spring, with communal baths often used for tea
ceremony cups

rotenburo – outdoor hot spring bath

ryokan – traditional Japanese inn, often associated with hot springs

Ryūkyū – indigenous name for Okinawa

sakaya – liquor shop

salary-man – businessman

sanshin (Okinawan) – traditional Okinawan string instrument

…*san* – honorific suffix used for adults of any gender

sen – an old Japanese currency denomination that was taken out of circulation in
1953. 100 sen was equivalent to 1 yen

sencha – a type of green tea

seppuku – a highly ritualised form of suicide (also known as *hara-kiri*) by self-
disembowelment, traditionally practiced by samurai as a way to restore their
own or their clan's lost honour according to the principles of the Bushidō, or
way of the warrior, a code of conduct for samurai

shamisen – traditional Japanese string instrument

shamoji – spatula used for serving rice

shide – a white paper streamer folded into zig-zags, often attached to shimenawa
ropes and used in Shintō religious rituals

shimenawa – twisted ropes made of either rice or hemp fibres used for purification
purposes in the Shintō religion

shinkansen – bullet train

Shintō – the indigenous, polytheistic religion of Japan. It is animistic (where
a spiritual essence is thought to inhabit all things – objects as well as
features of the natural world and animals) and pantheistic (where reality is
interchangeable with divinity and therefore infused throughout everything
that exists). Shinto rituals revere a multitude of gods and spirits

shīsā (Okinawan) – a protective lion-like creature often seen on the roof or at the
entrance of an Okinawan dwelling or shop

shōchu – strong Japanese liquor distilled from rice, barley, sweet potatoes, buckwheat
or brown sugar

shōjo manga – manga comics targeting a younger female demographic

soba – buckwheat noodles eaten hot or cold in a soup or dipped into sauce

suna-mushi – literally, 'hot sand steaming'. Specific to the southern island of
Kagoshima, those seeking relaxation, good health and beauty are buried to
their necks in black volcanic sand that is heated by the hot springs that well
up on the beach

taiko – traditional drum

tako rice – Okinawan dish inspired by food introduced by the American occupying
forces; it is a version of tacos, where the filling is served on rice instead of in
taco shells

takuan – yellow or white pickled radish

tatami – traditional Japanese floor covering made from woven rushes set in a
wooden or chipboard frame; each rectangular piece has a standard size for

different regions in Japan. A property's floor area is measured according to the number of tatami mats it can hold

tenugui – an elongated rectangular hand towel made of a thin cotton material, usually with a pattern. It has many uses including as a head covering, or rolled up into a headband. They can be decorative and are sold as souvenirs.

tonkatsu – a dish of sliced deep fried pork escalopes served with Bulldog sauce (a tangy brown sauce), finely shredded white cabbage and rice

torī – a gateway to a Shintō shrine, symbolically marking the transition between heavenly and earthly places

Uchinā – Okinawa, as spoken in Okinawan dialect

Uchināguchi – name for Okinawan dialect

Uchinanchū – name for indigenous Okinawan people

uchiwa – a traditional, non-folding fan, usually round or oval in shape

umeboshi – sour, salty pickled plum, usually served with hot rice

utaki (Okinawan) – a sacred place, usually a natural feature such as a mountain, a cave or a grove

wakasa lacquer – a decorative form of lacquer

weka (Okinawan) – Okinawan kinship

yakamashī – has various meanings, including 'shut up', 'noisy', 'nagging', 'critical'

Yamato – the dominant race of Japan, mainly based on the larger central islands

yukata – a simply cotton robe similar in shape to a traditional kimono, worn in summer

yunomi – tea cup, usually used with the honorific prefix 'o', as in *oyunomi*

zabuton – square, flat floor cushion

zengakuren – student protest group founded in the 1940s with communist and anarchist associations and active until the 1970s